"The best book I have read

down."

Doug Sprunt, One Way Ministries

"The most gripping account of the crucifixion I have ever read."

Wilf Wight, eastern Ontario district director, Canadian Bible Society

"I was at the foot of the cross. I stepped inside the empty tomb. This book took me there."

Robert DuBroy, cofounder of CHRI-FM, Ottawa, Ontario

"An awesome read: captivating, spellbinding, inspiring! Through the author's masterful writing, the centurion stood out as a real and personable individual. . . . The book also helped me visualize Jesus, my Savior, and his person and work for the forgiveness of my sins, for my daily walk, and for the eternal life he has in store for all who believe."

Cliff Kentel, Prince of Peace Lutheran Church, Regina, Saskatchewan

"A readable and accurate novel about Jesus Christ's last week on earth. David Kitz's portrayal of the collision between pagan Rome and temple Judaism is completely plausible. And as a perfect antidote to the faux expertise of Dan Brown's *The Da Vinci Code*, Kitz provides over a hundred endnotes and a handful of thumbnail biographies at the end of his book."

Joe Woodard, *Calgary Herald*

"Story has a way of capturing our attention and enabling truth to move from head to heart. David Kitz creatively unpacks the events of Passion Week as seen through a Roman centurion's eyes. Through vivid word pictures, we see the whip-sliced back of our Savior and hear the pounding of each nail that affixed him to the cross. We walk these last steps of Jesus's earthly ministry, leading to his death, burial, and triumphant resurrection from the dead. Kitz better helps us to do as the apostle John encourages: 'See what great love the Father has lavished on us, that we should be called children of God!' (1 John 3:1)."

Dean Ridings, author of *The Pray! Prayer Journal* and communications director of Navigator Church Ministries

"This engaging, hard-hitting narrative is a distillation of Kitz's study and prayer over fifty years as a pastor and educator, steeped in the wonder of this story. As a novelist, he reveals profound respect for the historical record through his characterization of Marcus Longinus, a Roman centurion who is unwillingly caught in the power struggles of the day. In contrast to the stench of these political machinations, the donkey-riding King emerges in the Roman world offering an entirely new way for humankind to be reborn. The Roman centurion is like us, caught between worlds. Who is king? Why? The Son of God shows unlimited compassion through healing the sick and feeding the hungry, and his purity catches the attention of the masses in a drama that still shakes the world, one aching, open, humble heart at a time."

Dr. Darlene L. Witte-Townsend, former professor of education, Johnson State College

"One of the most exceptional biblical fiction books I have ever read. I was struck by the everyday events and people affected by the dramatic climax of the cross, which Kitz presents on an equal level with Mel Gibson's *The Passion of the Christ.* Extremely well documented historically and biblically, the narrative transports you back in time and evokes both grief and thanksgiving as you follow the soldier's own emotional turmoil in grappling with the dramatic events of the darkest day in history. Like him you will be led to cry out in both despair and trust, 'Surely this was the Son of God!'"

Heather Goodwin, former manager of the Baptist Bookroom, New Brunswick

"David Kitz has written an intriguing book. Taking the point of view of the centurion who crucified Christ is new and fresh and gives the reader much to contemplate. Even though I knew the story, I felt compelled to read on to see how Kitz would unfold the drama. Excellently done!"

Tami Waring, Officers' Christian Fellowship, Maxwell-Gunter Air Force Base

The Soldier Who Killed a King

A True Retelling *of the* Passion

David Kitz

Kregel Publications

The Soldier Who Killed a King: A True Retelling of the Passion

Published by Kregel Publications, a division of Kregel, Inc., 2450 Oak Industrial Dr. NE, Grand Rapids, MI 49505.

Previously published as *The Soldier, the Terrorist and the Donkey King: The Other Perspective, A First Century Novel*, 2003.

ISBN 978-0-8254-4485-2

Printed in the United States of America
17 18 19 20 21 22 23 24 25 26 / 5 4 3 2 1

‡ ‡ ‡

Jesus did many other things as well. If every one of them were written down, I suppose that even the whole world would not have room for the books that would be written.

John 21:25

Foreword

WHAT WOULD IT have been like to live in the geopolitical center of the first-century world, when donkeys and camels were the cars and trucks, conversations over goblets of wine were the social media, and religious conflict influenced every facet of life? What would it have been like to live under the pagan, political domination of Roman tyranny, while also under the oppressive ritualistic control of hypocritical religious bigots? What would it have been like to live in the very week that this dark, confused world was invaded by heaven—a week when history shifted from BC to AD?

This gripping story offers its readers a front-row seat from which we can view the action. It's a hidden camera on the helmet of a primary witness of the history-altering drama when the Sovereign of the Universe, quietly riding a lowly donkey, overthrew the pomp and dominion of the most powerful kingdom this world had ever known. More than that, it's a look into the mind and heart of a man, not unlike you or me, who wrestled with the meaning and purpose of life.

As you read the thoughtful eyewitness account of Marcus Longinus, the Roman centurion, *the soldier who killed a king,* you'll feel his anxiety and anguish as well as exult in his ultimate answers because—despite the differences of time and culture—his story is our story.

DR. BARRY BUZZA
President Emeritus
Foursquare Gospel Church of Canada

Preface

YOU ARE ABOUT to set out on a journey through a pivotal week in human history—the week of Christ's suffering, death, and resurrection. On this journey you will notice time and date entries at the head of each chapter. These act as road markers as you make your way through the week. Most historians and biblical scholars situate this epic drama during the Passover week of AD 30. If this is so, then we can pinpoint many events to within minutes of their occurrence.

You will be seeing this slice of history through the eyes of Marcus Longinus, the Roman centurion who oversaw the crucifixion of Jesus. At the foot of the cross, this man made this startling confession: "Surely he was the Son of God!" (Matt. 27:54).

This is a work of historical fiction. Like other works in this genre, there are points where imagination is essential in order to round out the characters and to fill in details missing from the historical record. However, every effort has been made to tell this story in a biblically accurate manner. Frequently, when the story narrative intersects with the biblical account, direct quotes from the Bible are used. These quotes appear in italics and are cataloged by chapter in the endnotes. Quotations are drawn from the New International Version except where noted.

For navigational purposes, a map of first-century Jerusalem has been included.

With that said, and your seat belts fastened, I invite you to settle in for an amazing journey.

DAVID KITZ

Jerusalem AD 30

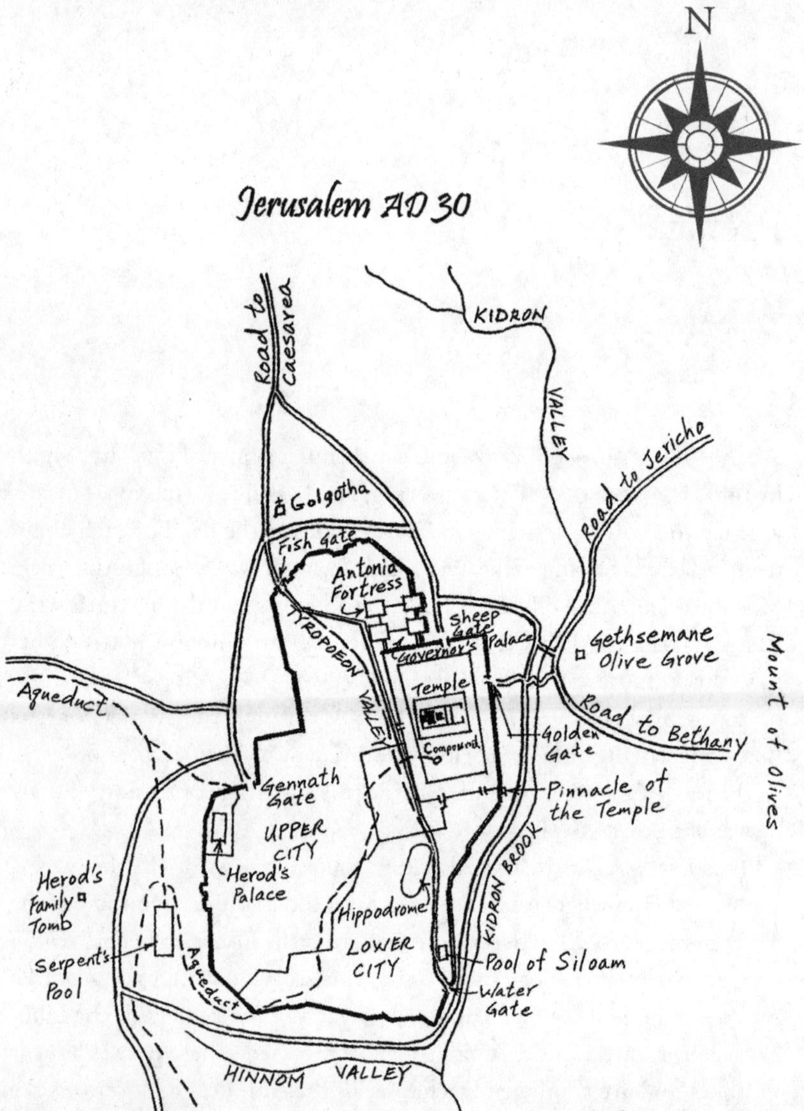

I

Four in the afternoon, Sunday, April 2, AD 30

IT WAS NEVER like this before.

I have been posted in Jerusalem for ten years now, but in all that time I had never seen a Passover crowd like this.

It wasn't the numbers. I had seen that before.

The Passover pilgrims always come plodding into the city in reverent caravans. Some of them chant psalms. Others are silent, looking bone-weary as they trudge, like fretful herdsmen with children in tow. Undoubtedly, many are relieved that their holy city is finally in view.

But this year it was different. There was this man—at the center of the whole procession. There had never been a central figure before. Every movement within that huge throng seemed focused on him.

Squinting in a futile attempt to get a better view, I gave Claudius a backhanded slap to the shoulder and demanded, "What are they doing?"

"They're climbing the trees, sir."

"I can see that!" I snapped. "But what are they doing?"

"They seem to be tearing off the palm branches, sir."

"What is going on here?" I said it more to myself than to any of the men standing near me. An uncomfortable feeling crept into me as the procession advanced.

"They don't usually do this?" Claudius questioned.

"No . . . They've never done this before." There was worry in my voice.

Claudius had been recently assigned to this place, the festering armpit of the empire, and I was at a loss to explain what was happening before us. We were standing on the wall above the gate of Jerusalem, and less than a half mile away, we could see the jubilant pilgrims surging toward us in alarming numbers.

"They're laying the palm branches on the road in front of that man—the man on the donkey."

Until Claudius said it, I hadn't noticed the donkey. Its small size and the frenzy of activity round about must have obscured this detail in the picture before me. What an odd way for this man to come. I could make no sense of it.

"They're throwing down their cloaks before him."

The sweat-glistened bodies of several men were clearly visible. Outer garments were being cast down before this man as a sign of homage. At the same time the rhythmic chanting of their voices became more distinct.

What were they singing? Could I pick up the words?

"Hosanna to the Son of David!"

"Blessed is he who comes in the name of the Lord!"

"Hosanna in the highest heaven!"

That's when it hit me like a barbarian's club. I realized what I was witnessing. It was a triumphal entry—the entry of a king.

It was the words. The words they were now boisterously shouting. He was their Messiah. The Son of David! The one they were waiting for! The one who would rid them of the Romans. He would set up his glorious Jewish kingdom, here, in Jerusalem! This is what I had been warned about since the day I first set foot on this cursed Judean soil.

And we, I and my men and the garrison in the city, were all that stood in their way.

This crowd of thousands was sweeping down the Mount of Olives into the Kidron Valley and then on toward us. They advanced like a huge human wave about to collide with the rock-hewn palisades on which we stood.

Would they sweep us away?

My initial curiosity had grown into worry. Now, in an instant, my worry turned to alarm. Instinctively, everything within me shouted, "Stand! Resist! Be a Roman!"

We had soldiers posted all about the city, especially along the pilgrim route. My own hundred men were among the first to be deployed. During Jewish feasts like this, we made certain we were highly visible. I dreaded what might happen if this crowd ran wild. Rioting could erupt, and with an impassioned throng such as this, riots have a way of quickly turning deadly.

For several moments a debate raged in my mind. Should I order the gate closed to keep this rabble with their pretender king out of the city? Or should I let everything proceed—let it proceed as though somehow we hadn't taken note of what was going on?

"Stand! Ready for orders!" I shouted above the swelling din. The sentinels on the wall snapped to attention.

I hastily scanned the crowd for any sign of weapons, any hint of armed treachery. To my surprise, I saw none. They were paying no attention to us. Everyone was caught up with hailing this man, the man on the donkey.

The front edges of the crowd reached the first platoon of eight men I had positioned by the roadside about four hundred yards before the gate. But they ignored them, sweeping past the clump of soldiers without so much as creating a ripple, like a swift-flowing stream around a stone.

At that moment I knew it made no sense to lower the gate. It would only enrage this crowd that was already fully aroused and moving as one.

Let them come. We'll handle them and their king inside the city.

Their king. On a donkey. I could only shake my head in disbelief.

I had watched many a triumphal entry while growing up in Rome, and the conquering hero always rode a gallant warhorse. And as a boy, I too had dreams of personal glory. But a donkey? It could only happen here, I thought with an incredulous grin.

I could see him clearly now. Donkey or not, he had the look of a man who knew exactly what he was doing. Those about him might not know or understand, but he knew. He had a destination in mind, a purpose. You could see it on his face.

"Hosanna to the Son of David!"

"Blessed is he who comes in the name of the Lord!"

"Hosanna in the highest heaven!"

There was something else different about him. At the time I didn't know what it was. I couldn't put it into words for a long time. I think I noticed it because I had watched all those other men come into Rome in their triumphal processionals. They were conquerors, but still they were hollow men, feeding off the adulation of the crowd, thirsting but never satisfied. You could see them vainly drink it in, hoping it would somehow fill the empty soul.

This donkey-riding king wasn't drinking from the crowd. I somehow sensed he was full already, and what he had within must have come from a different source.

"Hosanna in the highest heaven!"

"Hosanna to the Son of David!"

"Blessed is he who comes in the name of the Lord!"

Just at that moment a strange feeling seemed to rise within me. Maybe it was the joy of the crowd. I had expected anger. Maybe it was the children waving palm branches or the spontaneity of the singing? I don't know. For one moment it all seemed to come together. It seemed right somehow. Like heaven and earth had finally, for a moment, come into agreement—an agreement that had never been achieved before.

"Hosanna in the highest heaven!"

He was much closer now.

"Hosanna to the Son of David!"

He was now within the shadow of the gate.

"Blessed is he who comes in the name of the Lord!"

At that moment he looked up. For an instant our eyes met. Then I heard a voice—clearly heard a voice say, "I have a future for you."

I was confused.

I turned to Claudius and said, "What did you mean by that?"

"What did I mean by what?" He had a blank look on his face.

"By what you said about—about the future?"

"I didn't say anything about the future, sir. I didn't say anything."

I was totally baffled. Was I hearing voices? This whole thing was making no sense, no sense at all. Passover pilgrims weren't supposed to come into the city this way. We had a revolutionary on the loose—riding a donkey. And now I was hearing things?

I rubbed the sweat from my forehead, hoping for some clarity to emerge.

I had a hundred men whose lives were in danger from this Jewish Messiah and his horde of followers. That was what mattered.

By this time the donkey man had passed under the gate and was heading in the direction of the temple in the heart of the city.

I signaled for Claudius to follow as I raced down the stairs of the gatehouse. I emerged onto the street and grabbed the first two-legged bit of Jewish scum I saw. Pressing him against the stone wall, I demanded, "Who is that man?" I pointed at the retreating figure on the donkey.

The poor wretch was in shock and seemed quite unable to get out a word.

Claudius reached for his sword.

"Je-Jesus of Nazareth," he stammered and then quickly added, "the prophet from Nazareth in Galilee."

I loosened my grip.

Then in a voice loud enough for all near to hear, I announced, "Well, there is one thing I do know. We're going to have to keep an eye on that man."

2

One in the morning, Monday, April 3

SLEEP WAS IMPOSSIBLE. The events of the day kept playing through my mind.

He worried me. Donkey man. The donkey king. Jesus of Nazareth.

He could have turned that mob against us. They were in his hands. Why didn't he act?

Maybe it was the women and children in the crowd? Maybe it was a lack of weapons?

He must be waiting for his support to build. He obviously had his supporters from Galilee with him. Maybe he felt he needed to build his base of support here in Jerusalem before he attacked us.

I rolled over. The room felt unusually hot for a spring evening.

Maybe it just wasn't his time. He was a man with a purpose. I could see that. Of course that was it. He was working according to some plan, some script I could only guess at.

What was his next move?

The deep rhythmic breathing of my wife told me she was fast asleep. Zelda knew none of my worries. It was best that way. Our two young sons were also sleeping, in the adjoining room. Let them dream on.

But by the gods, it's hard to sleep when you feel your life is threatened.

I had doubled my men on duty for the nightly foot patrol through the city and put an additional man on as house guard. Maybe that idiot Arius wouldn't fall asleep if he had some company. I could faintly hear feet shuffling in the courtyard from time to time, so I knew they were on duty.

At least I knew our would-be Messiah wasn't in the city. As the sun was setting, I had watched him leave by the same gate by which he had arrived triumphant an hour earlier. Word on the street had it that he was going to spend the night with friends in Bethany. So an overnight coup was not in the works.

Then there was Claudius to worry about, my sister's son. I was so pleased when he first arrived from Antioch. I remembered him as a curly-haired boy back in Rome, but when he stepped off that galleon, I was looking at a man. I didn't even recognize him at that moment, though now I can see he has my sister's eyes.

Yes, there was Claudius. What had he stepped into if this thing erupted?

Hell-bent zealots. I hated them.

I could feel my body tense as the pictures raced through my mind.

There was Andreas, one of my lead men, dumped like a sack of refuse. I found him lying on the blood-drenched cobblestones. His throat was cut.

Then there was young Hermes, pinned to a wall by his own spear. His entrails were hanging to the ground.

Terrorists! Bloody terrorists! That's what they were. And there was no telling when they would strike. The incident last month was still fresh in my mind. Barabbas the Zealot, the ringleader, would pay for this!

These were isolated, random attacks by a few fanatics. For us Romans, the constant threat of terror was demoralizing. Each incident marshaled its own set of fears. But this prophet, this Jesus, with thousands adoring him and singing his praise, what could he do? Anything seemed possible. He put all of Jerusalem in a stir today. And this was only the first day of Passover Week. There was no doubt in my mind that we were in for a killer week, and it would be us or them.

I rolled over. My pillow was wet with sweat.

Then there was Flavio.

All this wouldn't leave me so fuming frustrated if it weren't for the leadership crisis. Late in the day, when Renaldo and I reported all we had seen to Flavio—our tribune, our commanding officer—he was drunk.

Drunk again. So here we were on the cusp of a mass rebellion, and our commander was so intoxicated he couldn't draw his sword to butter his own bread.

I threw back the flimsy cover, quietly pulled on a tunic, and slipped out the door.

Standing on the balcony, I could see the two guards start at my sudden appearance above them. One quickly moved to the street gate, anticipating a rebuke.

The still night air was refreshing as I drew in several long breaths. I reached for the balcony rail to anchor me in the darkness. It was a clear moonlit night. The stars were glorious.

I just needed time to think. All was quiet except for the incessant chirping of crickets.

I needed a plan.

How long I stood there I have no idea. Then it started to come. Slowly at first, and then my mind raced along.

I groped my way forward till I reached the stairs. Then, with the assurance of familiarity, I hurried down them. Beneath the stairs was a storage closet. The hinges creaked as I opened the crude door. I stooped to enter, turned a sharp left, and with fumbling hands reached for a small wooden trunk I knew should be on a shelf straight ahead of me at chest height. I smiled into the blackness as my fingers fell on a well-worn handle. I shifted the trunk's weight onto my hip and ducked back out the door. Moving out of the shadows, I set my trophy down in the center of the courtyard.

Arius shuffled toward me from the gate and in whispered tones asked, "Sir, do you need my help?"

I waved him off.

The clasps gave way before me, and the tight lid squeaked open. I pulled out the robe and held it up to the starlight. I did the same with the carefully folded prayer shawl. The pungent cedar smell of the chest had permeated the fabric. The scent revived me. I hastily stuffed both back into the trunk and carried the treasure up to my chamber.

For what was left of the night, I slept.

3

Six in the morning, Monday, April 3

THE FIRST STREAKS of dawn were just beginning to spread across the eastern sky when I left the house with the trunk tucked under my arm. In moments I was at Renaldo's gate. The gatekeeper immediately recognized me and granted entry.

Renaldo was a fellow centurion and a trusted friend. Our wives spent untold hours together, since our cramped Roman villas were joined one to another. For Zelda, female companionship of a Roman kind was hard to find in this outpost of the empire, so our wives found in each other a kinship that might never have flourished back home.

In the dim light I caught sight of a familiar toga-clad figure seated on the steps, stroking the head of a large dog. At the sound of my footsteps, Keeper swung free from his master and bounded about me in two great circles with his tail wagging furiously.

"He's such a great watchdog," I said in mock admiration. In fact, I knew he would be just that if a stranger entered.

"You're off to an early start," Renaldo offered as he rose, straightened, and we clasped forearms.

"Yes, well, it's not a regular week."

"No, it's not a regular week," he agreed, then shook his head. "What a show that was yesterday. Holy Jupiter! I thought we were history. That dog on the donkey could have had us trampled and served up as Passover lamb. That was too close. Way too close!"

"Don't I know it." I nodded my full agreement.

"We have to do something. This Jewish prophet is too dangerous."

"That's why I came over. I have a plan. It came to me last night."

"What about Flavio?" Renaldo resumed stroking Keeper. The dog's silky ears twitched beneath his gentle hand.

"Forget Flavio. He'll be drunk for the rest of the week. Herod's coming down about midweek. There'll be a big wine-swilling bash for the upper crust. He'll sober up just long enough so he can bow and scrape for Pilate at the right moment. Forget him. We have to save our own hides."

"All right. So what's this plan?"

"It's not some great master scheme, but I do have a few ideas."

"Yes, get on with it," he said with obvious interest.

"Well, the way I see it, we have way too little information about whatever is going on here. If there's some Passover plot being hatched, we need to be the first to know about it. Not like yesterday. I don't like surprises. Especially Jewish Messiah surprises."

Renaldo scowled in agreement.

"So why the trunk?" he asked.

I had set it down after our greeting, and now it was Keeper, sniffing about it, that brought it to Renaldo's attention.

"This is one way I can get some information."

I opened the trunk and pulled out several items of clothing, among them a Jewish prayer shawl and several phylacteries. Holding one of the fringed garments to myself, I announced, "Today I am Benjamin. Benjamin from Alexandria, and I've come to celebrate the Passover here, in the holy city, Jerusalem."

All this was done with a thick Aramaic accent and a mock reverence that left Renaldo slapping his thigh in laughter.

"Marcus, Marcus! Only you could pull this off!" Then he added in a more thoughtful tone, "I could look in on some of our usual sources. They're bound to know a thing or two about this donkey man."

"Now you're thinking." With a glance to the eastern sky, I added, "Look, we don't have much time. The sun's almost up. All my men know their assigned duties, so if you could just look in on them at the barracks, that would be great. I should be back in uniform by noon, and I could meet you there to discuss what we've found."

"No problem . . . Benjamin!" he said, shaking his head and grinning, no doubt contemplating the sight of me in religious garb.

I began to place the clothing back in the trunk, and then I turned to my friend.

"Oh, by the way, Renaldo, could you check in on Claudius at the Golden Gate? I expect our visiting prophet will be coming back into town by the same way today. Claudius might need a hand."

"No problem, Marcus." And then he added in a more serious tone, "Now, you be careful."

"Yes, well," I said, sighing, "I think we've all got to be careful."

I swung the trunk up under my arm. With a quick wave of my free hand, I said, "I'm off for an appointment with Jesus of Nazareth."

4

Seven in the morning, Monday, April 3

IN A FEW short minutes, Benjamin of Alexandria was on the streets of Jerusalem outfitted in flowing robes and phylacteries. He appeared at ease, in his element, like a devout fish enjoying a swim in a bowl of holy water.

At least I hoped that's how I looked to others. I was far less at ease within. I was making my way to the same city gate on which I had stood just yesterday.

I felt naked. Twice naked. First, I was on the street without my breastplate, my sword, and my armor, and second, I was beardless. Beardless in the bearded Jewish world. I had wrestled over this fact for some time last night. But then clean-shaven Jewish men are not so rare at Passover. Just yesterday I saw two such wretches, looking as I now felt. It's part of their purification rites, purification from the polluted Gentile world.

The city was beginning to stir.

Camels. The reek of camels was everywhere.

I wish by the gods they would keep those smelly, sullen beasts out of Jerusalem. I swear every Jew in town must have eight brothers who come with three camels each to stay at his house for Passover Week.

Just ahead of me, a boy of about fourteen was collecting dung from behind one of many beasts in his charge. The father overseeing his efforts overflowed with instruction. Suddenly the man turned in the narrow street, and we were face-to-face.

"Ah, a naked Jew!" He gestured at my face with a grin. "Shalom, my friend!"

"Shalom," I responded. His greeting put me at ease.

"Tell me, friend, do you know the best way to reach the Golden Gate from here?"

"I am going there now." I cast a hesitant glance at his camels. "You could follow me, or I could give you directions."

"Micah, get your brother to help you water the camels. I'm going with this gentleman. I'll be back soon for breakfast."

I had company whether I wanted it or not.

He turned again to me. "Did you see that prophet from Galilee come into the city yesterday?"

"I saw him. But who really is this man? See, I'm from Alexandria. I don't know anything about this man or why he would cause such a stir."

"I'm Timaeus from Damascus." He fixed his eyes on me and offered a tight smile in greeting.

"Benjamin." I nodded my greeting.

"Well, Benjamin, your accent tells me you're not from here, and neither am I, so we can talk like foreign experts."

We started to walk.

"As for this Jesus of Nazareth?" He shrugged. "I know only a little more than you. My brother here in Jerusalem knew nothing about him. Had never heard the name. But I heard of him once, about a year ago, in Damascus."

"In Damascus?"

"Yes. I'm in the linen trade." He put his hand to an elaborately embroidered sleeve and stroked the pattern. "We supply market stalls in Galilee. One of our sellers there told me of this prophet. He had seen him in Galilee."

"So what did he say about him?"

"Actually, he told me quite a lot, but I don't know how much I can believe. He said this Jesus worked miracles."

"Miracles? What do you mean, miracles?"

"He said Jesus drove out demons, healed the sick. He told me about this one time he went out to hear this prophet, if that's what he is. Jesus was on this hillside. Thousands had come to hear him speak.

Matthias—that's the man's name—he said he had never heard anyone speak like him. 'It was like heaven was talking.' He kept saying that. 'It was like heaven was talking.'"

Timaeus spread his arms heavenward in mock imitation. "Poor Matthias!" He shook his head.

"So was that the miracle? The way he talked?"

"No, no. It's not that, though Matthias kept going on about 'the kingdom of God.' Whatever that is. I suppose he got that from this Jesus. Anyway, after they had been there all day—he said there were more than five thousand people—this prophet told them all to sit down in groups of fifty or a hundred. Then he prayed and started breaking bread. He fed that whole crowd. Every last one of them."

"What's so miraculous about that?"

"Matthias said he only had five loaves and two fish when he started. He was watching him, and Jesus just kept on breaking bread until the whole crowd was fed. Five thousand people."

"Five thousand people?"

"More than five thousand people." He shrugged incredulously. "Look, I wasn't there. I'm just repeating this fool's story. Matthias kept saying, 'It was like he was giving himself to us! Like it came from inside him!'"

Now I was incredulous. I paused in my walk and asked, "What did he mean by that?"

"I swear by the altar, I have no idea."

"So what do you make of this Matthias and his story?"

"Matthias? He's a nutcase. And he's from a fine family in Capernaum." He frowned, shaking his head. "I know them well. It's hard to believe he'd get into something like this. He's following this prophet around the country. It's all he talks about. He was probably up some tree yesterday breaking off palm branches." He spat out the words in utter disgust.

"And Jesus of Nazareth?"

He raised a stout index finger and waved it in my face. "There's the real nutcase! There's no nut like a religious nut! And this kingdom of God talk. It'll end in disaster."

He glanced about to see if other ears were listening.

I continued in a more hushed voice. "How do you mean? Do you think the Romans will get involved?"

"Look, I'm no prophet, but by the throne I swear." He looked me square in the eyes. "You don't preach about a kingdom in this place and get away with it. Rome will see to that!"

"I was hoping to hear this prophet myself. Now I'm wondering if I should."

Timaeus sighed. "Go. Go hear the man," he said flatly. "Judge for yourself. I have better things to do with my time."

We were approaching the gate. There was a pause in our conversation. It seemed we had no more to say.

Suddenly Timaeus recognized a familiar face among the dozen or more men standing idly on either side of the customs booth. He waved and called the man by name. They clapped each other on the back, and I watched them shuffle back into the city with a heavily laden donkey in tow.

About thirty paces from me, Timaeus spun around, waved, gave a quick nod in my direction, and then he was gone.

5

Eight in the morning, Monday, April 3

AS I WAITED for Jesus to return to the city, I had time to collect my thoughts. I was feeling less naked, more at ease in my role.

I was on familiar ground now. This gate, the Golden Gate, was my own gate. Its security was one of my responsibilities. Yet here I was, incognito, whiling away the morning hours, waiting for a would-be messiah. The whole thing seemed preposterous. If I thought too much about it, my stomach knotted. The Jewish authorities would not look kindly on this bit of undercover espionage if I were discovered in this role. And my commanding officer knew nothing about this deception.

Nevertheless, in light of the risks as I saw them, I felt justified in my actions. After all, the Golden Gate was alternately called the Messiah Gate. According to legend, or prophecy, the Jewish Messiah would one day arrive and make his grand entry here. Perhaps he already had. Yesterday's crowd seemed convinced Jesus, this Galilean prophet, had done just that.

I felt my tactics were paying off. Meeting Timaeus was like finding a gold ring in a boar's snout. I could hardly believe my good luck. A dozen paid informers couldn't have netted me more information. The gods must be smiling on me, I reasoned. Why not press on?

As the rays of the early-morning sun cast long shadows into the valley below, I could see the first of many people making their way down the Mount of Olives on their way to the city. I had seen it a thousand times before. There was nothing unusual about it. This was not the frenzied pilgrim crowd of yesterday. It was more what you would expect on a market day, a busy market day, because this was Passover Week after all.

Soon the customs booth was particularly busy. Jonas, the tax collector, was in an almost jovial mood. His greedy eyes were smiling, though he struggled valiantly to maintain his tax collector's scowl. His eldest son and even his wife had been pressed into service, though she stayed in the back.

I was buoyed by the success of my conversation with Timaeus. My disguise had proven effective. I began to loiter about the entrance as I had seen so many other Jewish men do on so many other days. And I was not alone. Other men and sometimes entire families were obviously waiting to rendezvous with relatives, friends, or business partners. There was a good deal of hugging and greeting when these events occurred, and in most cases the party would then move on, into the city.

I was pleased to see my men carrying out their duties as prescribed. I had put Claudius in charge of the gate shortly after his arrival from Rome. He had a good mind and seemed to instinctively know what made for good security. In addition, he knew how to handle men—when to bark, when to bite, and when to wag his tail. Only time would tell if he also had a good nose for sniffing out trouble.

The sentries were in place, two on either side of the gatehouse exterior—that is, by the outside wall—two on the interior or city side of the gate, and two by the customs booth. I avoided eye contact with these men for fear of recognition. I tried not to worry too much about this possibility. Experience had taught me that all too often sentries have mastered the art of sleeping with their eyes wide open in broad daylight.

In addition to the sentries, a two-man foot patrol was now on a morning stroll down the Kidron Valley. Claudius also had dispatched four two-man patrols from this gate on to the city streets. Of course, there were the usual manpower assignments above the gate and along the western wall. All this was according to my instructions of the previous day.

But what about this prophet from Galilee? Would he be back?

Within an hour or so, it became apparent I wasn't the only one asking that question. The trickle of people arriving at the gate began to swell. Soon it became a crowd. From overheard fragments of conversation, I could tell that many of these people were in yesterday's pilgrim throng. Others were like me—the curious from the city. The entrance area of the gate became clogged with humanity.

Claudius came halfway down the gate stairway and bellowed, "Move on out! Move out!" while making a sweeping gesture with his arms as though shooing chickens out of the yard.

It worked. The crowd repositioned itself along the outside wall on either side of the gate.

Within minutes the gateway was clogged again with new arrivals, and Claudius descended once again for a repeat performance. There was a distinct sharpness to his voice this time.

Again the crowd responded well. The people on the outside wall made room for the newcomers, and all eyes were fixed toward the road coming from the Mount.

Would the prophet appear?

I was now in the thick of this wall crowd. The anticipation was palpable. More people were arriving every minute. Whole families appeared. A mother to my left busied herself organizing her brood of six to ensure none would be lost in the press of bodies. To my right, a father hoisted his young son onto his shoulders for a better view.

I glanced over my shoulder and up at the palisade above the gate. There, Claudius was in animated conversation with Renaldo. Claudius must have called Renaldo over from his position at the Sheep Gate, to see if anything should be done about this unexpected gathering. I knew he was worried.

Then someone ahead of me pointed and yelled, "That's him! He's coming!"

Necks craned. I raised my hand to shade my eyes. Just over the brow of the hill, a figure in white rabbinical robes was beginning his descent into the Kidron Valley. It soon became apparent he was not alone. A clutch of young bearded men surrounded him, and trailing behind was an assortment of wives, children, and barking dogs of both types, canine and human. The whole entourage may have numbered a hundred twenty. There was no donkey today and, to my relief, no thronging thousands. I'm sure there was a collective sigh of relief above the gate as well.

The near-giddy anticipation of these spectators was something I had not expected. I was surprised to find myself caught up in it. The front edges of the crowd by the wall surged forward to line the roadside. Meanwhile, others continued to pour through the gate.

The man to my left stepped forward, planting his foot on my toes. I grunted in pain and instinctively pushed my thumb and knuckles into his ribs. This brought the desired relief, and the man turned to face me. It was the man with the boy on his shoulders.

"My toes!" I gestured.

"Sorry, my friend."

I felt slightly embarrassed by the gruffness of my response. "You're waiting to see Jesus," I offered, stating the obvious.

"Yeah. The kids are crazy about him." He nodded in the direction of the brood to my right. "It's all they talked about since we came yesterday."

I could tell from his accent that he was from Galilee, so I continued. "Do you know much about him? See, I'm a Passover pilgrim from Alexandria in Egypt. All I know is what I saw yesterday."

"That was incredible!" he enthused. "Did you see him come in on the donkey? That's fulfillment of a prophecy."

Then he took on a more distant, thoughtful look, and he began to quote. *"Rejoice greatly, Daughter Zion! Shout, Daughter Jerusalem!"* And now his eyes brightened. *"See, your king comes to you, righteous and victorious."* He slowed for emphasis, and with his free hand stabbed the air. *"Lowly and riding on a donkey, on a colt, the foal of a donkey."*

It always amazed me how these people memorized their Scriptures.

"So, do you think he's"—I hesitated—"the Christ?"

"Shh!" He gestured with a finger to his lips and a glance to the wall. "Or the stones will hear."

He continued. "There is no one like him. He drives out demons. He heals the sick. Even the dead have been raised. And yesterday"—his voice raced with excitement—"yesterday I saw this with my own eyes. He healed a man born blind."

Seeing my interest, he pressed on.

"In the morning, we were leaving Jericho, the whole throng from Galilee, and by the side of the road was this blind beggar. He was yelling, *'Jesus, Son of David, have mercy on me!'* Jesus stopped and touched the man's eyes."

He made as though he would touch my eyes.

"And he was healed!" His own bright eyes beamed at me as he smiled broadly. The boy on his shoulders also joined in his father's enthusiasm as for the first time he smiled down at me.

We began to reposition ourselves, for the object of our conversation was now drawing near.

He nudged my shoulder. "And when he speaks, it's like God is talking to me. None of the rabbis speak like him. It's like he has seen heaven and heard the voice of the Holy One."

A girl in her teens near the front edge of the crowd shouted, "Hosanna to the Son of David!"

Soon others joined in. The masses surged around him, and together we squeezed through the Messiah Gate and pressed on toward the temple.

6

Nine in the morning, Monday, April 3

IT ONLY TOOK a few moments to reach the temple grounds. The Golden Gate granted the most direct access to the temple compound from outside the city. I was impressed by the sheer magnificence of the structure when I first arrived here ten years ago. The grandeur, the massive stones, the extensive gold ornamentation . . . taken together, they created an awe in the beholder that even now I find hard to express.

The western wall, which my men and I patrolled daily, directly overlooked the temple compound, so I knew this place like the back of my hand. I knew it, but yet I didn't. There was something veiled from me. Something I could not see, or maybe I would not see. The "could not see" part I vaguely understood. As a Gentile, I was permitted entry only to the Court of the Gentiles or outer yard of the great temple. To go beyond would be to risk death. The inscriptions in Greek and Latin warned of that. But the "would not see" of this veiling went much deeper. I didn't have time to consider it right then.

Another way in which entering the temple compound left me feeling exposed had to do with jurisdiction. Within the temple compound I was truly in Jewish territory. This was the last vestige of the Jewish state. I was within the high priest's domain. No uniformed Roman soldier entered here. Armed Jewish temple guards patrolled this precinct with the power to arrest at will. This was their place, and I was keenly aware of it.

Once again I felt naked. Fear of being exposed gnawed at my mind. At this point it was only the press of people around me that kept me moving forward. It was that and a nudge from the Galilean father—the man with his son on his shoulders. He definitely wanted me to see and hear Jesus.

There were more of this prophet's followers awaiting his arrival within the temple grounds. Our numbers may have swelled to well over a thousand at this point. Keeping him in view from within this multitude of craning necks was a challenge.

We poured into the Court of the Gentiles, with Jesus taking the lead. It quickly became clear that he did not like what he found there.

This whole area had been converted into a market for the duration of the Passover celebration. There were currency exchange tables, caged fowl available for sacrifice, and goods of various and sundry quality arranged for the pilgrims' perusal.

I could well imagine the eager anticipation among the merchants with the arrival of such a large crowd. But this prophet had no intention of leading a shopping expedition.

With a loud, anger-edged voice, he declared for all to hear, *"It is written, 'My house shall be called a house of prayer,' but you"*—his hand slashed through the air to encompass the assembled entrepreneurs—*"have made it a 'den of thieves'!"*

Then seizing the nearest table, he sent it, and all that was upon it, clattering onto the paving stones. The prophet swung around, and without stopping to admire the havoc he had caused, he grabbed a money changer's table, and with one quick move he sent a thousand coins rolling in every direction. The next banker's hoard met with the same fate.

Pandemonium and panic now fully broke loose.

Benches stacked eight feet high with dove cages were next in line. Cages toppled. Birds flapped. Feathers flew. Within moments scores of birds had been released by the prophet's followers.

Frightened merchants rushed for the exits, clutching all that their arms could hastily gather. Within short minutes the entire Gentile court had been cleared of both buyers and sellers.

The transformation was astonishing, the effect upon his followers electrifying. They were in his hands. They loved the sheer power of the moment. With single-handed raw courage he had swept aside the outward clutter of both wealth and religious tradition.

I was impressed. The man had convictions and would act on them.

Timid temple guards skittered about the perimeter of the courtyard, dumbfounded by what they had witnessed, yet fully knowing they were powerless to act before the prophet's adoring throng. This was a coup. In just moments they had lost control—lost it to the leader of a Galilean mob. Explaining this would not be easy.

The crowd pressed in closer, sensing Jesus was about to speak.

"My house," he said, and he gestured to the marble floors and columns that surrounded him. "*My house will be called a house of prayer for all nations.* This is why there is a temple. This is why I have come . . . that we might draw near."

There was no anger in his voice this time, just the sincerity borne of deeply held conviction. Then he turned from the crowd and faced the inner sanctuary, dropped to his knees, raised his hands to heaven, and began to pray.

Since arriving here I had daily seen Jews at prayer. But at no time had I seen anyone pray like this man. It wasn't his posture or his words. I didn't hear a word he said. It was something else. He wasn't praying for the crowd—to be seen or heard by them. I had this sense that he was praying to be connected. Connected to what lay beyond the great sanctuary doors, to what I'm told lies behind the veil in the Holy of Holies. He was connected to that, that part of this place I dare not see and would never dare to go. It was as though he knew the One who was there and was comfortable with him.

I found it odd how these thoughts came to me.

If he was comfortable, I most certainly was not! This was partly due to position. This prophet, Jesus, was too close. With all the movement and rushing to and fro as the merchants were evicted, by some quirk of fate it came about that Jesus stopped and was now kneeling in prayer just six paces away from where I stood. He made me nervous. This reverence for God stuff gave me an awed, eerie feeling. I didn't know how to respond. I never felt this strange unease with the Roman gods.

I glanced at the Galilean father for some direction. But he was gone. I don't mean physically gone. He was, in fact, kneeling beside me, completely lost in prayer. I turned to see how others were responding. Some were kneeling. Others were standing with hands lifted. Still others looked just as stunned and awkward as I felt.

I dropped to one knee to avoid looking conspicuous. How long I remained there, I really don't know. It couldn't have been long; it felt like eternity. I kept wondering what I had gotten myself into. This was not the conduct I had expected from a revolutionary.

The soothing murmur of a thousand spoken prayers filled the courtyard. The voices rose and fell like gentle waves on a shore. There was a quiet peace here, but I was afraid to let it touch me. The soft babble of voices reached a crescendo and then ebbed away.

Jesus rose to his feet. He turned to the multitude. He had the look of the satisfied on his face. Satisfied in prayer? That thought was a stranger in my mind.

Having witnessed the temple cleansing, this crowd had a strong sense of expectation. What would he do now? That was the unspoken question on everyone's mind.

In fact, for quite some time he did nothing. He simply stood there scanning the sea of faces. Then his eyes lit on a young lad, perhaps age twelve, standing to my far right. I had seen this beggar boy about the city many times. Their eyes engaged for a moment. The prophet gave a slight nod of his head—a signal for the boy to advance. He did so with haste. His right leg dangled loose like the limp rags he was wearing. The staccato scrape of his crutch on the stone floor echoed through the hushed courtyard. Eager determination marked his every move. In moments he stood before Jesus. His right leg was easily six inches shorter than the healthy left leg. The absence of any muscle in this stunted limb was painfully obvious, even at a distance.

Like a father, Jesus placed his hands on the boy's shoulders, looked into his eyes, and in a firm voice commanded, "Stretch out your leg!"

The boy's leg began to twitch and stir. Then it kicked forward. Once, twice, three times. With each kick the stone pavement grew closer. The toes stretched forward; the heel pressed down. On the fourth kick, contact was made. Two more kicks, and he had a solid footing. Now he began to jump up and down, up and down, on both feet. Muscle—muscle that hadn't been there moments before—began to appear in his leg. The wooden crutch clattered lifelessly to the floor. He was free.

With one voice the crowd began to cheer and applaud.

"Blessed is he who comes in the name of the Lord!"

The ecstatic smile on this lad's face I will never forget. He glowed. He danced. He danced on the spot a few more times, as if to confirm the miracle was real. Then he buried his head in Jesus's chest and clung to him in a thank-you hug that lasted a full minute. When he raised his head to look into the Galilean's eyes, tears streamed down his face. Joy tears. Thank-you tears.

"I can walk!"

"You can walk," Jesus confirmed.

In fact, for the rest of the morning, he did very little walking. He bounced, jumped, skipped, and ran, but seldom only walked.

I was astounded. I had never seen anything like this. I was seeing the impossible happen. It was happening in front of my eyes. I couldn't deny what I was seeing, but it was challenging my beliefs and everything I knew about the world around me. I kept rubbing my hand across the rough stubble on my chin. It was my way of checking in on reality. I was here. This was real. I wasn't dreaming.

A deep sense of awe began to invade my soul. I felt small—smaller than I had felt for a long time, maybe even smaller than the crippled boy—the formerly crippled boy. He was, in fact, a familiar boy. I saw him about the city on other occasions. Sometimes he would prop his crutch along the stone wall and sit and beg at the Fish Gate.

I was shaken out of my thoughts by a nudge from the Galilean father.

"Didn't I tell you he was amazing!"

"I've never seen anything like this," I confessed.

"When the Messiah comes, will he perform more signs than this man?" He shook his head to confirm the answer to his own question. Then in hushed tones he added, "I tell you, there has never been a prophet like him."

When we looked up toward Jesus again, another child had taken his place before the prophet. This was a younger boy, blind in one eye. Actually, from my vantage point there appeared to be no eye there at all, just a sunken hollow socket where the eye should be.

Quietly, Jesus addressed the boy's father. "How long has he been like this?"

"Since age five." Then he added with an aching tone in his voice, "It was an accident." He would have said more to explain, but Jesus raised his hand to stop him. It seemed no explanation was needed. The blaming, self-torturing thoughts could end.

Jesus placed his right hand on the boy's left shoulder. Then gently he placed his cupped left hand over the empty eye socket. He methodically took a deep breath, as though readying himself for some great exertion. As the breath slowly escaped his lips, he gazed down at the young lad, and with authority he commanded, "Be healed!"

Anxious moments passed. Then slowly Jesus drew back his cupped hand. Eyelashes blinked and fluttered in the harsh brilliance of light. The eye was there, clear and bright.

With two eyes the boy gazed up at Jesus. Then he spun around to his father and yelled, "I can see, Daddy! I can see!"

His father was overwhelmed. With trembling hands, he reached to touch his son's face—to see what wasn't there just moments ago. And seeing the miracle, he fell on his knees before his son and hugged him to himself. He rocked him to and fro, while his strong frame shook with emotion. Then with stammering lips he cried out to Jesus, "Thank you, master! Thank you!"

Jesus helped the man to his feet. But overcome with emotion, this man kept saying, "Thank you! Thank you!" over and over again.

A girl to my right began to sing, *"Hosanna to the Son of David!"*

Soon all the children had joined in her song.

"Hosanna to the Son of David!"

"Hosanna to the son of David!"

"Hosanna to the Son of David!"

Their chant echoed off the marble columns of the temple. The whole of the temple grounds resounded with their spontaneous enthusiasm. The ragged beggar boy, whose leg had been healed, began to skip and jump to the rhythm of their praise. A joyous pandemonium filled the sacred grounds. Everyone seemed caught up in it.

"Hosanna to the Son of David!"

"Hosanna to the Son of David!"

"Hosanna to the Son of David!"

I was, of course, reminded of what I had witnessed from the city gate just the day before. There was a power and energy in this swelling crowd that sent a chill through my body. Where was this all going? The momentum was building. Where would it end?

The jubilation continued.

Glancing to the edge of the crowd, I noticed a stir. An official delegation from the high priest had arrived. Their long, flowing robes were an excellent match for their long faces. There was no joy in that camp. Undoubtedly, they had been fully informed of the eviction of the merchants, and they had been assembled to come and to right that wrong. But now they were witnessing this mass hysteria, this indignity in the holy place. They were righteously disgusted by this public display of emotion and misdirected worship.

As the children's irrepressible enthusiasm began to wane, this high-powered delegation made its way to the front of the throng, where the prophet stood. With a pompous flourish their leader said, *"Do you hear what these children"*—he scowled in their direction—*"are saying?"*

Jesus of Nazareth nodded and smiled. *"Yes. Have you never read, 'From the lips of children and infants you, Lord, have called forth your praise'?"*

The prophet's words, though they were spoken calmly, stung like a slap in the face. Of course this learned scribe knew the Scriptures. To imply otherwise was an affront to his intelligence. But to insinuate that these children, the offspring of Northern rabble now allied with some of the scum of the city, somehow intuitively knew what was right? This was more than he could bear. The man turned purple with rage.

He began to sputter something about the ignorance of the masses but stopped mid sentence when he saw the reaction of those same masses standing directly before him. He and his kind retreated hastily, like humiliated dogs run out of town.

Seizing the moment, a young mother rushed forward, clutching a limp form in her arms.

Upon seeing this mother and child, I was stabbed by pain. Remembered pain. The dark sunken eyes glazed by fever, the pallid skin, the wheezing cough and raspy breath, I remembered it all. The child was racked with consumption. The disease was consuming her, consuming her body, and with it a mother's hope until none was left.

The toddler didn't stir a muscle as Jesus looked into her fevered young eyes.

Experience told me this gaunt daughter would be dead within a week. It was the mother who trembled and pleaded—pleaded for her who lacked even the strength to cry.

"Give me the child," Jesus gently urged.

The request took the mother completely by surprise. Instinctively she clutched the girl even more closely to herself.

"Give her to me."

There was tenderness in that deep voice.

The mother was visibly caught in an inner struggle. I suppose she had held on so long and so tightly that now it was hard to give this frail object of her affection to a stranger.

Their eyes met for an instant. He gave a short nod to his head as if to say, "Yes, it has to be this way." And the struggle was over.

She eased her slumping burden into Jesus's arms. The child's head drooped against his chest. He wrapped a big hand around the girl's head, brushed a wisp of hair from her eyes, rocked her side to side. Then with slow deliberation, he turned from the multitude and faced the great temple doorway.

An intense quiet engulfed the assembly. Moments passed.

"Father . . . Father . . ."

That's all I heard him whisper. He raised his gaze to heaven and then back to the little one in his arms. With the same slow deliberation he turned back to us.

She squirmed in his arms—eyes bright and clear. Two little hands shot out, reaching for her mommy. The smile spoke ten thousand words. The child was whole. Transformed! Completely healed!

The crowd was ecstatic.

"Blessed is he that comes in the name of the Lord!"

"Hosanna! Hosanna in the highest heaven!"

Then for a second time, our eyes met. He knew me. I could see it in his eyes. I don't mean Jesus recognized me. I mean he knew me. Knew me from front to back, from inside out, from my first day till now. It was a dreadful feeling—a naked feeling.

I turned abruptly from him. My heart hammered in my chest. I began fumbling my way through the crowd, desperate for an exit. I had to get away.

But my child . . . my daughter . . .

Why wasn't she healed? Why wasn't she spared?

7

One in the afternoon, Monday, April 3

"I KNOW IT'S hard to believe, but I saw it with my own eyes. His leg grew a full hand span. It happened right in front of me!" For emphasis I gestured at an imaginary spot a few feet ahead.

"Are you sure it was Lucas?"

"Who else could it be? What other kid hobbles along on a crutch and has a bum leg a hand span shorter than the other?"

"Lucas?" Renaldo snorted as he shook his head. He was incredulous.

"It was the same boy I've seen begging at the Fish Gate for the last six months."

"The one with the copper begging bowl?"

"The one with the copper begging bowl," I affirmed with a nod and then added, "Don't believe me? Check it out yourself. The last time I saw him, he was dancing around on both feet. He'll be back at your gate soon enough. But I don't think he'll be carrying his begging bowl or his crutch."

Renaldo looked thoughtful as his eyes scanned the streets of the city below. We were standing atop one of the four turrets of the Antonia Fortress, the hub for military command here in the city. We had finished a light noon meal and then, for sake of privacy, had climbed the stairs to the top of the northeast tower.

"Look, Renaldo, like I said, I wouldn't have believed any of this if I hadn't seen it myself."

"So let me get this straight. This Jesus of Nazareth does miracles, and you saw him do them?"

"That's right."

"He kicked the money changers and merchants out of the temple courts?"

"He went at 'em like a wild man."

"He defied the delegation from the high priest?" Renaldo questioned.

"Sent them scurrying for the exits like bugs under a rock."

"What do you make of this prophet, Marcus? This Messiah?"

Now it was my turn to be pensive. I was so awestruck by what I had witnessed that I was having a hard time sorting through all my thoughts and impressions. The words came to me slowly. "He's not at all like what I expected. He's not at all like a revolutionary."

"So he's not a revolutionary. Then we've got nothing to worry about," Renaldo said.

"I didn't say that." I paused but then added, "He's not like your common revolutionary." I put emphasis on the word "common."

"So, he is a revolutionary."

"His revolution, if that's what he's leading, doesn't seem to be against us, against Rome—at least not at this point." The vagueness of my answer left me feeling awkward.

"Then who is he fighting?"

"He's not exactly endeared himself to the religious establishment. Caiaphas is probably having a holy altar-kicking tantrum right now. Those merchants pay good money to set up shop in there"—I gestured with a sweep of my hand in the direction of the temple compound—"and they're going to be after him to get that Northern hick-town Messiah out of there. Now!" In imitation of their tactics, I made a downward stab with my index finger. "And I mean now."

"So we let the high priest and his clan handle it. They've got the authority and the manpower."

"Not at the moment. Jesus and his followers outnumber those temple guards maybe a hundred to one. I tell you he has the people—the crowd—in his hands. They don't dare move against him."

"Marcus, it's still up to Caiaphas. It's his problem. Let the Jews sort it out."

"I suppose you're right. He still scares me," I confessed. "Scares me like no man ever has."

"Why?" Renaldo queried.

"He's got power like no man I've ever seen." I shuddered inside at the thought of the unearthly nature of that power.

"This prophet really has you rattled, doesn't he?" Renaldo said. "You're still worried, aren't you?"

"Yeah, I'm still worried." Then to justify my concern, I added, "This talk about a kingdom bothers me. Besides, you didn't see what I saw today. It makes all the difference."

"With his grand entry yesterday, he had me scared spitless, so I hear you." After some moments of reflection Renaldo added, "You usually have a great nose for trouble. Let's hope we can head this off."

I appreciated those words. I found this whole experience unnerving. I needed the steady hand of a level-headed friend. In this whole situation, I felt like I was in unfamiliar territory and losing my bearings. I had never encountered anyone like Jesus of Nazareth. At least Renaldo showed some confidence in me.

"So how about you? Did you find anything out?"

"Well, Marcus," Renaldo began with a mischievous grin, "you've got good company. Pedrum is worried too. Scared and worried about Jesus of Nazareth."

"Pedrum!" I scoffed. "What's Pedrum got to worry about?"

"Seems our prophet from Galilee is bad for business."

"Bad for business?" My curiosity was piqued.

"Seems he's got a way with women." With eyebrows raised Renaldo added, "He's been messing with Pedrum's girls."

"Messing with Pedrum's girls?" I was keen to hear the details. Pedrum ran Jerusalem's biggest brothel.

"It's not what you're thinking." Renaldo winked at me as a broad smirk crossed his face. Then he began to elaborate.

"Apparently, Pedrum's lost two of his girls to this Jesus on his past visits to the city. Then last night he lost another one. That makes three now, and there may be more as the week wears on. Pedrum said he messes with their minds. The girls get religion, and the next thing you know, they're gone. They quit the business."

"Poor Pedrum!" I exclaimed in mock sincerity.

"And it's the busiest time of the year!"

"My heart bleeds for the fat bloodsucker."

"There are more troops on the way with Herod coming down," Renaldo said. "Those Northern boys will keep Pedrum's girls busy."

"I don't think it's our job to solve Pedrum's prostitute problems."

"Ah, there you have it!" Renaldo grandly exclaimed. "Pedrum has a problem with Jesus. Our high and mighty high priest has a problem with Jesus. The two need to get together. I'm sure they could cook up a solution."

"Who knows, they just might do that," I said with a wry smile. "And ah, what do we do in the meantime?"

"Nothing."

"Nothing but watch?"

"Nothing but watch," Renaldo stated flatly. But then on reflection he added, "I like what you're doing, Marcus. If Jesus is the people's Messiah, we've got to watch his every move. Then we move if we must. But why dirty our hands if we don't need to?"

"Yeah, I guess you're right." I paused and then said, "I just don't have a good feeling about how this might end."

"As long as our hides aren't in the stew, what does it matter? By next Monday this will all be over. The crowds will be on their way home. In the meantime, Herod arrives tomorrow. And for you"—he poked a bony finger in my direction—"there's Friday to look forward to." He spoke those last words with a lively nod and a wink.

"Yeah," I concurred with a vengeful grin, "there's Barabbas on Friday!"

The remainder of the afternoon was taken up with planning and preparation for Herod the tetrarch's processional from Caesarea. A messenger had confirmed the particulars of his expected arrival time and the size of the entourage. Two hundred horsemen, a hundred spearmen, and two hundred foot soldiers were accompanying a royal party of forty-eight. These details had been known for weeks, but in typical style

Flavio now called a hasty meeting of the centurions under his command to work out how to accommodate this influx.

The mood among the centurions soon turned sour. Space in the barracks was always at a premium. Then there was the problem of the stables. Flavio, of course, was expected to play the role of the gracious host, but how much do you inconvenience your own men to accommodate the troops of a visiting dignitary?

In the end it seemed the horses got better treatment than the men. I proposed tethering our mounts in a line along the outside of the east wall near the Serpent's Pool. That would free the stables at the hippodrome for the arriving cavalry.

The men presented more of a problem. Flavio wanted each of us to shift fifty of our men out of the barracks and into our own villa courtyards. When something nearing revolt broke out over that proposal, the number of men was reduced from fifty to twenty. The remaining thirty men would sleep in the open air along the top of the city walls—a rather chilling proposal given that we had just passed the spring equinox. Of course, it was left to us to inform our troops, and our own wives and families, of these new temporary arrangements.

The bowing and scraping before the powerful had begun.

8

Six in the evening, Monday, April 3

"YES, I SAW him leave. It was about an hour ago. Just like the other time, there must have been a hundred or more followers with the rabbi. They went back up the Mount of Olives," Claudius reported, and then he turned to me. "What's the story on this man? I've never seen anyone cause such a stir."

"He's dangerous," I stated emphatically. "More dangerous than any man I've ever met. Many think he's the Messiah."

"The Messiah? What's with this Messiah notion anyway? Ever since I got here, I've heard people talk about it. What's it about?"

"It's rooted in history—history and religion. It seems religion touches everything here. It's really about regaining past glory. The Jews once, for a short time, were a world power. They had their golden age under King David and his son Solomon. That was hundreds of years ago, but every Jewish child learns about it through the Scriptures. It's like they've never forgotten what that was like. The power, the glory—"

"And the Messiah?" interrupted Claudius.

"Ah, the Messiah!" My eyes glanced heavenward in mock imitation of Jews I had spoken with on this topic. "The Messiah will bring back the glory. That's the great hope—the hope promised in the Scriptures. He will arise, the promised Son of David. The people will rally round him, and together they will throw off the yoke of cruel oppression."

I couldn't help saying this with a melodramatic flourish. I was warming to the topic now and pressed on.

"Oh, and the kingdom? He'll restore the kingdom! There will be peace and prosperity, and every man will sit under his own fig tree and drink from the fruit of his own vine."

I paused in my theatrics.

"There's only one problem in all this." I cast my gaze on Claudius, inspecting him from head to toe, then turned on him in mock derision. "Why, it's you! You're the problem." And with those words I gave Claudius a playful, but aggressive shove. "You pagan Roman dog! Get your blood-sniffing nose out of here! This is our land."

After a snicker at Claudius's surprised reaction, I added, "Of course, they don't say that to your face, but that's what they mean. That's why you watch your backside. And why you watch prophets from Galilee. And why you have long ears like a mule. You never know what they're plotting." I paused. "Terrorists sprout up like weeds in this Judean soil."

"They're not all like that," Claudius said.

"Of course not. But there's enough of that nationalist, chosen-people mentality to affect everything. They have a sense of national history and national destiny. They're not like any other people we rule. They really are different."

There was a certain grudging respect in my words.

"The mistake I made when I first got here was thinking they were all out to get us. That just isn't true. When you think that way, you're bound to make mistakes." I gave a slow, thoughtful nod and then said, "I tell you, Claudius, there's no joy in crucifying an innocent man."

I paused to let the weight of my words sink in before going on. "In reality, most men don't care one iota about who rules over them. As long as their bellies are full and there's a woman in their bed at night, they're happy. It's the hungry young wolf you watch out for."

"So this prophet, this rabbi"—Claudius gestured with an open upraised hand—"is he one of these wolves?"

"What I saw and heard today makes me think so. He's the biggest, sharpest wolf I've ever seen. And that's why we're having this little talk. Tomorrow I want you to go and check out his teeth."

Eyebrows shot upward. I knew I had my nephew's full attention now.

"You're a new face around here. You're far less likely to be recognized.

You'll wait at the gate like those pilgrims this morning and then join with them as they head into the temple when Jesus arrives."

"Ah." He hesitated. "Are you sure I can do this?"

"I did it myself just this morning. I stood right down there." I pointed to a spot below us. "I watched you shoo the chickens out of the coop." I imitated the sweeping motion he had made with his arm. "And then I spent the morning with Jesus of Nazareth in the temple compound."

His mouth fell open. He was stunned by my words.

"Look, Claudius. We need to keep an eye on this man. I mean what I'm saying. All our lives could be in jeopardy.

"You're a natural choice," I reasoned. "Like I said, you're a new face around here. You speak Aramaic very well—better than I do. And you've got a brain in your head. Right now, you're the best man I have for the job."

I could see he was thinking.

"Couldn't we just get some paid informants or something?"

"Ha! In a case like this, paid informants will tell you whatever you want to hear and collect afterward. How do you think I managed to nail Barabbas? It wasn't with paid informants!" I scoffed at the idea. "No, he'll feel the spikes on Friday because I went out and got the facts on him—myself."

Determined to press home my point, I continued, "Look, there are times in this business when you've got to put your own life on the line. You got to dirty your own fingers. When good men like Hermes and Andreas go down, you don't sit and polish your brass. You get out there and sniff out the stinking truth for yourself. You owe it to your men."

I drew a deep breath and plunged on. "As for Barabbas, he's a tin-pot hooligan. A brainless bloody terrorist!" I spat the words out. "Now Jesus . . . Jesus, on the other hand, there's a different dog on the prowl. He's got followers. He's got a crowd around him. He's got heaven on his side. You don't let Jewish messiahs strut around under your nose and just ignore them."

"So how do I go about this?" There was a mixture of sincerity and trepidation in Claudius's voice.

"Tonight you're coming home with me. Zelda will have some great food waiting. I'll tell you all I know and give you all you need for the job. Then tomorrow you're on."

Still sensing uncertainty, I paused and looked straight into his eyes.

"Look, Claudius, if by the morning you don't feel you can do this, or if I don't think you're up to this, I'll pull you off. I just want you to give it a try. I know this takes a lot of nerve. Not just anyone can do it."

There was a pregnant pause.

"Fine. I'll give it a try."

He said it with a smile and a nod and enough conviction to give me considerable hope for success.

With the arrival of replacement guards, we headed home. We said little as we walked. As we rounded a street corner, our shadows became long titans striding across the gritty cobblestones. In moments the sun would set.

We passed the same sullen camels at the spot where I'd met Timaeus early in the morning.

On reaching the villa gate, the flitting movement of a sparrow caught my eye. It landed on a tangled nest among the lower level rafters. Tiny bobbing heads appeared with mouths agape.

Next thing I knew, two boys brandishing small wooden swords were charging at me.

"Papa's home!"

"Papa's home!"

9

Five in the morning, Tuesday, April 4

THE DREAM BOTHERED me. Bothered me a lot. It had come to me in that half-awake, half-asleep time before dawn.

At first I tried to block it from my mind. But the pain of it cut through like a branding iron searing my mind.

Then I tried to analyze it.

Maybe it was the time of year. After all, Tara died during Passover Week, two years ago.

Maybe it was going into her room last night. I was showing Claudius his bed for the night. It was Tara's bed. A thunderstorm had swept in from the west, so Zelda suggested he stay for the night. The moment I opened the door to Tara's room, the memories just flooded back—memories both happy and painful.

I found it odd how she came to dominate my affections.

When each of the boys was born, I was filled with all the pride common to every father. Above all, I wanted sons. Here were sons I could train. Sons who would be like me. Sons who were my own.

But then Tara came along. I was happy for Zelda. But I greeted Tara's birth with a certain casual indifference. A third child. A girl.

But she won me over. It was her laugh. Her smiles. The way she watched my every move, her greeting when I came home, the curl in her hair, and the lilt in her voice. It all brought joy to me—brought happiness at the core.

When she got sick, I became desperate. The doctors were useless. The remedies seemed to make her ill. As the months dragged by, her condition worsened. She was wasting away with consumption, too sick to cry.

I cried. I cried late at night.

I cried out to my Roman gods. I offered sacrifices at our household shrine.

Nothing helped.

Over and over again Zelda pleaded, "Ask the local god."

So reluctantly I went. I unpacked the wooden trunk. Retrieved it from under the stairway. Put on the local garb. Went to the temple.

I stood on almost the very spot I stood yesterday, the spot where I had watched Jesus heal the children.

I cried out, using all the phrases I had learned since coming to Jerusalem, to this Jewish center of worship. I cried to the God of heaven. The Maker of the universe. The one true God. The Lord God Almighty.

Quietly, I sobbed them out for my little girl.

She died the next day.

And now—now this dream—this cruel dream.

I was standing in the Gentile court of the temple again. Jesus was there. He was talking with the woman I saw yesterday, the one with the sick child. But she wasn't holding her own child. She was holding Tara.

Jesus said, "Give me the child."

But she said no.

She pulled Tara even closer to herself.

How this woman got Tara, I have no idea.

Jesus gently beckoned with his hands extended toward her.

But she was adamant. She would not give Tara up to him.

I was in turmoil. At first I tried yelling at her. But it was like she was deaf, unable to hear a word.

I was frozen to the spot. Transfixed, unable to move. Unable to even form the words. They wouldn't come out.

This struggle seemed to go on in an unending loop. Me, unable to speak—to tell her to give up the child. And she, unwilling to do so.

Finally, she turned away from Jesus. She nonchalantly sauntered over to me, where I stood. Dumped the slumping child into my arms. Turned and walked away.

She was dead. Dead in my arms.

Tara was dead!

I awoke like a drowning man gasping for air.

10

Ten in the morning, Tuesday, April 4

CLAUDIUS GOT OFF to a good start. He showed that natural confidence that comes from being at ease in your own skin. Over the years I have come to believe that you can't be comfortable being someone else until you first are comfortable being yourself. But Claudius demonstrated a certain inborn ease and bearing that is quite uncommon among young men of his age.

Claudius had the further advantage of being raised for the most part in the Syrian city of Antioch, hence his fluency in the Aramaic language, commonly spoken throughout this region. Last night I also discovered that despite his earlier questions, he was quite well acquainted with Jewish customs, thanks to the large Jewish community in that city.

Unlike me and the other centurions here, most of the regular Roman troops were, in fact, Syrians. Only a minority were from Rome itself, the largest segment of these true Romans being the governor's own Praetorian guard.

As for the Galilean prophet, he arrived right on schedule and in the prescribed manner. If anything, the crowds awaiting his entry were even larger today. Undoubtedly word had spread about yesterday's miraculous healings.

From the safety of my gate-top vantage point, it was with a certain sense of relief that I watched Claudius disappear into the press of pilgrims bound for the temple.

Better him than me.

Jesus so unnerved me that I couldn't bear the thought of going in there a second time with him. Everything about him set me on edge. The last straw came yesterday, in that brief instant when our eyes met. His eyes were double-edged daggers that penetrated my soul. It was as though my life was laid bare before him, like he grew up with me—knew me to this very moment.

What a stupid notion! Why was I even thinking these thoughts? Why did a momentary encounter leave me with such a soul-wrenching impression?

I was beginning to understand what Pedrum said about the prostitutes. Jesus messed with their minds, he'd said.

I firmly resolved not to let this prophet mess with my mind.

Fortunately, there was a great deal to occupy my thoughts. Preparations for Herod the tetrarch's arrival were now fully underway. The expected arrival time was late afternoon. The only thing still in doubt was the ceremonial route. Proper protocol would dictate that Herod be first welcomed to the city by Pontius Pilate. However, on his previous visits here, Herod Antipas was notorious for giving the governor the royal snub. Stooping before Rome was not something any of the Herods did particularly well.

Pilate, from my perspective, appeared to be in a rather conciliatory mood. Wishing to play the role of the gracious host, he had dispatched a messenger to formally invite the tetrarch to supper at the governor's palace. Herod's response would determine the final leg of the ceremonial route.

In the past Herod had always elected to proceed directly to his palace on the eastern perimeter of the city, making his grand entry through the Gennath Gate. But should Pilate's invitation be accepted, an alternate fork in the road would be taken, and the tetrarch would make his entry through the Fish Gate on the north end of the city.

I had orders from Flavio to make a thorough inspection of both possible routes. Midmorning found me thus engaged, on horseback, leading a party of six cavalrymen. Narrow, clogged streets presented a problem at the best of times, but funneling a royal party and an armed contingent of more than five hundred men through Jerusalem's maze of streets required plenty of advance work.

All appeared fine until we entered through the Fish Gate. Suddenly, the narrow street leading to the Praetorium turned into an impromptu market, clogged with sundry goods and bartering humanity.

I had never seen this street in such a state before. It must be cleared, I reasoned.

Apprehension was written on the faces ahead of us as we approached single file on our mounts.

Suddenly I saw it . . . him . . . and panic seized me. I spun around in my saddle. Instinctively my left heel dug into my horse's flank as I yanked sharply on the reins.

Startled by my actions, my horse reared and twisted.

It took all my strength and expertise to contain the beast beneath me and to wheel it around in the confined space. After considerable stamping and snorting from the horse, I succeeded.

The mounted soldier behind me threw up his free hand in a silent, questioning gesture.

"Retreat!" I ordered.

This was a feat not easily accomplished in these tight quarters. But to the credit of both the men and the horses, they mastered this tight reversal.

I felt like a cowardly fool in flight as the seven of us withdrew in awkward haste.

It was Timaeus. Timaeus the linen merchant.

I had suddenly recognized him, directly before me at the first merchant's booth. The shock of recognition had thrown me into panic as he turned to face me. He was standing not more than three paces away.

Fortunately, my men, at least the ones farther back in the line, had supposed that some sudden movement had spooked my horse. In fact, they were right, but the movement had been my own.

I now reasoned that Timaeus probably had no inkling of my identity, helmeted and armor-clad as I was. I might have been able to bluff my way onward, but in that instant, there had been no time for second thoughts.

I needed this informant, and I had no intention of blowing my cover in some accidental encounter.

We regrouped on the other side of the Fish Gate and then headed north on the Caesarea highway until we hit the fork heading to the Gennath Gate. It was a well-marked spot. Off to the right on a rock knoll, three roughhewn poles stabbed the sky: Golgotha, the place of the Skull, my Friday assignment, standing at the ready. It awaited the condemned.

We turned left at the fork and followed it down all the way to Herod's palace. Aside from dodging the odd puddle from last night's storm, there was nothing remarkable about this route, though it did provide more room to maneuver.

The next move lay in Herod's court. If he accepted Pilate's invitation, the merchants near the Fish Gate would have to be cleared. But that was not a mission I intended to lead.

II

Noon, Tuesday, April 4

IN DUE TIME my party and I arrived at the Antonia Fortress. I was there to report on the morning's reconnaissance work, but first I gave the six men with me their orders for the afternoon. To make room for Herod's cavalry, they were to begin setting up the tether lines for our horses along the east wall near the Serpent's Pool.

After surrendering my horse to one of my men, who took it to the stable, I climbed the first flight of stairs to the tribune's headquarters. The unmistakable smell of cooked cheese curd assaulted my senses. There was a certain familiar squalor to Flavio's briefing room. It was a fitting match with the state of the man. Only off in one corner, where a handsome bronze Apollo stood upon the god shelf, was there a semblance of order. A fresh offering of steaming food had been placed before it.

"Ah, Marcus, have a seat," Flavio called out when he spotted me at the door. Then he motioned to his personal servant and barked, "Get the man something to eat."

The tribune swabbed up a large glob of stringy cheese with a chunk of bread, stuffed it in his mouth, and slowly began speaking as he chewed. "So, Marcus, Renaldo tells me . . . you have your eye . . . on a subversive."

"As a matter of fact, I do."

"Tell me more," Flavio prompted as he reached for another plump barley loaf.

"It's a prophet, a rabbi from Galilee. Jesus, Jesus of Nazareth. That's his name." I stumbled about for words. Flavio didn't respond but kept right on eating, so I felt compelled to continue.

"He caused a huge stir Sunday, when he came into town. Came in like a king. Like he owned the place. The crowds—there were thousands around him—treated him like some conquering hero. It was bloody ridiculous!" I shook my head in disbelief, staring off into the distance, caught up in the memory. "I've never seen anything like it."

"So, what did you do?" Flavio asked.

"I talked with Renaldo, and we decided to have him followed. My nephew Claudius is on him right now."

I didn't want to reveal my direct personal involvement, since I had no idea what Flavio was thinking or where he was heading with his questions. In addition, I was in the dark about what Renaldo must have already revealed to Flavio.

"I knew we needed to do something," I said, justifying my actions. My use of the word "we" was quite deliberate. I wanted to be clear that this prophet was worthy of a group response, and I hadn't acted alone. Renaldo had been consulted.

"Sometimes I think you worry too much, Marcus."

"I worry because it's my job to worry," I shot back. "Barabbas is in prison because I worry."

Flavio appeared to consider my reply as he swallowed another stringy morsel. "So what do you know about this prophet?"

"A lot of people think he's the Messiah."

"May all the gods help us! Another Roman-killing messiah!" Flavio jeered.

"This one just might be the real thing," I said.

"Ha!" he scoffed. "Bring him on!"

He reached for his flagon. Finding it empty, he bellowed, "Where's my wine?"

"Bloody incompetent servants," he muttered. Then turning to me, he asked, "Does he have weapons?"

"No, not that I've seen."

"Has he threatened us?"

"Not exactly."

"Assaulted the tax collectors?"

"No."

"Then leave the Jewish dog alone."

The servant arrived with a bowl of hot, sticky cheese and placed it before me, along with two small barley loaves.

"Wine! Where's the ruddy wine?" Flavio demanded of his harried attendant.

"He is preaching about a kingdom—the kingdom of God," I countered.

"So let him preach."

"Who do you think will be the king of this kingdom?" I reasoned. When Flavio remained silent, I answered my own question. "I'm sure it will be none other than Jesus of Nazareth. I don't think there's room for two kings in this town, and a Roman governor too."

"I see your point," Flavio said.

He wiped a greasy hand across his mouth and then rubbed the three days of stubble on his chin. "So he talks about a kingdom?"

"The coming kingdom," I clarified. "It's the whole point—the core of his message. So I'm told."

The servant arrived with the wine. Flavio helped himself. Drank two-thirds of it in a massive gulp, then poured himself some more.

"And he has followers?" Flavio continued.

"Most of the Galilean pilgrims are firmly in his camp."

"Galilee?" Flavio questioned. "He's Herod's man." He paused to rub the tip of his nose. "I wonder what the Fox thinks of this Messiah."

"You may have a chance to ask him yourself."

"You're right on that." He straightened himself and cleared his throat. "I've been invited to the banquet." He spoke the words with a measure of hubris and then added, "Now, we'll just have to wait and see if Herod, the crafty Fox, takes the bait."

Flavio paused for a moment, then added, "Did you check the routes, Marcus?"

"Yes, the Gennath route is fine, but a market's been set up along the Fish Gate route, and it will have to be cleared if the governor's invitation is accepted."

"A market?"

"It seems that the merchants—the ones our visiting Messiah kicked out of the temple—have set up shop right along there."

"Humph!" Flavio huffed. "So he has caused quite a stir." Then after a pause he added, "Renaldo did mention that."

After another mighty gulp of wine, he announced, "Our messenger should be back from Herod anytime now. As soon as we get the word, we clear the street. But there's no sense stirring that hornet's nest unless we have to. Herod may yet turn Pilate down. So, till we know, we let the traders trade."

"Renaldo could clear that street, couldn't he?" I volunteered. "After all, it's in his sector. This afternoon I was planning to set up the tether lines for our horses along the east wall."

"Yes, I guess he could," Flavio said. "You can tell him that when you leave. Now, about this Messiah—back off. He's picked a fight with Caiaphas, and that weasel is in our back pocket. Caiaphas is nobody's fool, especially when there's money involved. He'll nail that Messiah's hands if he needs to. Don't forget, Marcus. He's the other big man in town."

As I broke bread, Flavio grew philosophical. He shifted back in his chair and then gazed down at his hand. He began playing with the gold ring on his finger.

"It's all about money and power. This world runs on money and power. The two fit together like a ring on a finger." Flavio meshed his fingers together and nodded. He seemed to think the metaphor particularly clever and repeated it for effect. "Like a ring on a finger."

"Don't forget that, Marcus."

Just then a messenger arrived from Pilate. In unison we fixed our attention on the young man standing in the open doorway. He cleared his throat and began, "His Excellency the governor sends word that His Majesty, Herod Antipas, tetrarch of Galilee and Perea, has accepted an invitation to dine at the Praetorium today. The tetrarch will arrive at the fourth hour. Let all be made ready."

Flavio's eyebrows shot up. He turned to me with a satisfied smile. "Marcus, you see to it. I'm off to the bathhouse."

12

One in the afternoon, Tuesday, April 4

"MONEY AND POWER. This world runs on money and power."

Flavio's words echoed in my mind as I left the fortress. That certainly was what Herod's trip to Jerusalem was all about.

It was the empire's worst-kept secret that Herod Antipas was engaged in an ongoing campaign to regain control of Judea. His father, Herod the Great, had built the magnificent gold-clad temple. The imposing palace constructed on the opposite side of the city was a further monument to his father's personal glory, or vanity, depending on your viewpoint. And it had all been lost after his death—squandered through constant family infighting and treachery.

Now the tetrarch of Galilee and Perea was reduced to a mere fourth of his own father's realm. How demeaning!

Tetrarch. Herod Antipas loathed the title. He despised the implied subservience to Rome.

King. Ah, King Herod, that was more to his liking, a title more in keeping with his heritage. Herod Antipas—King of the Jews. There was a title suited to the man.

But Herod was no son of David. He wasn't even a son of Jacob, the father of the Jewish nation. No. He was an Idumean, a descendant of Esau. But by some twist of fate, aided by nimble hands of murder and treason, his father had risen to the top. He had reversed the curse of a thousand years of Jewish history. This latter-day son of Esau had come to rule over his brother Jacob.

And how sweet it was.

But then there was Pontius Pilate. For Herod Antipas, Pilate's presence in Jerusalem served as a constant reminder of what should be his—what Rome had bequeathed to its own son, rather than to him, the rightful heir and successor to his father's throne.

And there was the temple. The temple was the fount of riches that had built his father's magnificent family palace. It had helped finance a thousand endeavors. Religion had its place. It had always served his family well. But now the temple, this focal point of Jewish piety, lay beyond his diminished borders, in another man's domain, under a petty Roman governor. The fount of wealth was no longer his.

Herod Antipas would not rest—could not rest—till justice, as he saw it, was done. A Herodian restoration was what was needed. Was not this his chief ambition, his one great goal in life?

What motivated this Herod was apparent to anyone who had eyes to see or ears to hear. Why, he had even financed his own party of followers to pursue these ends, to curry favor with the proper authorities and to lobby for the return of the whole kingdom.

A king in search of a kingdom. This was Herod Antipas coming to his Jerusalem, the capital that should be his own.

As for Pilate, what precipitated his unexpected move to improve relations with the sly Fox remained a mystery to me. But whatever it was, it undoubtedly had something to do with money and power. On that point Flavio was right. Despite his shortcomings Flavio understood this world and knew very well how it functioned.

As for me, I was concerned about Claudius. I knew I had to speak with Renaldo, to tell him to clear the merchants, but Claudius and I had agreed to meet at the Golden Gate just after the noon hour. I felt at this point that he was my first priority.

From the fortress I took the first stairway to the top of the city wall and proceeded along it. Coming first to the Sheep Gate, I hastily checked if Renaldo was anywhere in view. Not seeing him, I made no inquiries but quickened my pace, hoping I wouldn't miss my rendezvous with Claudius.

Another five hundred paces brought me to the Golden Gate, but

Claudius was nowhere to be seen. I questioned today's assigned gatekeeper, but he had not seen him. I had left very specific instructions with this man regarding Claudius, so he too had been expecting him. Since he was aware of this covert mission, he too was concerned. However, he pointed out that Jesus had not left the temple compound. So together we concluded that the prophet was still teaching his followers, and Claudius was so absorbed in the teaching that he couldn't pull himself away, or he was delayed for some other reason.

It was the possibility of some other reason that worried me.

At this point there was nothing further I could do about Claudius, so I turned my attention back to Renaldo. The mess at the Fish Gate still had to be cleared up. The tether lines had to be inspected, and Herod would be here in less than three hours. I was beginning to feel time pressure, and it was putting me in a foul mood. Worries about Claudius weren't helping matters.

Maybe Flavio was right. Maybe I did worry too much. But then, the drunken dolt should look after his own responsibilities. I resented picking up after him, covering for his drunken incompetence.

I hastily left instructions for anyone seeing Renaldo to send him my way. I was heading back to the Sheep Gate in hopes of meeting him there, and then proceeding on to the stables at the hippodrome.

As I retraced my steps, I brooded over Renaldo's apparent withdrawal of support for my initiative regarding Jesus. He seemed in full support when I began this investigation, and now it seemed he had pulled right back—had opposed me behind my back in his talk with Flavio. My point of view wasn't being heard.

Was I overreacting? I didn't think so. I was convinced this prophet was dangerous. The closer I got to him, the more firmly I held that conviction.

This time as I arrived at the Sheep Gate, I immediately asked if anyone had seen Renaldo. The gatekeeper reported he had been here a short while ago but had left. Again I left instructions that he should report to me immediately for an urgent message from Flavio. I turned to leave.

"Marcus! Marcus!"

I spun around to see Renaldo emerging from the gateway stairway.

"Hey, Marcus! You were right. That boy really was healed."

He voiced the words with such bald enthusiasm that I was completely disarmed.

"I just saw him. He was here—here at the gate." He gestured down the gateway parapet to a point below us. "I saw him. I examined his leg. It's completely healed. Just like the other one. It's incredible!" he enthused. "He can jump! And run!"

"I told you. I told you, Renaldo," I said while shaking my head.

"Yeah, but you don't expect it," he said as he justified his unbelief. "I mean, this kid's been like this from birth. You see him the same way, day after day. And then one day . . . Boom! He's completely different."

"I told you. You didn't believe me?" I uttered the words with a certain smug satisfaction.

"Well, you don't expect it," he repeated. "I mean, it's one thing to hear it, but it's quite something else to see it for yourself."

"That's exactly what I was trying to tell you. I said you've got to see this for yourself to understand."

I sighed. Now I was beginning to realize why I wasn't getting through.

"So it was Lucas," I stated.

"It was Lucas!" Renaldo confirmed, shaking his head in a state of incredulous wonderment.

I changed the topic.

"Look, Renaldo, I would like to talk with you more about this, but we've both got some work to do. Word has just come in to Flavio. Herod has accepted Pilate's invitation. He'll be going directly to the Praetorium. Arriving at four. The Fish Gate route needs to be cleared. You know those temple traders have set up shop in there, and you've got to get them out. And the sooner, the better. Flavio says that's your sector, so you're on."

Renaldo took all this in stride. "Sure, Marcus. I'll get right on it."

I turned from him, but he called after me.

"Marcus. We need to talk more about this Jesus—this Jesus of Nazareth."

13

Four in the afternoon, Tuesday, April 4

THE NEWS OF Herod's arrival spread like flies on a rotting corpse. Before long, people were streaming out of the city and lining the imperial highway from Caesarea in hopes of catching a glimpse of the royal party. Here was a bit of pomp and excitement during this solemn festive week.

Renaldo's assignment had gone smoothly, despite bitter complaints from the merchants. For the second consecutive day, they had been shunted aside by a would-be king. There was no joy among their ranks. In fact, the anger and hostility were palpable. Renaldo later told me you could sense it seething below the surface, ready to erupt—a volcano in search of a vent. But in the end, what could they do? They weren't about to take on the Roman army.

My inspection of the tether lines was uneventful. The men had done a fine job, though I would have preferred having the stakes driven about a horse-length closer to the east wall. This would have afforded at least an hour more shade from the afternoon sun. But there was no time to be fussy. Plenty of other things demanded urgent attention.

I and the cavalrymen with me hastily returned to the stables that encircled the hippodrome.

My groomsman had done his job well in preparation for this event. The time had come to don our ceremonial apparel, and all was laid out in orderly fashion. He began by helping me out of my everyday uniform, a stiff, multilayered, linen cuirass with accompanying greaves. After stripping down to nothing but a loincloth, I was ready to be outfitted in the best armor the empire had to offer.

First I was handed a burgundy linen tunic. This served as a kind of foundation garment over which the armor itself was mounted. Next came freshly polished footwear, followed by burnished bronze riding greaves.

Believe me, the groomsman's help in strapping these on and assuring a comfortable fit was much appreciated. Watching the other men struggle unassisted made me thankful for an extra pair of hands.

Next came the highly polished muscled cuirass of brilliant brass. It was rather like strapping on a tortoise shell. Its double hinges on either side joined the breastplate to the backplate. The left half of this hinged shell was commonly left open, thereby granting access. Having by this means slipped myself inside the cuirass, my groomsman slid a leather strap through the two rings on either side of the first hinge. By drawing the leather strap tight, he was able to align the two matching parts of the open hinge, and slide in the metal hinge pin, thus securing it. This process had to be repeated four times: one hinge just below the arm opening, another one at the waist, then one at the top of each shoulder.

The end result should be a tight yet comfortable fit, with the muscled cuirass fitting perfectly to the contour of the body. May the gods help the slovenly man who put on weight.

The time had now come to strap on my belt–the cingulum–with its loin-protecting strips of studded leather. The sword with its highly ornamented scabbard was also attached to the belt. The gold pattern found on the scabbard was incorporated into the hilt, the handle, and the pommel of the ceremonial sword.

Next, gold-fringed epaulets were fastened to the brass shoulder rings, which in turn were used to secure the scarlet riding cape. It was the epaulets and cape that above all else served to distinguish a mounted officer from the rank-and-file cavalrymen out on the field.

Finally came the highly embellished helmet, which by my own choice was capped with a jet-black horsehair crest.

We took pride not only in our military might, but also in our ability to impress. After all, what glory is there in triumph, if triumph is unseen?

Of course not only the horsemen needed ceremonial dress. The horses too were outfitted in the finest polished leather harnesses, embossed and adorned with silver studs.

I was just completing a walkabout inspection of my horse when I heard my name called from behind me. I swung around to see a very different-looking Flavio, resplendent in burnished bronze armor, mounted on his white charger.

"Get on your horse, centurion," he ordered. "We've got work to do."

The time had come to put into effect the decisions reached yesterday in our joint meeting with Flavio.

"Do a final inspection of the route from the Praetorium back to the Fish Gate," Flavio continued. "I'll lead the cavalry out to their positions along the highway, and then I'll come back to meet you at the gate. Then together we'll ride out to greet the old Fox."

Having said this, Flavio headed off in the direction of the parade grounds, where three hundred cavalrymen were already beginning to assemble.

I mounted my horse, and taking a contingent of ten horsemen with me, I headed to the grand stairs at the east end of the Praetorium. From there we followed the main street leading north to the Fish Gate.

Three hundred foot soldiers had been deployed at regular intervals on both sides of the street. Their job was to ensure the street was free of traffic and to limit the spectators to a single line on either side of the narrow street. Any excess humanity was either ordered off the street or told to move outside the city gate, where there was far more open space. In addition, two cavalrymen blocked every street intersecting with the tetrarch's route.

About halfway along the route, I spotted Renaldo on horseback, having a conversation with two such cavalrymen. I approached.

"All looks well," I said while motioning down the street with a jerk of my head.

He nodded.

"It's a far sight better than when I saw it this morning," I added.

"If we can just keep it this way, till that pompous little jackal gets through here," Renaldo deadpanned.

"You just do that!" I urged. "I'm counting on you."

My party and I moved on. Upon reaching the gate, I waited. Flavio's cavalrymen had taken their positions at regular intervals on either side of the highway, stretching off into the distance for about half a mile. The curious lined the route, up to five deep in places.

After a brief pause, I approached the closest cavalryman and inquired about the tribune's whereabouts. He reported that Flavio had proceeded up the highway as planned and should be returning shortly. Due to the curvature of the road and the rise and fall of the terrain, he was out of sight.

It was drawing close to the appointed time.

Flavio appeared, approaching on his mount. "Marcus, is all well?"

"Everything's clear, right up to the steps of the Praetorium."

"Then we'll be off to greet the tetrarch."

Except for the rhythmic clopping of the horses' hooves on the broad paving stones, we rode in silence, side by side, up the imperial highway. My contingent of ten cavalrymen trailed behind us. Opposite the victimless cross poles of Golgotha, at the fork in the road leading to the Gennath Gate, we stopped.

The road ahead dipped abruptly into a narrow valley, then emerged again on a ridge along the horizon. Within moments a messenger arrived and reported that Herod and his party were just beyond the ridge.

Minutes passed.

Then the tetrarch's standard-bearer appeared along the ridge, like a mirage in the shimmering heat of the sun. The foot soldiers appeared next, trudging in rows six abreast. They were followed by men on horseback four abreast, and then by spearmen. Row on row they appeared upon the ridge and then descended into the valley before them. The king's litter was briefly outlined against the horizon. Then came a cluster of porters, retainers, and court officials, more foot soldiers, more spearmen, more cavalry.

By this time the standard-bearer had arrived before us. A halt was called to the march. Herod's general, his legion commander, appeared before us on a fine chestnut steed.

Recognizing a familiar face, Flavio said, "Greetings, Caius."

"Flavio," Caius responded and nodded his welcome.

"All has been made ready. The route has been secured. The governor awaits His Majesty's arrival."

Again Caius nodded, then cast his gaze down the broad road leading to the city gate, lined with people and marked at regular intervals with mounted guards. He raised a furrowed brow. "Quite impressive, Flavio. I didn't think you were capable of this—this fine display," Caius conceded.

"Ah, you will know me better in the days to come," the tribune answered.

"Shall we inform the king of your fine welcome?"

"Let's." Flavio grinned, obviously pleased with himself and the general's proposal. "Let's do that."

Leaving my ten cavalrymen behind, Caius led Flavio and me back up the highway to his master. We squeezed our way down the right side of the road, past the general's weary troops.

Herod's litter was truly a sight to behold. Borne on two stout fourteen-foot poles by twelve semi-naked men, the luxurious compartment itself was six feet long. In it, both Herod and Herodias reclined, facing each other. The roof of the litter rose from each of the four Doric columned corners to form a peak in the center. On the crown of this peak rested an exquisitely carved golden, ruby-eyed cobra. Each top corner of the litter was spiked with the upturned sweep of a golden horn. Royal purple brocaded silk was used throughout.

The gold-fringed and tasseled drapes were drawn fully open when we arrived, and two short, hairy legs dangled from the litter—legs belonging to Herod the tetrarch.

"Get on your knees, you sons of harlotry!" he bellowed.

The litter bearers promptly responded.

"Now let's have some wine for my queen. And get the crest dusted off."

From behind the litter the wine steward quickly appeared, bearing a gold chalice for Herodias. A young female slave used something resembling a feather duster on a long pole to brush off any offending road dust from the gold cobra on the roof.

It was an odd choice for an adornment or family symbol. It was a choice that appeared even more incongruent because of the religious tradition of this ruler's subjects.

The clatter of our horses' hooves drew the king's attention. Spotting a familiar face among the three horsemen before him, he asked, "Ah, Caius, are we near?"

"Indeed, Your Majesty. The city lies directly before us."

The king poked a balding head out of the litter, but seeing little, he yelled, "On your feet, you swine."

In unison the litter bearers struggled to their feet from the kneeling position.

Herod again peered out, but still seeing very little, he yelled, "Higher, you swine!"

With valiant effort the hapless slaves lifted the carrying poles from above their shoulders, to a position above their heads. To go any higher they would need wings.

Still seeing nothing, Herod shook his head, and in utter disgust he glared at his attendants.

By way of explanation, Caius felt compelled to intervene. "The city is in plain view from the hill just ahead."

"Who asked you to speak?" Herod snapped. Then with an upward wave of the back of his hand, he ordered, "On with us then!"

Shaking off this rebuke, Caius barked out his command. "Forward . . . march!"

The caravan responded, slowly at first, as the message was relayed to the front of the column. We too moved forward, keeping pace with the royal litter.

I felt awkward–out of place. By not acknowledging our presence, Herod had left us hanging–ignored by the king. Flavio in particular must have felt the sting of this.

In a few moments the hilltop was gained. Caius called a halt. The king stuck his head out and peered down the highway to the city.

"Hmm!" He drew in a long, satisfied breath as he assessed what lay before him.

He slumped back into the litter and then began barking out a stream of rapid-fire orders to his attendants.

"My crown. Bring my crown.

"The jeweled robe. Get the jeweled robe.

"Get dressed, Herodias."

Then realizing the litter was still in midair, he ordered, "Down! Get me down, you swine!"

The slaves once again descended to their knees, then leaned fully forward, bringing the litter lower yet.

Herod hopped out, slipped out of a flimsy purple robe and into a gorgeous, jewel-encrusted, gold-trimmed fabrication. When the crown arrived, he snatched it from the cushion before him. Placing it on his bald head, he wailed, "The mirror—get the mirror, you harlots!"

Looking into it, he seemed suitably impressed with what he saw. And satisfied with his appearance, he perched himself on the edge of the litter and looked up.

Seeing his opportunity, Caius again ventured to speak. "The tribune, Flavio here"—he motioned with his hand—"has arrived with greetings from the governor."

"Yes, Your Highness." Flavio bowed. "His Excellency sends greetings. He awaits your arrival at the Praetorium. Marcus here"—he nodded in my direction as I bowed to the king—"has himself inspected and secured the route. We are at your service, ready to escort you to His Excellency."

For a moment Herod gathered his thoughts. Then he fixed his eyes on Flavio. "Appoint ten of your own men to go before us as heralds. Let them cry out, 'Make way for the king!' Many of my own subjects are here for the Passover, and to them I am king."

He spoke these last words as a kind of bitter justification.

Then looking to Caius, he asked, "Are the trumpeters ready with their fanfare? And my own heralds near the litter here, see that they cry out, 'Bow before the king!'"

"I'll see to it," Caius responded and rode ahead a few paces to fulfill these orders.

"As for you two," Herod said with a kind of shrill intensity, "you'll ride alongside the litter. If I cry halt, you will halt. If I say proceed, then proceed. There will be common riffraff along the way. If they touch the litter, kill them. If they touch me—you will die. I'll see to that myself. If a hand reaches out with a beggar's bowl, cut it off. I haven't come here to feed the dogs. Do you understand that?"

We both bowed stiffly from the waist. A moment of stunned silence followed. Flavio was first to recover. "By your leave, my lord the king, I will send Marcus here with the orders for our heralds. When he returns, we may proceed at your pleasure."

"Fine. Be off then." He sneered.

A distinct chill crept through my being as I spurred my horse to a brisk trot. My mind raced. How could I ensure Herod's requirements were met? Brute force may work, but there were no guarantees. Any deranged idiot could get through to the litter if he was determined enough. We had nowhere near enough men to form a wall along the entire route to prevent any such breakthrough.

My chief concern was that none of our troops knew of these new stringent crowd-control requirements that Herod had just dictated. I knew the ten men I was about to meet with could form part of my response, but I needed twelve.

My ten cavalrymen were waiting at the front of Herod's column, just as Flavio and I had left them. I ignored them and rode past. I then beckoned the first two mounted guards beyond them to meet me in the middle of the highway.

"You have new orders. You are now messengers. Hear me. Quickly move along the route from here all the way to the Praetorium. Order each of our men to keep the people off the road—on the threat of death. Have them announce it immediately. Tell them to chase any beggars away. Order them out of sight. Herod wants any hand reaching out with a beggar's bowl cut off. So chase the beggars off. Why should we be that jackal's butcher?"

Looking intently at them, I said, "Did you get that? Repeat it back."

When the man on my left succeeded in repeating the essence of the message they were to transmit, I sent them off.

I returned to my own ten cavalrymen and gathered them around me. "You are no longer armed escorts. Herod wants you as his royal heralds," I reported.

This news was greeted by some with looks of disdain.

"You are to call out, 'Make way for the king! Make way for the king!'"

Even more looks of disdain.

"You need to do that. Call it out. But your real job here is to make sure no one gets on the road or steps out of line back in the city—not so much as a young child wandering onto the route. I have orders to kill anyone who touches the royal litter.

"And no beggars," I continued. "If Herod sees a hand reaching out with a beggar's bowl, he wants it cut off. So watch for them. If you see even one beggar, tell them, 'Herod's men will cut your hand off. Get away! Out of sight, before he comes!' If they refuse to listen or move, draw your sword and chase them off." Once again I added, "I don't want to be Herod's butcher. So do your job well.

"Now I want you to advance in groups of two when we start out." I signaled this with two fingers raised. "Leave about twenty or thirty paces between each pair. Have you got all that?"

I again had one of them repeat their instructions and then had them arrange themselves in teams of two. I wanted no room left for error.

"I'm going back to Herod. When he's ready, he'll give the word, and you'll start." I pointed to the first two conscripted heralds in the processional.

Giving all these instructions had taken more time than I had anticipated, so I stormed back to Herod's litter, fully expecting a rebuke.

I arrived to find the slave with the duster busy fussing over the gold horns on the corners of the litter's roof. Another slave was combing and pinning the queen's hair. As for Herod, he was holding a mirror and cursing the young female slave who was trimming his beard. On seeing me arrive, he brusquely pushed her aside, but then he followed that with a well-aimed leering smile in her direction.

"Your Majesty"—I bowed forward from the waist—"the heralds have been appointed. All is ready. We await your pleasure."

"It took you bloody long enough!" he barked. Then motioning with his hand, he directed, "You'll ride there, on the left side of the litter, just a bit behind me. Don't block my view, or I'll have you castrated. You hear that?"

"Yes, Your Highness."

I would soon discover that Herod's threats were not mere bluff and bluster.

I maneuvered my horse to the back of the litter. Flavio was already in his assigned position, slightly ahead of the open litter, right alongside the front set of litter bearers. I would ride parallel with the rear set of litter bearers. Immediately alongside me was posted a tall brutish-looking foot soldier, apparently one of Herod's personal bodyguards. A bodyguard of equal stature stood alongside Flavio. These men were closest to the edge of the highway and served as the first line of defense should any unruly person from the crowd dare to advance toward the king.

On the right side of the litter, the same pattern was repeated. Caius rode alongside the front of the litter, with an accompanying bodyguard to his immediate right. At the rear right of the litter rode a centurion under his command, flanked by the fourth bodyguard to complete the array.

A further array of twenty-four swordsmen would walk with swords drawn immediately before and behind the litter in ranks six abreast.

The start of the procession was delayed, despite the urgent haste that Herod had called for. Herodias needed more time with her hair, and a perfumer was called to anoint the royal couple. Soon the heavy scent of nard blended with the reek of human sweat.

To while away the time, the muscular bodyguard to my left amused himself by slashing away with his drawn sword at some imaginary foe. At last the Herods were ready. The litter bearers stood erect, and Caius called out the order to advance.

"Now walk like men—not like camels—you swine," Herod hollered out to his bearers.

The first few hundred yards were uneventful. The trumpeters blew their fanfare. The heralds near the litter shouted, "Bow before the king!" And the cowed populace dutifully responded. There were no beggars in sight, and no one dared venture onto the imperial highway. I was confident my own advance men had done their job well.

About two hundred yards from the Fish Gate, Herod caught sight of a white-robed delegation off to his right. Perhaps it was the glint of gold embroidered thread and jeweled adornments that caught his attention. He called a halt to our advance. The litter was lowered, and three of the plumpest white robes were beckoned by the king to come forward. One of them I immediately recognized as Timaeus of Damascus.

I strained desperately to hear the full conversation, but since this delegation stood on the opposite side of the highway, I could only make out a few words. I overheard something about impediments to commerce and so-called prophets misusing the great temple. To this Herod responded with the only words I heard distinctly. "I will meet with you Thursday."

In moments we were off again, only to be halted once more by another delegation on the right. We stopped just before the city gate. It was Caiaphas, the high priest himself, along with several of his family members. They made a great show of bowing low in their elaborate finery. Undoubtedly they were here to welcome this Herod to the city and perhaps to invite him to visit the great temple his father had built.

Herod called them over. But try as I might, I could not make out a single word, though I could distinguish the high priest's voice from the others. His voice always reminded me of the sound of rusty hinges. The creaking somehow cut through the other noises in the air. But I was still unable to decipher what was spoken.

The litter rose once again. We passed through the Fish Gate. I could feel my body relaxing somewhat from the tension. We were over halfway to the Praetorium without incident.

Suddenly, just ahead, among the bowing throng, a small copper bowl flashed in the sun. I sucked in a shallow breath and hoped it had gone unnoticed.

Herod's hand shot out from the left side of the litter, just a few feet above and ahead of my horse's ears.

"There! There!" he yelled. "Stop the litter!"

Flavio bellowed, "Halt!"

"Bring the boy over." Herod gestured to the bodyguard next to me.

The guard beckoned with his hand, and the once crippled Lucas stepped forward. He wore a shy smile, but there was an eager glint in his eye.

"Is that a beggar's bowl in your hand?" the king inquired.

"Yes, sir."

"I didn't come to feed beggars," Herod said coldly. "Now, teach this boy not to beg from a king." Herod again gestured to the guard.

With one hand the guard grabbed the boy's free hand. With the other hand he raised his gleaming sword above his head.

With sudden terror in his eyes, Lucas instinctively yanked back.

The blade flashed down.

The boy fell back into the crowd as the guard triumphantly raised the severed, dripping hand above his head.

"Well done, Cestas!" Herod cheered. "Well done!"

I saw Lucas flee, white-faced and stumbling, clutching tight the bleeding stump.

"There are no beggars in Galilee," the Fox announced to the crowd. "And if I ruled here, there would be none in Jerusalem."

The onlookers were stunned—riveted to the spot.

Herod paused, and after a brief search he pulled out the flimsy purple robe from among the cushions behind him. He made a great show of folding it carefully several times.

"Bring me your trophy."

Cestas came forward and placed the small, severed hand in the folds of the purple robe, bowing graciously to his monarch.

"Ah, tribute for the governor." Herod laughed coarsely. "Let's be off!"

The remainder of the processional was uneventful. Following the trumpeters' fanfare, Pontius Pilate and his wife, Claudia Procula, received the tetrarch graciously, with considerable pomp. The Roman governor politely inquired about the journey and made flattering comments about Herodias and her attire.

As for Herod, he seemed perfectly jovial and invigorated. He commented about wishing to make a presentation of a wee item at the banquet that evening. He committed the purple bundle to one of his attendants, and then arm in arm with Herodias, he accompanied the governor up the grand stairway to the Praetorium.

My duties as a royal escort had come to an end.

14

Six in the evening, Tuesday, April 4

WHEN I RETURNED after my assignment with Herod the tetrarch, I found Claudius at the Golden Gate. He was positively effusive. I had to slow him down so I could understand what he was saying, and I insisted he start at the beginning.

"When we got into the temple compound, Jesus spotted some men carrying goods through the temple courts. He immediately stopped them. I think this was all just a ruse. It was just an attempt by those same merchants to set up shop in there again. He saw right through it and sent them packing.

"Then he began teaching," Claudius continued. "I've never heard anyone teach like him. It was so different."

"How?" I asked. "How was it different?"

He thought a moment before answering. "I guess it was the examples—the parables he used. I didn't always fully understand what he meant. I guess it's because I'm not a Jew, but when I understood, I really understood. I suppose it's because his parables would take a certain truth and make it simple, something you could grasp. He talked a lot about the kingdom of God."

"The kingdom of God," I huffed. "So, tell me about this kingdom of God."

I spoke the words with a certain disdain. After what I had witnessed in the past few hours, kings and their kingdoms had lost their appeal. I was in no mood to be regaled with accounts of conquest and might, not from some power-hungry would-be Jewish Messiah.

Claudius could sense my reticence, but brimming with enthusiasm, he pressed on anyway. "I'm really not sure that the kingdom he's talking about is anything like what we call a kingdom. Actually, the more I listened to him, the more I became convinced he's talking about something totally different."

"So what's so different about this Jesus and his kingdom?"

I could tell I really had him thinking now.

"Well, Jesus?" He was struggling for words. "I've never heard anyone like him. It's like he knows God. I mean really knows God—the God who made everything—like they sat down and planned the world together."

I couldn't help but chuckle at this notion, but at the same time I understood exactly what he meant. I had watched Jesus pray. I had sensed both the power and the mystery of those moments.

"Did you notice that too?" he asked.

"I guess I did," I admitted. "But . . . he just gave me this eerie, uneasy feeling, like he was connected to someone or something far bigger. And I was small—smaller than I've ever been."

"Hmm," he mused. "I know what you mean. I felt that way too." But then he was struck by another thought.

"But he talked about God like a father—not far away, but near—near as the next breath. And as though he cares, really cares about us, not like our Roman gods. He said we shouldn't worry, because our heavenly Father knows what we need. He even knows if a sparrow falls, and he knows the number of hairs on our head." He impulsively ran his fingers through his dark brown hair and then added, "I heard him say that."

I fell silent. But I wanted to snap back at him. Snap back about what I had just seen happen to Lucas. Snap back about my daughter, Tara. Snap back about a thousand and one injustices I saw in this botched-up world. Caring? Where was this caring God? But after a long pause, I just changed the topic.

"Yeah, but this Jewish dog talks about a kingdom. You still haven't told me about his plans for this glorious kingdom."

Claudius must have noticed the hard edge to my voice, because he began more tentatively. "If I understood him correctly, it's where God rules. It's where his will—God's will—is done. I don't think it's so much a place, a physical place, as it is a state of the heart—a place where people know God and love and obey him. I'm really not sure that he's here to overthrow Rome."

"Then why is he here?"

"I'm not sure I really know," Claudius said. "I guess he wants to somehow connect people with God—get them together. Connected—like he is connected with God."

"Humph!" I sniffed at this notion.

Claudius went on. "One thing I do know for sure: those fancy-robed religious leaders don't like him much. Jesus had taught for a while this morning, when all of a sudden the high priest, along with maybe ten other officials, came marching in. They demanded to know by what authority he was doing these things. He didn't answer them, but instead he asked them a question. He asked them, 'By what authority did John baptize?' They talked it over and then said, *'We don't know.'* So he said he wouldn't answer their question either. They just turned around and left in a holy huff. You could really tell the crowd around Jesus just loved the way he handled these high and mighty holy types."

Claudius abruptly turned to me and asked, "Who was this John anyway?"

"A few years back he caused quite a stir. Thousands of people went out to the Jordan River to hear him. He insisted that people repent, turn from their sins, and then he would baptize them in the river. Even some of my own men went out to hear him. In the end, Herod the tetrarch had him beheaded."

After reflecting a moment on the day's events, I caustically commented, "That bloody old Fox hasn't changed much."

"Anyway," Claudius continued, "from then on Jesus would teach for a while, and then some new high-powered delegation would arrive to question him. They weren't sincere in their questions. It was like they were trying to trap him into saying something they could later use against him. That's all I think they were after. But in the end Jesus always turned the tables on them. He exposed their real motives. He saw right through them."

I felt a certain remembered discomfort when Claudius said those words. After all, Jesus's eyes had shone a light on the darkness of my own soul. I don't know why I felt so naked, so transparent before this man.

"But, Claudius, what makes you so sure he's not here to kick out the Romans?"

"It was the way he answered one of those fancy-robed delegations. They asked him if it was lawful to pay taxes to Caesar. He called them hypocrites right to their faces. He accused them of trying to trap him. Then he asked for a coin. He demanded to know whose portrait and inscription were on it. When they answered, 'Caesar's,' he jumped on them—like a cat onto a nest of mice. *'So give back to Caesar what is Caesar's, and to God what is God's,'* he told them. Even at a distance, I could see their mouths drop and their ears catch fire. They left like cowering dogs with their tails between their legs."

Claudius became even more animated as he said, "The crowd—the crowd loved it. You could really tell the people loved seeing those phony religious officials get a taste of a little humility. I'm sure they haven't tasted it for a good long while."

Then to conclude, he said, "That's why I don't think he's a threat to us. He's not opposed to paying taxes. Nothing he said all day makes me think he's got a quarrel with Rome. But he's sure got the religious leaders worried and bothered. Later in the day he went after them full force. Called them hypocrites, blind guides, a brood of vipers!"

"Ooo! I'm sure they were pleased," I said sarcastically.

This assessment confirmed what Renaldo and I had been thinking. I had heard the same thing reflected back to me by Flavio. This latest evidence on taxes lent considerable weight to the conclusion Claudius had drawn. But I still felt uneasy. Jesus simply struck me as such a huge, larger-than-life figure—the kind of person you don't dismiss lightly, no matter what others say. I somehow felt that all we had done thus far was scratch the surface. I'm not sure I really understood him at all. How could I begin to fathom what he was trying to accomplish?

But Claudius wasn't done.

"You know about this kingdom notion," he said. "Jesus told another story, and it helped me catch what he was driving at. He talked about a landowner who planted a vineyard and then went away. He rented the land out to farmers, but when he sent servants to collect the rent, the farmers would beat the servants or kill them. Finally, in desperation he sent his own son to collect the rent, thinking the farmers would respect him. But the renters said, 'Let's kill him and the land will be ours.' So they took the son outside the vineyard and killed him.

"Then Jesus asked the people around him what would happen to those renters when the owner came back. They answered that the landowner would kill those miserable renters and give the vineyard to someone else who would pay him on time.

"Jesus said they were right. And then he said, now catch this"—Claudius gestured with an upraised index finger—"'*The kingdom of God will be taken away from you and given to a people who will produce its fruit.*' Those were his very words."

"So what did he mean by that?" I asked, quite mystified.

"I wasn't too sure myself at first. I knew he said this as a rebuke to the high priest and the religious establishment. Everyone there knew he was telling this story against them. But later I asked the man beside me what he thought Jesus meant by this parable. He said the landowner was God, the religious leaders were the renters, and the servants who came to collect the rent were the prophets of the past. We just weren't sure who the son was. I suggested that Jesus himself might be the son. But he just looked at me like I was a complete idiot, shook his head, and said, 'God doesn't have a son.' I kept my mouth shut after that."

"Well then," I surmised, "this prophet, this Jesus, really has set himself up in opposition to the religious authorities. If he's publicly predicting the end of their rule, he has picked a fight with them."

I sucked in a long, slow breath. "And, Claudius"—I nodded in his direction—"it'll be a fight to the finish."

I continued as my mind caught the implications of my own words. "Jesus may have the people or at least a good number of the common people on his side. But Caiaphas is nobody's fool. He's got money and power behind him. The son in that story, if that's who Jesus is"–I gestured with an upraised open palm–"he might yet be taken out and killed."

15

Seven in the evening, Tuesday, April 4

MOST OF MY conversation with Claudius had taken place as we slowly ambled along the top of the city wall, from the Golden Gate, past the Sheep Gate, and on to the Antonia Fortress.

An official reception, complete with a hearty meal, had been planned for the arriving troops. While Pontius Pilate entertained Flavio, Herod Antipas, and the tetrarch's general, Caius, inside the governor's palace apartment, the common soldiers feasted in the central courtyard of the fortress. Huge cauldrons of thick stew had been simmering over charcoal fires for a good part of the day. By the time we arrived, they were almost empty. Their contents had been ladled into the soldiers' pewter bowls, and the men were now scattered about the courtyard, some sitting on crude benches, while others ate, bowl in hand, standing in diverse clumps.

Claudius hurried off to retrieve his own bowl from within the barracks, while I made my way to a kind of second-level dais overlooking the courtyard from the north side. This is where the centurions dined.

A long table had been set up, and on either side of this table, the centurions were already seated. Most had just begun their meal, which unlike that of the common soldier, consisted largely of roast lamb.

I took a seat at the only spot left open. It was at the far end of the table, across from one of Herod's centurions. To my left sat Marius, one of the centurions from our own legion.

There was a fine bit of good-natured banter going on when I arrived. At a suitable moment, Marius introduced me to the two men across from us, and I bowed in greeting.

There was something vaguely familiar about the man across from me, but at first I didn't recognize him. Perhaps it was due to the lighting. By this time the sun had gone down. Even as we arrived, torches were being lit and then fastened to brackets in the stone walls along the perimeter of the courtyard. Due to his seating position, this centurion was turned away from one of these torches, and very little light hit his face.

Soon a servant arrived with my meal, and I began to dine.

Wine flowed freely. Voices became more boisterous. Bouts of hearty masculine laughter echoed through the night air.

At one point the man seated across from me turned his head sideways, so I clearly saw his profile. I recognized him as the centurion who rode escort duty across from the litter bearers and me during Herod's entry just a few hours earlier.

The conversation grew more coarse as discussion turned to women and their ways, then on to feats of strength, then feats in battle. I was attentive, but brooded in silence, partially distracted by the events of the day.

Then with his lips loosened by ample wine, the bellicose man across from me piped up. "Did you see Cestas today? He sliced off that little beggar's hand like he was cutting through butter. Sure taught him not to beg. Did a freakin' fine job! I couldn't have done it better myself. Taught a real fine lesson. A mighty fine lesson."

My left hand shot out across the table. I seized him by the metal collar of his breastplate, yanked his body fully across the width of the table, slammed my right fist full into his face, and then flipped the stunned brute off the side of the table.

I pinned him to the floor and yelled, "I'll teach you to keep your bloody butchers out of our town!"

I hammered him once more. And I would have done it again, but Marius restrained me, shoving me back on my heels.

I shot to my feet and pressed forward, shaking with blind rage.

Voices were yelling all around me.

I shook free of Marius and his hold on me. Then I stormed down the stairs and out of the military compound.

Out . . . out into the night.

16

One in the morning, Wednesday, April 5

AFTER I KNOCKED repeatedly, Arius the gatekeeper finally arrived and opened the barred wooden gate.

"Master!" His voice betrayed a measure of surprise. "Welcome home."

I acknowledged him with a hasty nod, then began briskly striding across the courtyard. Suddenly I stumbled and nearly fell over the feet of a sleeping soldier.

Ah yes. Thanks to Herod, or was it Flavio, I had twenty men camped out in my villa courtyard. In the moonlight I threaded my way around them to reach the stairway leading to the family bedrooms on the second level.

I passed by our own bedroom and quietly moved on to our sons' room. Gently taking hold of the worn leather strap that lifted the latch, I slowly eased the door open. I was amazed that for once, the hinges didn't creak. I lightly inched my way into the room.

The boys slept on two separate beds on either side of the room. A full moon was visible through the broad, open window directly ahead of me. I listened for their steady breathing and waited a few moments for my eyes to adjust to the light level. Then with slow, deliberate steps, I moved to the bed on the right side of the room. I stooped and ever so gently grasped the hand of my older son, Julius. I heard him swallow, but he didn't wake. His breathing continued with that soothing rhythm common to a sleeping child.

His hand was warm . . . small . . . a perfect hand.

Perfect fingers.

A perfect little hand resting on the palm of my own large, rough hand.

I let go of his hand, straightened, turned, and with the same slow, deliberate steps, I moved to the other side of the room.

I took the hand of my younger son, Andrew. Held it in mine. Felt its warmth and life. Laid it gently down.

I turned to go, then felt impressed to stop in the middle of the room, between my two sons. I raised both of my hands about shoulder height, palms open, much as I had seen Jewish men do. While slowly raising my head, I whispered, "God of heaven, take care of my sons. Take care of my sons."

I eased the door shut behind me and through the dark shadows, shuffled to my own bedroom.

This time the door creaked when I opened it.

"Marcus?" Zelda whispered into the darkness. There was worry in her voice.

"Yeah, it's me." I sighed. I began to undress.

"Marcus, I was so worried. Are you all right?"

"Yeah, I'm fine." I paused a moment or two. "I nearly killed a man, but I'm fine."

"Marcus!" Now I really knew she was worried. She threw back the covers and bounded out of bed. She was at my side in an instant, pulling me close to herself.

"Are you sure you're all right? Come to the window so I can see you." She tugged lightly on my sleeve.

"Just let me get this off," I said, referring to my tunic.

I knew she wouldn't be satisfied without a full inspection, so I pulled the garment over my head and tossed it on a bench. I was glad to be free of it after such a long day.

"Come. Come now to the window," she urged.

"See? I'm fine." I began to speak the words before we even arrived at the window, before she had a chance to look.

She reached her hand to my chin and turned my face from side to side in the moonlight, searching for the bruise or cut that wasn't there.

"Your 'all right' isn't always all right," she chided.

"I'm fine. See?" I said, reaching out to place my hands on her shoulders.

"You're fine all over?" she asked, quite in earnest.

"I'm fine all over."

I drew her close and wrapped my arms around her as a form of proof.

"I was so worried," she said, looking up at me. "You said you would come home with the other men. They started coming, and you weren't with them. Claudius didn't know where you were. Nobody knew. You know I don't like being alone with all those rowdy men down there."

I heard more than a hint of anger in her voice, and she drew back a step.

"I know. I know," I said, trying to be reassuring. "I just had a horrible night—a horrible day. It was awful."

"So you got in a fight?"

"I guess you could call it that. I beat somebody up."

"I hope he deserved it."

"Oh!" I nodded my head. "Oh, he deserved it. Deserved far more than he got."

Then changing the topic, I added, "You know I'm getting cold standing by this window." I hugged her warm body close to me again. "And furthermore, I'm tired, very tired. I think we should go to bed before I collapse in a heap."

"Ah, you poor man," she said with a deep, melodramatic sigh.

We crawled under the covers. And she received me gladly. We loved each other. In her arms I found happiness.

It was the only good thing about the day. Like so many other days, she and the boys often were the only good things about my day—about this life.

17

Four thirty in the morning, Wednesday, April 5

IT STARTED RAINING about two hours before sunrise.

I heard curses—men cursing in my dreams. It took a while to realize the curses were coming from the men downstairs in the open courtyard. It seems soldiers are never fond of getting soaked while they sleep.

The rain had started sporadically at first. It almost stopped but then began in earnest. That's when it roused all the men. Arius had the good sense to open the kitchen door and let some of the wet and irritated soldiers sleep on the floor in there. More room was found in a storage shed near the gate and even in the hallway of the servants' quarters. Nevertheless, when I got up in the morning, I found four men sleeping on mats on the second-level balcony just outside our door.

The rain was steady and the sky uniformly gray from horizon to zenith and down to the distant horizon again.

Our household cook was summoned. He reported that breakfast was ready as planned. Any men still sleeping were roused. A thick, heavy porridge was dispensed into tin bowls using a wooden hand paddle. The men ate in grim silence.

Together we slogged off through the pouring rain to the barracks at the Antonia Fortress. My men assigned to sleep along the top of the wall were already there.

They had not fared much better. When the downpour started, most of them had left the wall and had crowded into the city gates at ground level. Until sunrise, they were forced to make do with the meager shelter the gates afforded.

Due to the weather it was an equipment day. Swords were sharpened. Spears were repointed. Shields were oiled. Bridles and halters were tended to. Footwear was repaired, and clothing was mended. The legion's smiths and cobblers were a busy lot.

I called for an equipment inspection in the early afternoon, all the while hoping the rain would stop and the sky would clear. It was a faint hope. This weather had all the earmarks of a two- or three-day general rain, something we hadn't yet had this spring. With their crops freshly planted, there would be many a happy farmer in the land, but I was left feeling anxious.

What worried me most was a chance encounter with Herod's centurion, the one whose face my fist encountered the night before. I worried about a revenge attack, or worse yet, that he might bring the matter before Caius, or, may the gods have mercy, before the gold-crowned Fox himself. The threat Herod made yesterday still rang in my ears. Over the years I had become affectionately attached to every part of my anatomy. I would fight any loss to the point of death.

I was beginning to think I liked the pretend-king on a donkey far better than the pretend-king carried on a gold-encrusted litter.

I had planned to send Claudius back into the temple compound to continue his undercover education at the feet of Jesus of Nazareth, but the rain killed that plan. Hardly a soul stirred from the homes, and the temple area with its broad open-air courtyard was largely deserted.

I busied myself in the stable workshop attaching some silver adornments to my horse's ceremonial bridle. It was the kind of work I could have easily left to my groomsman, who was employed alongside me, tending to other cavalrymen's needs. But throughout my twenty years as a soldier, I have always enjoyed this type of leatherwork, and furthermore, I was occupying a spot where a chance meeting with my prime rival from Herod's ranks was highly unlikely.

Due to the menial nature of the work, I soon found my thoughts turning back to last night's events. For a time after my fight with Herod's centurion, I had wandered aimlessly about the city streets. I was so filled with rage, I could barely control myself. I clenched my fists over and over, digging my fingernails into the palms of my hands. Even today I could see the red marks left in my palms. I knew I needed time to calm down or I would kill someone. I was so incensed. I needed to get out of the city, to get alone.

I wandered out of the Golden Gate and down into the Kidron Valley. An olive grove ran along the slope of the Mount of Olives. In the Aramaic language, it was called Gethsemane. I had gone there before to think or to clear my mind after a particularly difficult day. I felt drawn there now.

Fortunately, there was sufficient moonlight to guide me. I avoided the dark shadows and moved slowly, not fully trusting my footing on the uneven path that led into the grove. Soon, off to the right, I heard male voices speaking in quiet tones. Instinctively my right hand came to rest on the pommel of my sword. I need not have worried. Possibly a dozen men were sitting or reclining around a white-robed figure in the shadows about twenty paces off the path. They ignored my passing as I hurried by.

I made my way farther up the slope, finally stopping at a bare rock outcropping from which I could faintly perceive the outline of the city walls and the silhouette of the great temple on the opposite slope. Here I sat down.

Just getting out of the city brought a measure of calm to my spirit, but almost immediately anxious thoughts flooded in. Beating up a fellow officer in an unprovoked fight as I had just done could result in dire consequences. There were consequences I didn't even want to think about. If I were called to account for my conduct, running off, as I also had just done, would do little to advance my case. All these thoughts troubled me.

For a time, I seriously considered returning to the city, considered getting thoroughly drunk to forget my troubles, even considered visiting Pedrum's brothel for a little physical pleasure to ease the anguish in my soul.

Briefly I even considered ending it all by jumping from the Pinnacle of the temple, that high point on my section of the wall that dropped cliff-like into the Kidron.

I got up to do one or all of these, when suddenly I remembered Jesus. I remembered the words Claudius had attributed to him—about the Jewish God knowing if even a sparrow falls, and about him knowing the number of hairs on my head.

Was this God watching me now?

Did he care even one wit about what happened to me? About what happened to Lucas? About what happened to Tara?

The crickets chirped. A million stars illumined the sky. Every breath I drew was filled with the moist, fresh scent of life—the life of spring. A gentle breeze stirred the leaves of the nearby trees. Even in this darkness, stark, quiet beauty surrounded me—assaulted all my senses.

I thought of death—thought of life—thought of family. I thought about all the apparent contradictions in this life, thought about this God who cares, and yet somehow terrible things happen to innocent people.

How could this almighty God, working through a mortal man, heal a crippled boy one day and on the very next day allow the same boy's hand to be cut off by some demon in human flesh?

I shook my head in bewilderment.

Then I thought about the deep contradictions in my own life, about my own actions, the darkness in my own past.

Does anything make sense?

I sat down again.

I prayed, bowing forward in the direction of the temple. Poured out all my troubles, all my frustration. Prayed for the beggar boy. Prayed as though someone would hear.

After a long while, I got up and went home.

I didn't understand it. I didn't understand life or God or this man called Jesus. I understood the mess I was in, and it felt good just to speak out my frustration.

Maybe I didn't just speak my words into the night air. Maybe someone in the broad, starry expanse above did hear me. In any case, I left the hillside strangely at peace, more willing to face tomorrow and whatever anguish or joy it might bring.

✣ ✣ ✣

"So how's our banquet table warrior?"

Renaldo's voice cut through my thoughts, bringing me sharply back to the present.

"Oh, I'm fine," I answered with a quizzical grin as I looked up from my work. "Banquet table warrior? Is that what I'm called now?"

"That's your new name, Marcus. Banquet Table Warrior. Marius thought up your new title. We all think it has a certain ring to it, a certain flare." He gestured grandly with his right hand as he beamed. He was obviously enjoying some good-natured humor at my expense. Then he added, "You did a mighty fine job on that bigmouthed idiot. A mighty fine job! All our men were quite impressed."

"I wasn't trying to impress our men. It was Herod's man who needed his brain rearranged."

"Oh, you did a fine job of that. A fine job. I couldn't have done better myself."

I hadn't expected this jocular admiration from any of my fellow centurions. But Renaldo continued. "Look, those strutting cocks needed their tail feathers kicked good and hard, and the sooner, the better. If this hadn't happened, they'd be running the place by the end of the week. They need to know their place. They're our guests, not our bloody masters."

"So what happened after I left?"

"That bigmouthed idiot screamed for your head. Marius told him he'd be dead before sunrise if he opened his mouth about this to Caius. He told him he was in our fortress now. Told him to sit down and shut up. And he did. He sat down with his fat bloody lip and drank until he was so drunk that they had to carry him down the stairs. I don't expect we'll see him at all today. If he's smart, he'll keep his head down all week."

My eyebrows shot up when he said these words. I nodded and smiled, knowing that a camel's load of worry had just been lifted from my mind.

"No, Marcus, you did us all a big favor last night. A huge favor. The whole week will go better because of it."

"Do you know why I clobbered the bonehead? It was 'cause of Lucas. They cut off his hand yesterday. During the entry."

"Cut off Lucas's hand?"

"Yeah, cut off his hand." I spoke each word with slow, emphatic deliberation. Then I made a downward chopping motion with my right hand, as though I were hacking off my own left hand at the wrist.

"They did it right in front of me. Right in front of Herod. It was at his orders. The bloody butchers! Thought it was great fun. It was Cestas—Herod's bodyguard. He did the job. Then that boneheaded centurion bragged about it last night at the banquet. That's when I let him have it. Bloody butchers!"

"The man's lucky he's alive." Renaldo's eyes narrowed. "I'd have cut him to pieces," he declared through clenched teeth.

I had no reason to doubt his declaration. Renaldo knew Lucas far better than I did. On occasion he had used him to run small errands, despite his stubby crippled leg. Afterward he would drop a copper coin into his beggar's bowl.

"I can't believe it." Renaldo shook his head. "What kind of bloody idiot would cut off a kid's hand! Why? Whatever for?"

"Because Herod hates beggars—hates the poor." I seethed. "He told me, 'Cut off every beggar's hand, everyone with a beggar's bowl.' I sent ten of our men ahead to chase off the beggars, but they must have missed Lucas. Maybe he wasn't even there when my men passed by. Anyway, Herod spotted him. And wham! It was over."

Again I made the slashing motion. Again my blood was beginning to boil. The rage I felt last night came surging right back. I turned from Renaldo and hammered the flat of my fist down on the workbench behind me. Tools and rivets bounced and rattled. The sharp pain of this action shot through me.

At least I had a hand I could abuse.

Renaldo was silent for several moments. I turned back to face him. He stood with his head bowed. He pinched his eyes closed several times, sighed deeply, and repeatedly clenched his right fist. I half expected him to do the same as I had just done. Instead, with a determined, calm voice, he asked, "What did Lucas do after this happened to him?"

"He just ran off, holding the bleeding stump. It happened so fast. There was nothing I could do."

"He'll be at Pedrum's," he said, "if he didn't bleed to death—if he's still alive."

"Pedrum's?"

"Yeah, Pedrum's." He sighed and rubbed a big hand across his chin. "His mom is one of Pedrum's girls. After his father died, they lost everything. Some moneylender—a Pharisee—took it all. They moved into the city, and she got a roof over her head by selling the only thing a woman like her has left to sell."

Again he pinched his eyes shut, shook his head, and said, "Lucas will be there."

He turned from me and began walking away. But he called back, "I'm going to get him. I'll have the legion doctor take a look at him."

He stepped out into the rain and was gone.

I stood in silence. The steady patter of rain on the crude workshop roof seemed to calm my mind. After a few moments I let out a deep sigh and then shrugged. Maybe on the hillside last night, my words didn't just drift into the still night air. Maybe they were heard?

Maybe . . .

18

Seven in the evening, Wednesday, April 5

"BELIEVE ME. HE'S one tough kid." Renaldo let his breath escape with a low whistle. "He took it like a man—like a true soldier. I told him to, and he did. Took it a far sight better than many men I've seen."

Renaldo was responding to my question regarding Lucas and his treatment at the hands of the legion's doctor. We were relaxing around the pool at the Roman bathhouse at the close of the day.

"There's no way he would have survived if I hadn't got him out of there. No way! Pedrum said he wrapped the stump the moment he got to the house. His mom was busy with a customer, so he said he did the best he could. Wrapped some dirty rag around it and tied it tight with twine. Because it was tight, I guess it probably saved his life. But an amputation like that needs proper care. Not what you get at a brothel." Renaldo sniffed in disgust.

"So what did the doctor say?" I probed.

"First he cauterized the wound—and wow, that really was quite the ordeal!" Renaldo cradled his own left hand as though he himself had endured this assault to his flesh. "Then the doctor soaked the stump in some good strong wine, and he told me to bring the boy back tomorrow. He said he'll probably pull through, but he needs proper care and good food. The wound needs daily cleansing with wine and later with oil."

He paused and combed his fingers through his wet hair before he continued. "I took him home. He's at our house now. Junia managed to get some broth into him before he fell asleep. Tomorrow she'll give him a bath, and I'll take him back to the doctor. That brothel is no place for him."

"I won't argue with you on that point. What did his mom say? Did you talk to her?"

"Yeah. I think she was relieved. She was crying the whole time. I told her we'd look after him until he was better. But she just cried harder. I think it bothers her that she can't really do anything for Lucas. I said she could come see him at our house if Pedrum would let her come. Pedrum agreed, and that seemed to settle her a bit. When I picked Lucas up in my arms to leave, she fell at my feet bawling. She said, 'Thank you. Take care of him.'"

Then after a moment's reflection, Renaldo said, "I guess time will tell if she comes to see him."

"Or if Pedrum actually lets her leave," I caustically added. "I wouldn't trust that slithering snake. Remember, for him and his kind, it's the busiest time of the year. He'll let her go see Lucas if it's to his benefit to let her go, not because of some great sense of compassion."

"Sometimes I think you're too hard on dear old Pedrum. He's probably got a heap more compassion than the Pharisee that seized their land. At least he doesn't cover up his greed by standing and praying in the marketplace by day and then sneak off at night for some fun with the nearest harlot."

Renaldo turned to face me as he continued. I could tell by the intensity in his eyes that he was warming to his topic. "You know that Pedrum tells me some of those fancy-robed religious men are his most regular customers. They're Jewish experts in the law by day, and then come dressed as Gentile whore hunters at night. A real fine bunch! If there is a hell in the afterlife, like these Pharisees so confidently claim, I'm sure it was made just for them."

"Oh, oh, oh!" I laughed and waved a cautionary finger in his direction. "How can you say that? Why, I always thought they were holier than God himself." There was an ample supply of sarcasm in my voice.

"Holy! If that's holy, I'll drink all this bath water! It's all show, and you know it. From start to finish! If you're rich and can parade around in fancy clothes, heaven's gates are open wide." He gestured by throwing his own strong arms wide open. "But may the Almighty help the poor working dog. They'll cheat him out of the rags on his back, steal the crumbs off his table, and then they'll stand and brag about it in front of all the other fat swine. Fat swine!" He spat out the words and shook his head in disgust. "That's all they are. Fat swine in long, fringed robes showing off their fat phylacteries."

"Now you're beginning to sound like Jesus of Nazareth," I said.

"Jesus?" he asked. "What did he say about them?"

"Called them a brood of vipers. Called them blind guides and hypocrites. Said it right in the temple courts. That's what Claudius told me."

"Well then, there's one Jew who's got them pegged. There are no bigger hypocrites in this world. Say one thing and then do the opposite. That's what they're all about."

He drew a deep breath and grew reflective. "You know, I half believe in their one true God. It makes more sense than our Roman concoction of deities. But I won't bow before him so that pack of bloodsuckers can lord it over me. Besides which, to them we're just Gentile dogs, the filth of the world, untouchable and unclean. They would never take us in if we even wanted to follow their God. And who'd want them to?" he scoffed. "If they did accept us, we might become just like them."

"You know, Renaldo"—I quickly scanned his towel-clad frame and then winked as I said—"I think you would look really handsome in some fancy flowing robes."

He whipped the towel from around his waist and gave it a vicious flick that cracked against my hip. I laughed, stepped back, and planted my feet, ready to counterattack with my own towel, but a second assault never came.

I waved a hand in surrender and said, "Look, I understand what you mean."

Though he smiled weakly, I could tell he was genuinely annoyed by my levity. To show my sincerity I added, "I've been thinking about my own beliefs since that donkey-riding prophet rode into town. He seems to have a way of getting my attention."

"Hey, Marcus, you've got to tell me how that prophet healed Lucas. How did that leg grow like that?" He gestured in bewildered amazement with an open, upraised hand.

"It was incredible! It was just like I told you the last time. Somehow Jesus signaled for Lucas to come up. He put his hands on the boy's shoulders and then told him to stretch out his leg. It was like that limp rag of a leg came to life. The leg started to move. It was as though Lucas kicked downward, and with each kick the leg grew longer. Then he was touching the ground, and he started to jump—to bounce up and down."

I found myself mimicking these movements. I reached down and ran my hand along the back of my calf as I said, "Suddenly there was muscle in that leg—muscle that wasn't there just a moment ago. It was incredible! Just incredible!"

Renaldo shook his head, and then he rubbed his hand across his brow as he absorbed this account.

"You know, Marcus, all Lucas would say while the doctor was working on his stump was, 'I wish Jesus was here!' He whispered it over and over again. I think it's what kept him going through the agony of that treatment. I honestly think the boy believes Jesus could heal his hand. I don't mean heal his stump. I mean give him a new hand. Grow it right onto that stump."

I threw up my hands in a questioning gesture. "Who knows? Who knows what Jesus can do? I thought I knew what was possible and what was impossible, but I don't anymore. Not after what I've seen."

Renaldo hung his head in thought, then raised it to look me in the eye and ask, "So do you think he could heal him?"

"I said I don't know. I don't know a lot of things I was sure of before. There's a power there I've never seen before. It's a power that's not from this world. I'm not even sure if he's from this world." I paused and then added, "And I have no idea where this will all end."

I sat down again beside the pool and let my feet dangle in the tepid water. Renaldo put his hand on my shoulder as he eased himself down into a similar position.

"So what do you mean by that? How do you think this will end?" he asked.

"This Galilean prophet's days may be numbered. He's stirred up a hornet's nest by kicking those merchants and money changers out of the temple. He's offended and humiliated the high priest and his clan. He's cut off a major source of their temple revenue. He called the Pharisees a brood of vipers. And if that's not enough, he predicted that their power, their kingdom as he calls it, will be taken from them and then given to others."

I paused and kicked my right foot out straight, scattering a shower of drops onto the flat surface of the water. "You don't say and do those kinds of things without creating some enemies. I'd say he's sealed his own fate."

With a furrowed brow, Renaldo asked, "Where'd you get this information?"

"Claudius. Claudius told me. Yesterday I had him sit in on one of the prophet's teaching sessions. It was quite an eye-opener. Jesus doesn't just heal the poor; he takes a skewer to the bloated rich. He's publicly opposed the rich and powerful in this town, and his opposition has been right to their face. If nothing else, the man's got courage."

I drummed my fingers on the poolside tiles and then continued. "I tell you, Renaldo, they won't stand for it. They're probably hatching some plot to do away with him right now, as we're sitting here talking."

"Yeah, but he healed all those kids," he said. "Doesn't that show that the God of heaven is working through him?"

"The God of heaven? Do you honestly think that matters to them? This is all about money and power. That's their real god. Jesus is a threat to their money and their positions of power. Healing a few poor kids, the offspring of the unclean—that isn't going to mean a thing to them. You're right. You hit the nail on the head. They're puffed-up swine that care only about themselves. There isn't a drop of mercy in them." Then with scathing irony I added, "But they're right. They're always right. Right to the letter of the law."

"So what do you think they'll do?"

"I'm not sure. But I know what they won't do. They won't arrest him with that crowd around him. They know better than that. They'd have a bloody riot on their hands. There's no doubt about that."

Thought after thought came racing in as I considered the implications of my own words.

"They might wait till after Passover when the crowds leave, but then Jesus would probably leave with the crowds and head right back to Galilee. Then he'd be out of their hands. No." I hesitated and then briskly snapped my fingers. "I think they'll try to act now, if they can. He's humiliated them in front of the people. They won't stand for that. Caiaphas won't stand for it. Jesus has co-opted the high priest's authority right within the temple courts. Blood will flow because of it. Mark my words. It will flow."

"But what could they do to him? What crime has he committed?" Renaldo reasoned. "You know the Jews can't condemn a man to death. They can't have him crucified. They would have to bring him before Pilate."

"Yes," I said, "but accidents happen in the dark of the night. And Renaldo, I think you underestimate the old Weasel. If anyone can twist the law to his own liking, Caiaphas can. That Weasel can kill his prey in more than one way. The big question is, can he get his hands on the prophet?"

"So you really think there'll be a confrontation?"

"Absolutely. From what I saw on Monday, the confrontation has already started. It started when Jesus kicked out the merchants. Later, when I was there, the high priest's men questioned him, but he wouldn't back down. Then yesterday, according to Claudius, he humiliated Caiaphas and his delegation right in front of the crowd. Like I said, he called the Pharisees and the teachers of the law a pack of hypocrites and a brood of vipers. I'd call that a confrontation. And he didn't do it out in the desert; he did it right in front of them, in front of the pilgrims, and right in their holy place. I tell you, the man's got guts."

"But"—I paused to emphasize my point—"I'm just waiting for the other side to strike back. And they will."

I made a long, sweeping motion with a pointed index finger and then stabbed down spear-like into my friend's bare ribs. "I'm sure they will."

Instinctively Renaldo recoiled, shrugged off my antics, and then said, "But you don't think he's a threat to Rome?"

"Not from what I've seen or heard. But he is a threat to Caiaphas. Right now he's their problem. And that's where I want to leave him. If blood's going to flow, I don't want it getting on these hands."

19

One in the morning, Thursday, April 6

My feet felt the sharp bite of cold, wet snow the instant I dismounted. Our military objective was spread out before us, nestled along a wooded valley beneath lead-gray skies. A light haze of woodsmoke hung over the village, hinting at places of warmth in this bleak winter world.

The clustered huts were now surrounded. Their fate was sealed.

With an upraised wave of my sword, I signaled our position and our readiness to my centurion commander stationed on the dark forested slope on the opposing side of the valley. His own signaled response called us forward.

The noose was in place. Now we tighten it so none can escape.

In unison we rushed forward, swords drawn, bucklers held at the ready, swift but silent. Surprise was our sharpest weapon.

Our orders were clear. Spare none. Vengeance must be swift, utter, complete. Barbaric justice for barbarians. Nothing else would do.

I rounded the corner of the first hut, and all but collided with a child—a girl.

Thhuuck!

My sweeping blade caught her just below the ribs, slicing three-quarters through her slim torso.

Her blond head snapped back in shock.

Questioning blue eyes shot upward, looking me full in the face.

I felt a hot, red gush cover my sword hand.

‡ ‡ ‡

I sat bolt upright in bed. Trembling. Sweat drenched. Chest heaving. Heart pounding.

I fumbled to bring my two hands together, expecting to touch blood. But I felt none—none that I could see in the blackness of our bedroom.

Zelda's hand touched my shoulder. I pulled away, swung out of bed, and stumbled to the window.

Again I wiped my left palm across my right. In desperation I squinted and strained as I tried to focus. But even here at the window on this dull overcast night, only the faint outline of my hand was visible. I brought my trembling right hand—my sword hand—to my face. I touched my nose and mouth. I anticipated feeling the warm stickiness of blood.

It was dry.

My shoulders heaved. My breath came in enormous gulps. I sank down, clutching the windowsill for support.

"What's wrong? Marcus, are you all right?"

Zelda was at my side. She touched my brow. Wiped away the sweat. Called my name again. "Marcus?"

Though present with me, Zelda seemed far away, beckoning me from another world.

"It's . . . It's Germania!" I gasped.

She cradled my head in her arms.

For Zelda and me, Germania had become a code word. It signified everything that had gone wrong in my past as a single young man. It was the living hell I endured for eight long years as a common soldier.

Germania was cold destitution wedded to the hot depravity of war. All of it ended in futility with the agony of defeat and a shameful withdrawal across the Rhine. These were wasted years, years spent in the brutality of slaughter. I saw young men—my companions, close as brothers—hacked to death. And for what?

For no lasting purpose.

Germania. The lost province.

I lost more than a Roman province there.

I lost peace. I lost innocence. I lost a province, a part of my being, at the very core of my own soul.

During saner moments, in daylight hours, I could console myself over Germania. Germania brought promotion. It brought rank. I was now a centurion because of my conduct, my combat experience in Germania. But at night when the blond-haired girl visited, this meant nothing. Less than nothing. Rank, position, and this world's honor turned into dross, mere dross, discarded, soul-searing dross.

For long minutes Zelda rocked me, both of us sitting on the floor with our backs against the wall. My throat stinging. My eyes moist.

"Tell me what happened?"

I shook my head. Shook it hard. Shook it over and over.

How could I tell her? What could I say?

The stain was on my soul, though I couldn't find it on my hands. Nothing in this world could remove it.

And heaven knew about Germania.

Heaven knew about the blond-haired girl.

Heaven knew about me. Knew all about me. Knew me to the core.

Isn't that why my own girl—my daughter, my Tara—was dead?

20

Five thirty in the morning, Thursday, April 6

AT THE FIRST hint of morning light, Zelda offered herself to me. She loved me. She had always loved me, even in the worst of times. Why, I'll never know. I drank more deeply from her than ever. It was an aching feast of pure pleasure. Her love was a blanket covering over my guilt-ridden night of despair.

If there is a God, and he made me to experience a woman like this, he must be good. He must be very good.

But why did he make us to know pain?

I lay exhausted but satisfied by her side. She was the anchor that held me. Loving her sustained me. In times like this she kept me from falling into the chasm at the center of my own soul, a chasm that had opened up in Germania and had grown wider ever since.

I met Zelda back in Rome after my eight hellish years in Germania. My mother and her mother were close friends. It wasn't an arranged marriage. It was a suggested marriage. My mother suggested I meet Zelda. After that first meeting I was the one who did all the suggesting.

As I dressed, Andreas came to mind. Why, I don't fully know. Maybe it was the memory of all the blood spilled in that nightmare. Maybe it was because he was simply another good man lost, and my hideous dream had reminded me of all those other good men lost in Germania. But Andreas was a good young man lost right here in Jerusalem.

I'll never forget finding his body dumped on the street, just a few steps from our front gate. An early-morning wake-up gift, courtesy of our local terrorists.

Bloody Zealots.

I had worried about my sons discovering the huge bloodstain on the cobblestones, so I covered it with sand and then had Arius sweep it up. Even so, a discolored patch remained. Perhaps all this rain had finally washed it away.

Remembering Andreas reminded me that I had Friday to look forward to. Tomorrow Barabbas would finally get his due. I had the blacksmith make a special set of spikes just for him. I personally planned to do the honors. Both Andreas and Hermes would be avenged. Rome would answer back, blood for blood. We would have the last say.

Breakfast was a more cheery affair. The rain had stopped during the night, and there were beginning to be some breaks in the cloud cover. Our twenty-man crew from the previous night had been reduced to only eleven as additional shelter had been found in every nook and cranny of the Antonia Fortress. The same had been done here within our villa. Last evening the courtyard was still being soaked by an intermittent drizzle, and there was a sizable puddle in a depression near its center, so space had been found for the men indoors.

My two sons were up early, and they made a happy nuisance of themselves as they plied the soldiers with questions. Claudius was great with the boys. They soon were the center of attention, a position my older son, Julius, particularly enjoyed.

The boys followed us out onto the street as once again we set out for the Fortress. I gave each of them a boost so they could see into the sparrow's nest. The bobbing bald heads of the hatchlings peeked out, expectant mouths wide open.

I sent the boys back to their mother and turned to quickly scan the cobblestones where Andreas had fallen. The dark stain was finally gone.

The day was looking far more promising, but within me I felt a certain unease. I couldn't put my finger on it at first, but then we passed a gaudily clad man. It was Timaeus as he emerged from his brother's home. I immediately remembered where he was going. He was on his way to his prearranged audience with Herod.

Perhaps this was the cause of my unease?

As I fully expected, Timaeus turned and headed in the direction of Herod's palace. There was no fear of recognition this time. I was on foot with my men, and he paid scant attention to us. He was intent on his destination.

Was the noose being drawn around the prophet from Galilee? I couldn't help but think so. I expected Timaeus to get a sympathetic hearing before Herod. When money talked, Herod always listened, and Timaeus represented money, international trade, commerce, all the fine things this life offered.

I could well understand the linen merchant's frustration. For the first two days of the week, Jesus of Nazareth had co-opted his market space—the best market space in town. On the third day, the Roman army shut down his street stall so Herod Antipas could parade into town. Then yesterday the Almighty joined the conspiracy against him by sending a deluge. And today? Today was the first day of the Feast of Unleavened Bread, the day to slaughter the Passover lamb. Everyone was occupied with the preparations, which meant it was hardly a suitable day for much buying and selling.

From a business standpoint, the week thus far had been an unmitigated disaster. Only Friday remained before the Sabbath, and Timaeus and his associates were determined to get the temple compound back into business for Friday, thereby salvaging at least a small portion of this wreck of a week.

Only this Galilean prophet, this rabbi of the rabble, stood in their way.

I knew Timaeus would never go before Herod alone. He'd be part of a well-dressed, well-prepared delegation. They would make their case before the Fox, and as sure as the sun rose this morning, the Fox would lament that if he were king here in Jerusalem, this travesty would never have taken place. His righteous indignation would be stirred. But that's all he could stir since he had no authority here. This was Pilate's playground.

But Jesus was from Herod's jurisdiction, and the conniving tetrarch was well aware of the prophet's effect upon the masses. He had heard of his miraculous powers and had hoped he might somehow harness them to serve his own kingly purpose. If the reports he had heard were true, then this roving rabbi could turn water into wine. If this were so, then perhaps he could also turn lead into gold. If he could feed five thousand, why couldn't he feed an army bent on conquest? If he healed the lame and the blind, and it had been the talk of the whole region, why not have this miracle worker heal those wounded in battle? The possibilities seemed limitless.

Herod's desire to meet Jesus was genuine, but that desire extended beyond mere curiosity. After all, what good is a royal subject if he isn't subject to his king? Perhaps this prophet could be useful. As in everything he did, the Fox had a purpose, an overriding purpose, a kingdom-gaining purpose.

A flock of bleating sheep came streaming toward us, distracting my thoughts and bringing me back to present Passover realities. Four foul-smelling shepherds were directing their flock down the street at the north end of the temple compound. The male yearling lambs were on their last journey. Their fate too was sealed.

The morning was uneventful. I had Claudius back in uniform at the Golden Gate. I had him watching for the arrival of the Northern Messiah. But there would be no activity today. For the second consecutive day the prophet was a no-show. Even if he had arrived, I fully resolved to leave Jesus to the temple authorities. He was their problem. I had enough problems of my own.

As I descended the stairs of the gate, I caught sight of Jonas and his son, unoccupied at the customs booth. With a quick wave of my hand, I signaled my intention to speak with him, and after taking the salute of the sentinels at the gate, I headed straight to the booth.

"Good morning, you old goat!" I called out as I approached.

"Well, if it isn't the top dog himself," he shot back.

"It's always good to see a man standing around doing nothing. It sets me at ease," I said.

"Ease?" His eyebrows shot up. "Oh yeah." He nodded emphatically. "It's been a week of ease all right. I've had my feet up all week."

Of course, just the opposite was true, and it was true for both of us.

"Do you think we could have a short word?" With a jerk of my head, I motioned in the direction of the road leading down the Kidron Valley.

"Sure," he answered, and then with a glance and a nod to his son, he transferred responsibility to him.

A light mist still hung over the lowest reaches of the valley, but the early-morning sun was promising to burn it off. The swallows nesting along the crevices in the city wall were engaged in a full-throated competition with the songbirds in the trees along the brook. Traffic to and from the city was just beginning to stir.

When we had gone a few paces beyond the gate, I spoke. "I just wanted to say thanks for the help with the Barabbas case."

"Oh, don't mention it." There was relief in his voice. "I thought you were going to warn me about some new plot."

"No, there's no new plot." I hesitated. "Let me rephrase that. There's no new plot that I know about. You never can be sure what's being hatched in this crazy city."

"Yeah, you're right about that. I guess we learned that with Barabbas." Jonas nervously bit on the corner whiskers of his mustache, and then continued. "Now, that Galilean prophet? I've been losing sleep over him all week."

"Harmless as a dove," I said. "Harmless as a dove."

"How do you know?"

"I checked him out myself on Monday, right back there in the temple courts." I made a quick double-pump motion with my upraised thumb aimed over my shoulder. "Then on Tuesday I had Claudius in there with the prophet."

"You Romans have more nerve than brains." He kicked a loose pebble off the pathway, looked up at me with a quizzical grin, and then with an incredulous shake of his head, he repeated, "More nerve than brains, that's all I can say."

"If we didn't have nerve, we wouldn't be running this place. Or any other place for that matter."

He shrugged, furrowed his brow, and then cocked his head to one side. It was his way of reluctantly conceding my point.

"So he's harmless?"

"Harmless to us." With my index finger, I pointed first at myself, then at Jonas, and then back again. "Caiaphas, on the other hand"—I paused for effect—"now there's a man who I'm sure hasn't slept well all week."

"So you think the old rusty gate has lost some sleep? Over what?"

"Money. Money and prestige. It can't look too good having some roving up-country rabbi come in and take over your temple at the religious high point of the year."

"I suppose not," Jonas said. But then he added, "You know this prophet, Jesus of Nazareth, he's been here before. He kicked out the money changers a few years back. Caused quite a stir then. But nothing like this. He's got the temple guards running scared. That's what my uncle told me."

"Your uncle's right. I saw that firsthand on Monday. So what else do you know about this Galilean?"

"My wife tells me he's a friend of tax collectors and sinners. She told me one of his disciples was a tax collector before he met the prophet."

"Ah, tax collectors and sinners?" I responded with a wink and a nod. "Maybe there is hope for the two of us yet."

Jonas smiled back at me. "So, Marcus, where is this all headed? Some people think he's the Messiah. You know that, don't you?"

"Yes, we're well aware of that. But he doesn't oppose paying taxes to Caesar." I gave my tax collector a supportive thumbs-up signal. "And he hasn't spoken a word against Rome since he's been here."

"That's not a surprise. He knows better. You and your boys would have him nailed up on Golgotha the moment he did."

"You're right about that," I agreed. "But I honestly don't think he's got a quarrel with us. He's going after the parading hypocrites in long, flowing robes, those killjoy Pharisees and teachers of the law. You know the ones—the religious police who run this place."

Jonas blew a sharp breath of air through his graying mustache. "Oh, I know the ones. The pure ones! The ones who kicked me out of the synagogue the moment I got this job. But they'll travel Roman roads to seize a widow's house in the next town. They'll expect Roman soldiers to protect them from bandits on the way to Jericho. They'll connect their fancy homes to the Roman aqueduct, and every evening they'll bathe their stinking rumps in its water."

I nodded in agreement. My words had obviously struck a nerve. But Jonas wasn't finished.

"Every day they'll curse the Gentiles and their influence. With their mouths they lust for the good old days, the days before Rome." He gestured expansively and then shrugged. "Ha! They don't talk about the rotten poverty of those good old days, 'cause while their mouths talk, their filthy hands rake in the money the empire has brought in here. Oh, I know the ones! Believe me. I know them well."

"Spoken like a true son of the empire," I said with an exaggerated nod.

Over the years Jonas and I had developed a working relationship that allowed me to speak to him in a certain way. I could say things I would never repeat to another Jew. He was observant—a Jew with his religious blinders off. He put his life on the line when he took on this occupation. I respected him for it.

"Look," I said. "Jesus of Nazareth is the high priest's problem. He's not ours." Jonas and his family were fully included in the scope of my statement. They fell under our protection. They were part of us. Then I added, "If we're lucky, this will all blow over, and the prophet will be back in Galilee sometime next week. Then he'll be Herod's problem."

"Herod?" Jonas huffed. "There'll be another head on a platter soon if Herod gets ahold of him."

"Jesus and what happens to him is out of our hands. But Barabbas isn't, and tomorrow he'll get what's coming to him. And it's thanks to you." I spoke my appreciation with genuine sincerity. "We would never have landed that fish without your help."

"I didn't expect catching Thaddaeus would lead us where it did. I mean, he's just a petty tax thief. I really had no idea Barabbas was the ringleader behind all this stuff—the theft, the tax booth vandalism, the murder of the soldiers." Even now Jonas gestured his surprise with upraised open hands. "I thought he was harmless. A little hotheaded, but harmless. It wasn't until you showed me that weapons stash—that pile of swords you found in his house—that's when things began to fall into place." He sniffed and shook his head. "I guess you can't tell what's in the soup until you taste it."

"If Barabbas is the soup we're talking about, I'd say there's a good-sized dash of poison hemlock in there. It's too bad Hermes and Andreas had to taste it. Oh well. Tomorrow I'm going to spill that soup all over Golgotha. And the world will be a better place because of it."

We reached the Kidron Brook. There was a lively babbling flow, thanks to all the rain. I've often seen it bone-dry. I glanced back up the road to the city. "I guess it's time we headed back. You've got taxes to collect. I've got a tribune I should see."

21

Eleven thirty in the morning, Thursday, April 6

BACK AT THE fortress, true to my prediction earlier in the week, Flavio was nowhere to be found. None of the centurions had seen him since Herod's arrival. Caius, on the other hand, had been active and visible, providing leadership for his troops within both the city and the fortress.

Just before noon a red-faced, bulgy-eyed Flavio put in an appearance at the fortress. He brought word that Herod intended to tour the temple area. The high priest's invitation, offered during the tetrarch's arrival on Tuesday, had been accepted.

Flavio hastily convened a council of centurions. After some debate it was decided that Renaldo and Marius would provide the manpower needed to secure the route from Herod's palace on the western edge of the city, on through the heart of the capital, to the temple compound on the east side. Here was a route fraught with hazards—a security nightmare. After my previous experience with the tetrarch, I was eager to avoid any personal involvement. I volunteered my men to provide cover duty so Renaldo's men could be reassigned for the task.

As before, we assumed Caius and his troops would lead the march. A messenger was dispatched to Caius, outlining the outcome of our deliberations and offering our services. The general was staying with his master at the Herod family palace.

We received a reply that was both prompt and curt. Reading from a prepared statement, the messenger intoned, "His Majesty, tetrarch of Galilee and Perea, will not traverse the city of Jerusalem, but rather, following the custom of his grandfather, Herod the First, he will take the southern perimeter route and enter the temple compound through the glorious Golden Gate. His own soldiers will provide escort. We have need of no others."

Here was a royal snub. That's how Flavio perceived it. His neck and face turned beet red. For a moment I thought he might kill the messenger.

"We might just as well kneel before the king—the bloody Fox—and kiss his stinking feet!" he raged. "Why not hand him the city on a silver platter? Silver? Pah!" He spat. "That wouldn't be good enough for him. Gold. Only gold will do!" Then with acid in his voice, he added, "Oh, I forgot. Silver platters are for prophets' heads. And beggar boys' hands."

Then with teeth clenched, he rapped his knuckles three times on the table before him. "What do we do?" He glowered as he shook his head.

It was a question no one dared answer. But Flavio didn't expect an answer from us. The tribune turned from his assembled centurions, took a few steps to the nearest window, and looked out across the tile roofs of the city. He stroked his chin, and then with both hands grasped hold of the window ledge as he gazed straight ahead.

After a few moments he turned to the fidgeting messenger. He yanked the rolled parchment from the messenger's hand, seized a writing quill from the table, and began jotting furiously. In due time he spoke.

"We'll meet the Fox at the Golden Gate. He won't walk in there alone. This is our city, not his. He'll see us first."

Flavio rolled the document up once again and handed it back to the waiting messenger.

He scowled. "Off with you."

But the tribune wasn't finished with his dispatches. He again seized the quill and with an air of urgency began writing on a fresh sheet of parchment. His final strokes were executed with a confident, dramatic flourish.

My curiosity was intense, but neither I nor any of the other men present dared speak.

"Messenger!" Flavio bellowed.

One of our young recruits straightaway stepped into the briefing room.

"To the governor! With haste," Flavio ordered as he handed the soldier this new missive.

Then turning to us, he continued. "We'll see what Pilate says about Herod's sudden turn to religion."

I was relieved about the news of Herod's chosen route to the temple. There were no crowded streets, encounters with beggars were less likely, and best of all, there was little direct responsibility on our part. The true reason for this circuitous route was obvious after a moment's thought. The route through the city would bring the Fox to the back side of the temple compound. From there he could choose one of several rear or side entries. But this was no way for a king to come. He would enter by the main gate, the Golden Gate, or he would not enter at all.

If the route was no cause for alarm, Herod's apparent rapprochement with Caiaphas certainly was. Herod would leverage any friendship, any alliance with the rich and powerful to his own advantage. Caiaphas certainly was both rich and powerful. His mansion spoke volumes. I had repeatedly been told that the opulent interior made the governor's palace apartment look shabby.

Once again the litter bearers would be pressed into service. In my mind's eye I could see the regular cadence of their steps, smell the sweat from their bodies, hear Herod's curses over some imagined misstep. However, the tetrarch's arrival was at least two hours off. Until then there were ample preparations to be made, and once again Flavio tapped me for service.

Tuesday's arrival procedure for Herod would again be employed. There were, of course, some obvious differences. The distance our troops would be covering was vastly reduced. Herod would be following a U-shaped route, starting from the Herod family palace on the west side of the city, traveling south past the Serpent's Pool, then east across the southern perimeter of the city wall, the bottom of the U, and finally heading north to the Golden Gate at the top of the U. Flavio and Marius would greet the tetrarch as he turned north on the final leg of the journey, just opposite the Pinnacle of the temple. The Pinnacle is the high point on the wall at the south end of the temple compound.

The fortifications at this point soar two hundred feet above the Kidron Valley below.

Once again I was asked to inspect the route before the king's arrival—the distance from the Golden Gate to the point on the road opposite the Pinnacle. Traveling along the top of the city wall, this distance amounted to only a few hundred yards, but at ground level the official route multiplied this distance by at least a factor of four. About four hundred yards from the Golden Gate, the road to the Mount of Olives was intersected by a north-south road running parallel to the Kidron Brook. Herod would be coming north along this road and then turning to face the Golden Gate and the massive gold-clad temple directly behind it.

My groomsman was dispatched to bring my horse back to the Antonia Fortress from the tether lines near the Serpent's Pool. In fact, all the horses were brought back and conscripted for duty. Once again we would give Herod a show. He would know who was in charge here.

I was just getting into my brass-muscled cuirass when my groomsman returned. With some quick assistance from him, I was in the saddle in minutes. Again I called on a half dozen cavalrymen to accompany me on this reconnaissance mission. It took only a few moments for us to ride from the fortress to the Golden Gate.

A constant stream of bearded men was being channeled in both directions through the wide arched gateway. Most of those leaving through the gate were carrying freshly slain year-old lambs. With their throats cut, the bloodied heads dangled limply. The Passover lamb would be made ready for the great feast.

Aside from the heavy traffic, no particular security concerns were readily apparent. From past experience I knew that at this hour the bulk of the slaughter had already taken place. Though the killing would continue until sunset, most families would try to have this job done by early afternoon, even if it meant standing in line from the early morning. Here was slaughterhouse religion at peak performance.

With the heavy focus on the Passover celebration, my hope was that fanatics and religious zealots would have their minds fully occupied on this sacred event, rather than being distracted by Herod's sudden appearance here, or by the activities of the Roman army near this city gate.

We continued on down the road into the valley, the same road Jonas and I had walked that morning. Before reaching the Kidron Brook, I gently tugged right on my horse's reins, and with that my party turned south onto the road that led around the city. We had not gone far when we came to the bloody discharge. A veritable river of blood gushed from a three-foot diameter clay pipe that emerged on the left side of the road. Here was the outflow from the slaughter in the temple. From there this red stream of gore flowed another two hundred yards before it joined the Kidron Brook. To be accurate, this stream was not pure lambs' blood. It was supplemented by water from the main city aqueduct, enough water to keep the solution moving freely.

A stream of blood—blood flowing between fertile grassy banks dotted with the flowers of spring. It was a disturbing sight on a sunny day, one not easily forgotten.

The air was thick with a constant buzz of flies. Swallows swooped low to enjoy this flying insect feast. There was a continual wheeling and diving in what amounted to a winged acrobatic frenzy. A colony of swallows' nests lay upon the steep adjacent wall. I worried that their careening flight might spook the horses.

How the blood of a lamb could bring freedom to a nation remained a mystery to me. I heard the whole story: the plagues on Egypt, the lamb's blood sprinkled upon the door of each home, bringing escape for the firstborn from the angel of death. Jonas had told all of it to me. And for me there was a certain resonance to this tale. I was a firstborn son. Three years ago, before Tara's death, my family had eaten the Seder meal with Jonas and his family. He was a believer. Though the synagogue would not have him, this tax collector took us in and taught us the rudiments of his faith.

We reached the point on the road opposite the Pinnacle without incident. Two-way traffic on the road was more brisk and purposeful than usual. The populace by and large ignored us as they went about their business and we went about ours.

We returned to the gate. As I approached, I looked up to see Claudius looking down at me from atop the gate. I returned his salute and was instantly reminded of Jesus of Nazareth. Though in reverse position, I was right now at that point where our eyes had first met. The words—the words I heard at that instant of meeting—came echoing back forcefully into my mind.

"I have a future for you."

The voice was soft, even gentle, but somehow terrible.

I shuddered. I looked about me half expecting to see him by my side. There was no one—no one but my own cavalrymen.

A gray-bearded man approached. He held the back legs of a freshly slain lamb as his son clutched the front legs. They walked by me with their burden, passing on the left. Behind them, drops of lamb's blood dotted the paving stones.

It was my mind. It must be my own mind playing back the earlier incident, I reasoned. That's why I heard his words. But why? Why did this man, this prophet, unnerve me like this?

We continued on to the fortress, but my mind was on the Northern Messiah. His penetrating eyes haunted my thoughts. There was a power there that I had no ability to fathom. I was reminded of Ruth's words. Ruth was one of our household servants, a Jewish girl. When at the supper table I had told Zelda about Jesus and his miraculous powers, Ruth's eyes brightened. I asked her if she knew anything about this man.

"Oh, yes," she'd said. "Almost a year ago he healed a blind beggar from the Lower City. Jesus made some mud, put it on the beggar's eyes, and sent him to wash in the Pool of Siloam. When he washed, he could see. It was a miracle. I've seen this man myself. I know it's true," she earnestly avowed.

When I'd asked her about this power Jesus had and where it came from, she bowed her head and answered, "From God." But she seemed somehow uncomfortable with her answer. She added, "It must be from God. He does good things. But our leaders aren't sure. They think it may be demon power. But demons don't heal the sick."

Maybe the religious leaders were right. Maybe it was demonic power that made the blind see. It seemed preposterous. But why had I heard this voice? Why did this man trouble me so? Thinking of him seemed to stir up nothing but torment within me, and I didn't even know why. I felt strangely attracted to him, yet at the same time repelled.

Then there was this talk about the kingdom of God. Maybe Timaeus was right about this prophet. The words of the wealthy merchant came back to me: "You don't talk about a kingdom in this place and get away with it. Rome will see to that!"

Maybe we would see to it. Maybe we should see to it soon.

But Jesus's enemies were the same pompous, self-serving leaders I despised. He had aligned himself with the common man, with the poor, the oppressed, the sick and suffering. And he didn't just champion their cause for personal benefit like some crass politician lobbying for the emperor's favor. No, he healed them. He fed them. He walked with them, ate with them. He was one of them. He was their king, whether he wore a crown or not. I saw that clearly when he entered on the donkey. He was the donkey king. A horse would have put him above the crowd. A horse would have meant elevating himself like all the other egotistical men who led in this upside-down world.

In his case others would have to do the elevating.

The meaning of his entry on Sunday came clear to me now. It was a perspective gained from my comfortable perch on the back of my own noble steed.

By the time I reached the fortress for the second time in the week, I resolved to shut this Messiah out of my mind. He didn't fit any of my categories for human behavior or religious thought. He was beyond understanding, an unwelcome intruder into my city and my thought life.

Flavio was already mounted and attired in gleaming brass. I immediately reported my observations on the route. He seemed little interested. The decisions had already been made. A higher authority had determined our response to Herod's visit.

"Pontius Pilate will meet him at the gate," Flavio crowed. "They'll both know Rome runs this world."

By "both" Flavio meant, of course, the high priest and the tetrarch.

Ambition and treachery formed a blend that pulsed strongly in both their veins, too strongly to be left unchecked.

"He's already passed the Serpent's Pool. He'll be here within the hour," Flavio reported. Then he added his orders. "It's your gate. You'll wait there with the governor until the Fox comes. I'll greet him at the Pinnacle and escort him to the gate. After that he's in the governor's hands. Off with you then."

I saluted and turned. Meanwhile Flavio wheeled his horse around to face the cavalry assembling on the parade ground. Within minutes they would ride out of the fortress and begin their deployment along the route to the Golden Gate.

I ordered the six horsemen who had accompanied me to join the ranks of the other cavalrymen. Then with considerable haste I returned to the gate. I dismounted and clambered up the steps of the gatehouse. I ordered Claudius to quickly assemble all the men under my command from their positions along the wall. Within short minutes I reported on the unfolding events, Herod's expected arrival, Pilate's coming to greet the tetrarch, and the high priest's plan for a royal tour of the temple compound. In all my years on this assignment, there had never been such an assemblage of the high and the mighty at this gate. I wanted everything and everyone looking their best, fit for a king, whether genuine or a pretender. I was grateful for the troop inspection I had undertaken on the previous afternoon. Armor and equipment had been freshened up and repaired; nevertheless, a frenzy of purposeful activity followed.

I returned to ground level and mounted my horse just in time to salute Flavio as he led row upon row of cavalry past the gate and out along the route to the point opposite the Pinnacle. Renaldo and Marius were among the centurions who joined in this display of military might. Five hundred pikemen followed the cavalrymen. They formed up on either side of the final four hundred yards leading to the gate. They stood erect with the butt end of their spears planted in the ground directly in front of them. With their right arms fully extended straight out in front of them, they grasped the shaft of their twelve-foot-long pikes. Arrayed in this manner they formed a bristling arch between which Herod's litter would pass. Finally, close by the gate, the trumpeters held their instruments by their sides as they awaited the signal for the imperial fanfare.

When all were in position, I called for the lowering of the heavy, grated iron gate. From now on, the Passover celebrants would be forced to use an alternate entrance or exit.

In short order the toga-clad governor, Pontius Pilate, arrived on his gold-ornamented chariot. The gate was raised. By the governor's side stood Claudia Procula lavishly dressed in full-length scarlet. Her bejeweled opulence contrasted sharply with the poverty common to most women of this province. The chariot took a position allowing the ruling couple to look out to the Mount of Olives, in readiness for the approaching king.

The only missing player was Caiaphas. In due time his delegation arrived, and the enormous gate was hauled up once more on creaking chains, only to be lowered again when the priestly party had exited.

Pilate had been gazing down the road stretched out before him when Caiaphas arrived, and it was only the coarse rattle coming from the gate chains behind him that alerted him to the approach of the high priest and his delegation. He turned, stepped down from the chariot, and briskly strode over to the dumbfounded cleric. The expression on Caiaphas's face said it all. He clearly did not expect to see Pilate here. He had intended this to be a discreet, private tour and consultation.

"You're expecting someone?" Pilate brusquely inquired.

An uncomfortable pause followed. Caiaphas cast a hasty glance at those accompanying him, adjusted the folds in his robe, cleared his rusty throat, and replied, "Yes, King Herod requested a tour of the great temple."

"Did he now?" There was a coldness in Pilate's voice that betrayed the utter contempt he felt toward this Jewish leader. "Ahh!" He gestured grandly. "There is no king in these parts. I know of no king." Then spotting me on horseback nearby, the governor turned and in mock sincerity called out, "Centurion. Is there a king around here?"

"We have no king here but Caesar," I answered, joining in the sport.

"The centurion says there is no king but Caesar. Do you have some other king I'm unaware of? Perhaps I should meet this king."

By now the high priest was well beyond flustered. He had stepped into a trap. Surrounded by Roman troops and cut off from the safety of the temple's hallowed sanctum, he was now being hectored by his chief political rival. It seemed more than he could endure. He began to tremble uncontrollably, whether from fear or anger I could not tell.

"Your Excellency"—he swallowed hard—"I was referring to the . . . te-tetrarch of Galilee."

"The te-tetrarch?" Pilate mimicked not only the high priest's tremulous stammer, but also the rusty-gate scratch of his voice. "Is that so? Well, the tetrarch is no king. And he certainly isn't your king." Then with slow, icy deliberation, Pilate said, "There is no king here but Caesar. Did you hear that?"

This was no rhetorical question.

"Yes, Your Excellency. I heard."

"Do you, any of you"—he scanned the delegation—"have any other king?"

The cowering dogs dutifully answered, "No, we have no other king."

Caiaphas, however, was silent. A fact well noted by the governor.

Then Pilate took a step closer to the trembling priest, pointed a bony finger in his face, and hissed, "Now don't forget that, you old goat, or your blood will be running down the Kidron! Did you hear that?"

"I . . . I am your servant, Your Excellency," Caiaphas rasped.

"Ha!" Pilate laughed an icy laugh in a show of disdain for that remark. Then he turned on his heels and marched back to his chariot, where once more he joined his wife.

For a full minute there was stunned silence from the religious delegation, and then suddenly they all began to speak at once in a huddle of hushed tones like schoolboys after a tongue-lashing from the headmaster.

But there was murder in the high priest's eye. Nothing childish there. From my vantage point I could see that. He didn't have the means, but he most certainly had the intent.

I am sure that if the gate had been open, the delegation would have returned to the safety of the sanctuary to plot their revenge, but that option was not open to them. They were trapped in this pocket, surrounded by hated foreign troops, subject to the whim and ridicule of their enemy, awaiting the arrival of their pretentious savior king.

Long, awkward moments passed. But they were saved from this interminable purgatory by Herod's arrival.

Caius and Flavio led the procession with the royal litter following close behind. One by one, the pikemen drew back their extended arms, bringing their long, angled spears into the fully upright position. This synchronized motion continued up the length of the column as the royal party advanced along it—a truly impressive display as viewed from the back of a horse. For a moment I was envious of Claudius, who had an even better view from the top of the gate.

At last the two mounted commanders arrived before Pilate's chariot. They were motioned to take their position on either side. After a brief confusion of feet, the royal litter managed to turn sideways so the royal couple could face the governor as he stood upon his imperial chariot. The trumpeters sounded the fanfare. When the last note had echoed off the marble wall, Pilate unrolled the parchment handed to him by an attendant. He cleared his throat and began his oration.

"It was under the rule of the great and wise Emperor Caesar Augustus that this magnificent temple behind us began to take shape. He recognized the desire of the Jewish people for a central place to worship. It was Herod the great Idumean king who oversaw the construction of this masterpiece of the empire, and today it stands as a symbol of Roman respect for the unity and diversity of all the peoples of the empire. It is only fitting today that I, as the emperor's representative, welcome the son of this master builder, Herod Antipas, the tetrarch of Galilee and Perea."

With a wave of his hand, Pilate signaled the sounding of a second trumpet fanfare. As the first note was sounded, he stepped off the chariot and then graciously lent a hand to his wife. Thus accompanied by his mate, he swaggered over to the royal litter to personally greet Herod and Herodias, who both stood to meet them.

Greetings were exchanged, none of which I could discern from a distance. After a brief discussion Claudia joined Herodias in the royal litter. Herod barked out some orders. The litter bearers stood to their feet and headed off in the direction of the governor's residence. Apparently the ladies would have their own time together.

At a leisurely pace Pilate escorted Herod over to where the priestly delegation waited.

It was an unusual sight, these three hostile, inflated men exchanging greetings and meaningless pleasantries. Herod Antipas, Pontius Pilate, and Joseph Caiaphas; the Fox, the Badger, and the Weasel. All three were kings in their own right, within their own jurisdiction. All three craved more power, absolute power, while fiercely holding one another in check.

Pilate turned to me and gave a quick, tight nod. I signaled up to Claudius, and the great Golden Gate, the Messiah Gate, was hoisted, granting entrance to the three competing kings.

Only the fourth king, the people's king—the donkey king—only he was absent.

22

Seven in the evening, Thursday, April 6

IT WAS ALREADY dark when I trudged, lantern in hand, up the stairs of the southeast turret of the fortress, the prison sector. Octavio the jailer greeted me warmly. He knew well why I had come. Each of the three prisoners on this particular level, the highest level, would be crucified tomorrow, and I was charged with their execution.

"So you'll join me tomorrow on the Skull?" I asked.

"Of course," he said. "I wouldn't miss that party for all the emperor's wine and women."

"Good." I smiled. "I'll need your help. It's been a while since I've been to a hammering. I guess you could say I'm a bit rusty."

"Marcus"—he shrugged—"don't worry. You'll do fine. I'll bring my crew. They're experts now. We'll have 'em up there before they know what hit 'em."

"Sounds good to me."

His words put to rest some hidden doubts and misgivings. I usually avoided parties of the hammering kind. But this one, this was a party I was throwing. And I had a score I needed to settle with the head guest.

"Now, Octavio, I would like a little visit with our three fine friends."

"Let's go then."

The heavy plank door creaked open, and I stooped to enter the first dank cell. The combined stench of urine and sweat assaulted my nostrils. Barabbas was in a sitting position with his back to the far wall. His feet, which stretched out before him, were secured in a well-worn set of wooden stocks.

The fat pig hadn't lost much weight despite his prison diet. His eyes were as cold and belligerent as ever. No contrition there—not that I expected any.

I handed the lantern to Octavio, who had entered right behind me. I drew a five-inch, four-cornered spike from a pouch attached to my belt. I examined it carefully before the prisoner. I stood the head of the spike on my thumb and gently pressed its iron point into the fleshy ball at the tip of my middle finger. I drew the prisoner's attention to the sharpness of the point, admired the nail's considerable length, and then asked Barabbas if he thought it would be adequate for the task at hand.

He glared at me, rattled his chains, and called down upon me all manner of curses in the name of Jehovah. When he began going on about the glories of the Maccabean revolt two centuries ago, I turned my back on him.

Narrow, religious zealots like him made me sick. Here was an advocate for a brand of exclusive, race-based religion that holds the rest of humanity in contempt. He would have us all back living in caves so he could preserve the pure faith. If he had his way, the streets would flow rivers of blood just so he could take us back to his narrow world. The stain on the cobblestones near my house had only been a small token of his intent.

Arguing with men of his kind was utterly pointless.

When his rant ended, I calmly smiled back at him and wished him a good night's sleep. Tomorrow I would hammer home a few points of my own.

"I'll see you in the morning," I called out as I pulled his cell door shut.

Of course, this insurrectionist had not acted alone—hence the two other men on their way to the Skull. The Skull, Golgotha, what a fitting name for the hill of execution. The bare, rounded rock crown of the hill mirrored the ultimate fate of all who walked up its slope. Their heads would become white skulls much like that barren knoll.

The man behind the next door went berserk the moment I stepped into his cell. Here was a trapped animal spitting venom on any who approached. I needed no theatrics to gain his attention. He provided his own.

While this human sewer spewed curses, I placed the point of the spike at the base of my left palm and shouted back at him, "Tomorrow! Tomorrow!"

He got the message.

While he continued his raving, I slammed the cell door shut. This man was capable of anything. There was little doubt in my mind which one of these three was the butcher.

The last man presented a sharp contrast. Thaddaeus, dear Thaddaeus. His tongue had come loose under duress, which culminated in the arrest of the other two. He appeared reflective, even resigned to his fate. Or was it only fear that I saw stamped upon his lean and lanky frame?

He glanced up at me when I entered his cell and then hung his head as though in shame.

"We're going to Golgotha tomorrow," I stated in a matter-of-fact manner.

He sucked in a short, tight breath and squeezed his lips together as though I had punched him in the stomach.

"Tonight will be your last night . . . here."

I added the word "here" to soften the finality of my statement. His lowered head began to weave from side to side. I could clearly see his mind absorbing what his body would feel.

My announcement was no new revelation. The execution date for all three men had been set last week, immediately after the trial. But I came confirming an eventuality that the whole of this man's being wished to deny. It was plain that my words came as a staggering shock to his system. It was a shock that left him reeling.

After my encounter with the last two prisoners, I was unprepared for the long silence that followed.

"Do you have any questions?" I asked.

He began to rock back and forth, head down, hands nervously clenching and releasing, clenching and releasing. He swallowed hard and then stammered, "Wi-will there be myrrh?"

"Yes. I'll make sure there's myrrh." I paused and then justified the use of pain remedies by adding, "We're not barbarians."

He continued his rocking. A brief glance up at me and a quick, tight nod, I took as his way of thanking me.

Then he was overcome. Unable to look ahead, to face me or the future, Thaddaeus turned from me, face to the wall.

I turned from him. I had nothing more to say.

The door creaked shut. The metal latch bar clicked down.

Tomorrow waited . . . Golgotha awaited. The Skull awaited its prey.

23

Five forty-five in the morning, Friday, April 7

"MASTER. THERE'S A messenger at the gate wanting to see you. He says it's urgent."

"Already? We haven't even had breakfast yet." I sighed, straightened, and reached for a towel to dry my dripping face. "Arius, tell him I'll be there in a minute. I still need to wash up."

In fact, although I was freshly shaven, I wasn't yet fully dressed. In due time I strapped on my sword, stuffed three dried dates in my mouth, and then slowly ambled across our villa courtyard, crowded with cranky, early-morning soldiers. They were reluctantly setting their day into motion.

A visibly agitated messenger saluted me as Arius opened the gate. It was the same young man I had seen Flavio send off yesterday with an urgent dispatch for Pilate.

"Sir, I have just come from the governor. You are to report to the Praetorium immediately. Jesus of Nazareth has been arrested. The high priest has brought him before the governor for judgment."

"Is that so?" I said in a state of consternation. "Who sent you?"

"The governor himself. He said you were familiar with the Galilean."

I blew a short puff of air through my nostrils. All of Jerusalem was somewhat familiar with the Galilean.

"So he wants me there immediately?"

"Immediately, sir." He shifted from one foot to the other and then, as if to justify this response, he added, "The high priest and a big delegation, maybe three hundred men, maybe more, arrived at the palace door at first light. They had the prisoner—Jesus—with them."

"Tell the governor I'm on my way."

With a quick nod of my head, I dismissed the messenger. Instantly he turned and began his run back to the governor's residence. I took one step back inside the gate and began barking orders.

"You, you, and you!" I stabbed my index finger in the direction of the most dressed and prepared-looking soldiers. "Strap on your swords and follow me. Now!"

Then, addressing the other soldiers, I announced, "The rest of you, meet me at the Praetorium as soon as you are ready."

"Claudius"—I nodded in his direction—"you are in charge. I'll give everyone their assignment for the day when they get there."

I stepped back through the gate and began covering the ground with long, quick strides. My three recruits had to run to catch up.

With each stride a new thought came jogging into my head.

Stupid Arius! Why didn't he tell me the messenger was from Pilate? I would have moved a good deal faster.

Obviously my concerns about the prophet had moved up the chain of command. Flavio must have informed Pilate about my worries and the actions I had taken, hence this unusual move—a direct summons by the governor. I harbored the hope that he would consult directly with me on the matter.

Three hundred men! Three hundred men at first light? The Weasel must have had a busy night. It takes a good deal of effort to set your troops in array. Caiaphas must have been hatching this plot for a good long while.

But the Weasel caught his prey! What a sweet bit of treachery that must have been. I wondered how he pulled that off. Now the high priest would move in for the kill. We would see if he could slaughter his own Passover lamb.

The people! If the pilgrims, especially the Galilean pilgrims, knew their Messiah had been seized, there could be a mass revolt. That must be why the Weasel had done his dirty work in the dark of the night.

And furthermore, he had played out this drama at the zenith of the festival, while minds and hearts were on faith, home, and family. Here was a cunning scheme worthy of the Fox, played out by the Weasel.

Undoubtedly most of the population would still be unaware of these developments, even as I had been caught off guard. Off guard but not surprised. I could smell this coming.

My conversation with Renaldo at the bathhouse came echoing back. It gave me an eerie feeling knowing I had spoken like some prophetic oracle. It made me wonder from where that insight had really come.

"By Jupiter! I forgot the spikes." I wheeled around while reaching out my hand to halt the soldier at my side. Addressing him directly, I said, "I forgot them—the spikes. They're in a pouch hanging on a peg in my bedchamber. My wife, she'll know where they are. Ask her to get the pouch for you. Then bring it to me at the Praetorium. Oh, and tell the other men to hurry. This is urgent." I fixed my eyes on him to stress the importance of this last statement and then added, "Now run."

I swung around and resumed my steady pace. The loping slap of his sandals on the pavement told me that he took my words to heart. The two men remaining with me sensed the gravity of the situation and quickened their own pace. In a few moments we reached the governor's residence, the stately columned palace adjoining the rear, southeast side of the Antonia Fortress.

The sight before me contrasted sharply with what I saw when I had escorted Herod to this very location three days earlier. My early-morning messenger was wrong. There must have been five hundred men crowded into the street fronting on the fortress. A cordon of Roman soldiers had already been thrown around this crowd. The street was blocked in both directions. Pikemen, with their menacing spears lowered for attack, formed a solid wall before me. Only the foolhardy would dare approach.

Off to the right I spotted their commander. It was Marius. I signaled my approach with a wave.

"A fine mess we have here!"

"Yes, Marcus, a fine mess," he agreed. "The high priest has his man. I only hope we can keep the crowds away."

"Your boys are doing a fine job of that. Look, I've got twenty more men on the way. They'll be here in a few minutes. Claudius will be leading them. They can form a second line of swordsmen immediately behind your pikemen."

"That would be excellent, Marcus," he said with a thumbs-up signal. "Not a soul will get through here. I'll see to that."

There was determination in his voice—determination stiffened by a whiff of fear. He too remembered the surging crowds of Sunday, adoring their Messiah king. The latent power of the masses could break forth at any time. At this moment defensive vigilance was paramount.

"Tell Claudius and his men to fall in behind you then," I said. Then I added, "The governor sent for me. I need to get through."

"By all means."

Marius stepped forward, faced his bristling pikemen, and with a short horizontal move of his right hand he parted them, allowing access for me and the two men who followed.

I moved to the Praetorium entrance as quickly as the milling throng would permit. They were packed in so tightly that progress was slow and fitful. I repeatedly yelled out, "Make way! Make way!"

They did make way when they saw they were facing a centurion, but due to the press there was little space they could grant me. I was sorely tempted to draw my sword and then use the flat of it on the recalcitrant. But though I was armed, I could become an easy target in this inflamed crowd. I let that temptation pass.

At last we reached the stairs fronting the Praetorium. Here again a line of pikemen faced the crowd. Their spears, however, were raised upright, forming a respectful barrier for this hasty assembly. The contrasting stance of this array of pikemen was striking.

A quick glance over my shoulder confirmed the composition of this crowd. These were the high priest's men. There were at least fifty temple guards present, some with swords drawn. Then there were perhaps two hundred priests, Sadducees, and members of the Jewish high council, the Sanhedrin. Finally, there were the leading merchants and traders of the city—an irate bunch, thirsty for blood.

No women. No pilgrims. No disciples. No Galileans save one, and I had yet to set eyes on him.

I turned back and locked my eyes on the pikeman directly before me. I raised my hand as a signal, and he stepped back smartly, granting access to the six broad stairs leading to the governor's residence.

These stairs were unoccupied except for three men: Caiaphas, Annas, and Jonathon.

Jonathon was chief of the temple guards. I knew him well enough. We had words on more than one occasion. He liked to throw his weight around, considered me of no account, well below his own station. I responded by treating him in like manner.

Annas formerly held the position of high priest, and he was also the father-in-law of Caiaphas. Undoubtedly he was here as an adviser on points of law and protocol.

Then there was Caiaphas, the Weasel himself. His long, narrow face was made longer yet by his grizzled beard. I always thought he had a rather hungry look. He seemed rather satisfied this morning though. The hint of a smile was on his face.

At the top of the stairs, on either side of the grand cedar doors, twelve sentinels stood guard. Pilate was nowhere to be seen. The great doors emblazoned with the imperial eagle crest remained firmly closed to the restive horde out front.

Leaving my two men on the first step, I approached the doors. I nodded a greeting in the direction of the three temple officials as I passed them. I had reached the fifth step when both the doors directly in front of me burst open. Pilate strode through, flanked by Flavio and an assessor, a lawyer well acquainted with Roman law. Instantly the sentinels' arms shot upward in salute.

I froze in my tracks and saluted.

Pilate's furrowed brow marked his surprise at seeing me here on the stairs. He swept by me, but with a quick, beckoning motion of his hand, he indicated that I fall in behind him, something I was quite willing to do.

Pilate was dressed in his procurator's robes, the robes of judgment.

In his left hand he held a tightly wrapped scroll. I was curious as to its contents. He took his position on the fourth step before the three-man temple delegation. Flavio and the assessor took their positions on either side of the governor, while I stood to the left of my commanding officer.

A hush fell over the throng. This is what they came to see. Every ear strained to hear the proceedings.

The governor peered over the heads of the men directly in front of him. He scanned the assemblage on the street, took in the significance of it all, and then cleared his throat.

"Where is the man?"

Jonathon turned quickly. On reaching the first step, he beckoned beyond our pikemen to three of his own temple guards, who then advanced with their prisoner—Jesus of Nazareth.

He was a mess, almost unrecognizable. His hair was matted. He had been spat upon. The spittle was drying in his beard. There were red welts on his face and neck, a blood-oozing gash above his left eye, a discernable limp to his gait.

It was apparent that during the night they'd had their way with him.

He was escorted to a position directly before me. Intuitively I knew he was my man now, my charge.

A twitch of Pilate's eyebrow hinted his surprise at the condition of the man.

"Loose him," he directed with a slight wave of his hand.

Two temple guards hastened to unfasten the leather strap binding Jesus's arms to his torso. The third man freed the prisoner's hands. With a second wave of his hand, Pilate dismissed the temple guards, who repositioned themselves on the first step and stood facing the proceedings.

Pilate took a seat on the throne of judgment, which had been brought out for him by two attendants. Raising the scroll in his left hand, he asked, *"What charges are you bringing against this man?"*

It was clear from this gesture that he was referring to the charges written on the scroll he now clutched in his hand. Undoubtedly he had read these charges himself, and in all likelihood had discussed them with the assessor standing to his right. But he wanted the high priest to articulate them.

"If he were not a criminal, we would not have handed him over to you," Caiaphas said with a huff.

A rather cheeky response, I thought.

"Take him yourselves and judge him by your own law," Pilate answered.

Here Annas interjected, *"But we have no right to execute anyone."*

A devious response if there ever was one. The temple, in fact, routinely acted as both judge and executioner in religious matters and had been granted full authority to do so. Death by stoning was commonplace. I had witnessed Annas himself cast the first stone at some hapless adulteress within the first week of my arrival here ten years ago. No, the temple had the right to execute, and these crafty fellows could surely find grounds to execute this man. They just didn't want the blood on their hands. They did not want to be blamed for the death of this rabbi. For many he had become the hope of the nation. No, they wanted us to do the job, to act as their executioners. They wanted him judged and executed under Roman law. What Caiaphas said next made this abundantly clear.

"We have found this man"—he aimed a bony finger at Jesus—*"subverting our nation. He opposes payment of taxes to Caesar and claims to be Messiah, a king."*

Now here was a capital offense—a capital offense under Roman law.

The Weasel had backed the Badger into a corner, and he was relishing the moment.

These charges would need further examination. But Pilate would not proceed in full view of a gloating high priest, urged on by his consorts and a handpicked audience. He retreated.

He abruptly arose from his throne, fixed his eyes on me, and said, "Bring the man." He motioned with a jerk of his head toward the great doors behind us and then marched off into his residence.

I stepped down to escort Jesus, but he was already in motion. It became clear that the steps were painful for him. I put my hand to his elbow.

Despite the pain, he moved with the quick determination of a man with a destination in mind—the very thing I had noted on his arrival to the city.

I avoided his eyes. By the gods, I avoided his eyes! I couldn't help think that out of some great mercy he was avoiding my eyes too.

For some strange reason there was the fading smell of fine perfume about him. It hinted of far better evenings than the last.

Just before passing through the doors, I looked up and saw Pilate's wife, Claudia Procula, granddaughter of Augustus Caesar, gazing down at us from a second-floor window. Undoubtedly she had been watching the unfolding events with considerable interest. She knew only too well the missteps her husband was capable of.

When we entered the judgment hall, the dark-eyed Badger was seething. He knew Caiaphas was using him. He had said so to the assessor. He let fly a string of profanity. "He has me trapped!" he snarled. "Trapped like a rat in a stone water jar." And with that he tossed the list of charges onto his desk.

Then he turned to Jesus in the center of the room. He looked him over, walked fully around him. Pilate sighed and nervously ran his fingers through his thinning hair. He made a smacking sound with his lips and asked, *"Are you the king of the Jews?"*

"You have said so," came his equivocal answer.

This answer left the governor rocking on his heels. He brought a finger to his lips in pensive thought.

Jesus was not making an acquittal any easier.

But after a moment Jesus continued. *"Is that your own idea, or did others talk to you about me?"*

"Am I a Jew?" Pilate shot back with an ample measure of haughty contempt. *"Your own people and chief priests handed you over to me."* He continued the questioning. *"What is it you have done?"*

"My kingdom is not of this world," Jesus said, and to drive home this point, he added, *"If it were, my servants would fight to prevent my arrest by the Jewish leaders. But now my kingdom is from another place."*

Certain words that Claudius had spoken came echoing back into my mind. He had been convinced that this kingdom Jesus spoke of was somehow different from kingdoms as we know them. Now I heard it from this would-be Messiah's mouth. He was no armed insurrectionist, and he had offered the actions of his followers as proof.

But Pilate seized on that word—kingdom. "*You* are *a king, then!*" Pilate deduced.

With calm, clear deliberation the prophet spoke. *"You say that I am a king. In fact, the reason I was born and came into the world is to testify to the truth. Everyone on the side of truth listens to me."*

It almost seemed from this response that Jesus was operating from, and speaking on, some higher plane—a dimension I had witnessed him operate from during the healings at the temple. He was inviting Pilate to join him in discovering this higher ground of truth.

Pilate would not be moved. They were speaking past each other.

"What is truth?" Pilate shrugged. The question was rhetorical. He had no intention of being dragged into a philosophical discussion with this prophet of the Jewish masses. Once again, the Badger retreated.

Grabbing the list of charges from off his desk, he motioned for us to follow him back outside.

I quickly scanned the crowd as I emerged into morning sunlight with Jesus at my side. The crowd had not grown. Marius and his men had kept the general public at bay. His ranks had been augmented by a contingent of my own men. I spotted Claudius off to my far left.

I felt more at ease.

In due course we all resumed our previous positions. At this point I fully expected Pilate to pronounce the prisoner guilty of high treason. After all, this Messiah had freely confessed to being a king. But I can only guess that Jesus's words did have an impact on the governor. Upon taking his seat, Pilate announced, *"I find no basis for a charge against him."*

A murmur arose from beyond the pikemen.

Caiaphas was livid. He let fly with a torrent of accusations, the last of these being that Jesus had threatened to destroy the temple and then rebuild it in three days.

Showing extraordinary patience, Pilate let the high priest rage. When

Caiaphas's fury was spent, Pilate turned to Jesus and asked, *"Don't you hear the testimony they are bringing against you?"*

But Jesus answered him not a word. His silence itself became a challenge. Pilate had cleared him. Why should he answer to these further allegations?

Though stunned by this silence, Pilate repeated his position. "I find no basis for a charge against him."

Once again discontent began to rumble through the crowd on the street.

At this point I expected the trial to end and the prisoner to be released. Let the crowds rage. Rome had spoken.

But Annas stepped smartly into the breach. *"He stirs up the people all over Judea by his teaching. He started in Galilee and has come all the way here."*

"Is he a Galilean?" Pilate asked. "Under Herod's jurisdiction?"

"Yes," the flustered Caiaphas confessed, not knowing where this questioning might lead.

"Then to Herod he should go," was Pilate's prompt response. "Why drag me into this?" He sneered at the high priest.

The governor seemed weary of the whole affair, and for the third time that morning, he found a way to dodge and retreat.

This trial was over.

The dark-eyed Badger rose from his judgment seat. He walked over to Jesus, the accused, and with a rather cunning smile and a nod, he said, "Off to Herod you will go, man of truth."

24

Seven ten in the morning, Friday, April 7

PILATE CALLED FOR a scribe. He dictated a short description of the early-morning proceedings. He explained that when he discovered the accused was from Galilee, he felt it only proper that the tetrarch should judge the man. "Since he is your subject, I defer to you in this matter," he stated.

He included this letter with the roll of charges the high priest had prepared. After affixing the imperial seal to this missive, he handed it to me.

I viewed these developments with growing alarm. I had no desire to parade our prisoner across the city to Herod's palace in full public view—a public that would surely include a large number of pilgrims, fellow Galileans, and disciples of this man. I could think of no better way to advertise his arrest and thereby foment turmoil. I could easily envision a pitched battle out on the street between the Messiah's followers and the high priest's temple guards, supported as they were by the Weasel's merchant-class allies.

"Now, centurion, take that message and your man here to Herod. I'm sure Jonathon can accompany you. The high priest certainly won't."

In a flash it occurred to me—Herod wasn't at his palace across town. He was here. He and Herodias had spent the night here with the governor and his wife. The governor's next words confirmed this sudden insight.

"He's in the guest apartment. You and the tribune, Flavio, can work out the details with these gentlemen." He motioned with a jerk of his head in the direction of the three-man delegation. He showed little concern for these details. The Messiah was, after all, the high priest's problem. With that he turned from me and strode back into his residence.

The dark-eyed Badger had scurried off. Of course, we didn't nickname the governor "the Badger" without cause. Initially it was because of his eyes. He had dark-brown eyes. By that I do not mean the color of the iris of the eyes—they were a rather standard, unremarkable brown—it was the skin about the eyes that had a dark-brown hue. This was his distinguishing feature. It gave him his badger look.

It now became clear to me that Caiaphas and his crowd out front were not moving anywhere. Caiaphas, Annas, and Jonathon were in a hushed but heated discussion a few feet away. They were clearly caught off guard by these sudden developments.

Flavio turned to me. "You may yet have a fourth man on Golgotha. Herod won't take kindly to a second king—a man from his own domain."

I sniffed and then scowled at the thought of his expected reaction. "No, he won't," I said. Visions of brutal torture galloped to mind.

"This thing may get very ugly." I motioned beyond my prisoner to the throng on the street. "I have twenty of my men backing up Marius and his pikemen. I may need all my men if Caiaphas gets a conviction."

"You're right there, Marcus." Flavio nodded. "We need to keep this contained. I'll send a messenger and have them brought up. They can form a second line around the perimeter of the crowd." Then to my relief he added, "I won't be moving from here until this matter is settled."

Flavio showed a measure of early-morning sobriety I had not witnessed in weeks. Maybe heaven was working on our side in this. He stepped back into the shadow of the Praetorium entrance and in short order dispatched messengers. The entire legion was placed on high alert, troops were redeployed, street patrols were doubled.

Seeing the temple officials still in discussion, I beckoned my three-man party on the first step to come forward. My third man, with the retrieved nail pouch in hand, had rejoined his partners.

While accepting the pouch, I said, "You three will be coming with me. We'll be taking the prisoner to Herod inside the fortress."

Throughout this time Jesus stood in sublime silence. I could only imagine what was going through his mind. Terror would be logical. But it was not to be seen in his face or his posture.

He puzzled me. No—troubled me. Once again he was beyond my understanding.

Flavio returned. He motioned to me, and we approached the temple delegation.

"The centurion here has the written charges you have brought against the man, and he has the letter from the governor. He will take them and the prisoner to the tetrarch inside the fortress."

"In the fortress?" Caiaphas objected.

"Yes, in the fortress," Flavio said. "The tetrarch is here." He motioned over his right shoulder.

This news was greeted with dismay. The high priest would not enter the fortress, even as he would not enter the Praetorium. If he did so, he would become defiled—unclean during this high point of the Jewish calendar. That he would even venture out onto the street was an indication of the gravity he attached to this matter.

Again they huddled to discuss this among themselves. It was clear that Caiaphas was furious because Pilate had not simply ratified the decision of the Sanhedrin and then ordered Jesus crucified. I am certain he believed Pilate had acted out of spite, and perhaps he had. Now Caiaphas was forced to rely on Herod's erratic judgment to convict this man who had dared to challenge his authority. This meant he would now be unable to personally present his case before the king.

Things turned out just as Pilate had predicted. Jonathon was chosen to accompany me. But Caiaphas and Annas elected to stay and await the outcome. In their place they selected two men from among the coterie of priests and teachers of the law assembled behind our line of pikemen. Jonathon called on his three guards, who once again bound the prisoner, and together as a party of eleven, we set off.

It's only a few paces from the front steps of the Praetorium, around the southwest turret of the fortress, and then into the fortress itself. But the milling throng didn't make our passage easy. The moment they saw us move Jesus in that direction, there was a corresponding surge from the crowd toward him. They wanted blood. I hastily pressed a half dozen pikemen into service. They worked a certain magic. When their spears came down, aiming directly ahead, the way suddenly opened before us. Even so, I was relieved to reach my sanctuary—the fortress.

The guest apartment to which Pilate referred formed the entire second level of the southwest turret. It connected directly to the governor's residence by a canopied catwalk, but there was also a second entrance from the inside of the fortress. This was the entrance we would use.

I reasoned that there must have been a dramatic thaw in relations between the governor and the tetrarch. Perhaps the first ladies had something to do with this. Claudia Procula often invited Roman friends and relations to her home. These guests, like Claudia herself, came from the upper echelons of Roman society. For weeks on end they would stay in this lavishly furnished tower suite. But this overnight stay was a first for the Herods. In my mind it was an ominous development.

We reached the steeply rising stairs leading to the apartment. Without a moment's hesitation I again reached out a hand to support the limping Messiah.

He nodded his appreciation. A wisp of a smile crossed his lips.

It's strange how the mind works. In an instant I was transported back to my childhood. In a moment of rough play, my younger brother had stumbled, snapping his ankle. It was the kind of accident that could just as easily have happened to me. For weeks I supported him. I became his living crutch while the bone mended. Every night I helped him up the stairs.

It was like that now. In my mind I was back helping my brother. For twelve steps I supported him—the Messiah.

On the balcony above, Cestas, Herod's brooding bodyguard, waited. His well-muscled arms were folded across his chest. The brute's encounter with Lucas flashed into mind. Now here he stood guarding the entrance to his master's suite.

A mixture of anger and loathing welled up within me. I fixed my eyes on him and then addressed him.

"We have come with an urgent message for the king from His Excellency the governor, and the high priest." I spoke with a glance toward Jonathon.

"He's not to be disturbed," Cestas replied impassively.

"I said it's urgent." There was insistence in my tone.

"I said he's not to be disturbed."

He didn't flinch or look me in the eye.

Seeing the impasse and the anger beginning to burn in my eyes, Jonathon intervened. "Look, man. We have just come from the high priest and His Excellency the governor. This is a matter of importance."

Cestas was unmoved.

"We have a prisoner. A Galilean," I said. "The king is to render judgment."

The word "prisoner" seemed to spark this butcher's interest. What this man did with prisoners I dreaded to imagine. He stared at Jesus. A thin smile crossed his lips.

"Who is the prisoner?" he asked.

"Jesus, the prophet from Nazareth," I answered.

"Jesus of Nazareth?" His eyebrows shot up. He snickered. "Yes, my master will see him." Then with a full grin he said, "He has wanted to see him for quite some time."

He turned and rapped his knuckles three times on the door.

No response.

He rapped again.

"Cestas!" came the gruff response. "Send them away!"

He knocked once more and said, "They have a prisoner. Jesus of Nazareth."

I could hear the muffled sound of movement from within. The door latch clicked and then opened. It was Herod, bleary-eyed, unkempt. An open purple robe hung loosely around his shoulders. In all other respects he was naked and exposed.

"You have a prisoner," he growled as he looked beyond me.

"Yes, Your Majesty," I answered with a bow. "We have just come from the governor and the high priest. The accused is with us, Jesus of Nazareth. Here are the charges against him."

I bowed again and offered him the rolled parchments. He ignored them completely.

"Bring him in," he ordered. He stepped back inside and adjusted the robe about himself.

"Herodias!" he bellowed. "We have a guest. Jesus of Nazareth."

It took a few moments for my eyes to adjust to the dim light of the room and then to fully realize where I was. This was the royal bedchamber. On the far side of the room, Herodias lay on her side in an enormous four-poster bed. She propped her head up as she watched our men bring in the prisoner. A magnificently carved table, inlaid with ivory, stood in the center of the room. Off to the wall on the right stood two enormous thrones of a similar style. On the left a doorway led to what I guessed were the servants' quarters.

Jesus stumbled slightly as he crossed the threshold. This rather large room soon became small with the arrival of eleven men.

"Untie him," Herod instructed as he perched himself on one of the thrones.

Jonathon's men expeditiously followed through.

I instructed two of my soldiers to wait outside and the last man to wait just inside, at the door. Jonathon followed the same formula with his men.

Addressing Cestas, Herod said, "I will call you if you are needed."

I was relieved with his departure, though I sensed a certain reluctance on his part to leave.

"Jesus of Nazareth," the Fox pompously intoned. "The prophet of Galilee. I've longed to see you, my most noteworthy subject."

With that Herod arose, and holding his robe shut, he approached the Messiah. He inspected the taller man, walked fully around him. Noticing the welts and the dried spittle, he looked my way and asked, "Is this your work, centurion?"

"No, Your Majesty." My eyes darted to Jonathon and back to Herod again.

"Ah, the high priest's work!" the Fox remarked grandly as he turned to Jonathon. "I didn't think you temple boys were capable."

This bit of sarcasm drew an acknowledging nod and a slight smile from the chief temple guard. Here was a backhanded compliment from the pretentious Fox.

"Your Majesty, I have here a letter from His Excellency the governor and certain charges brought by–"

The king halted me with an uplifted hand and a shake of his head.

"That can wait, centurion." He paused, and then with a certain dramatic flourish, he began. "We have here a man of rare talent. He makes the lame to walk, the blind to see, has cured the leper. I have heard reports that he has raised the dead." And then spotting a gold chalice on the inlaid table, he seized it by the stem and with relish declared, "He has even turned water into wine."

He lifted the chalice before the Messiah and grandly asked, "Isn't that so, Jesus?"

The Messiah did not answer him a word.

If Herod was perturbed by this silence, he didn't show it. "Servant girl!" he hollered. "Servant girl!"

An attractive young woman entered from the door on the left, and with short, quick steps, she made her way before the tetrarch. She bowed low.

"Fill this chalice with water and bring it back."

He stared after her as she left.

I noticed Herodias following his hungry gaze.

"Soon we will see if this prophet can perform the works of which we heard." He nodded his head with an eager enthusiasm. Then addressing Jesus, he asked, "Tell us of your magic arts."

The Messiah fixed his eyes straight ahead. He looked beyond the Fox and did not answer him a word. His silence was challenging enough.

Herod's gaze flitted to me, to Jonathon and his men, back to Jesus, over to Herodias.

The servant girl returned, brimming chalice in hand. This time as she bowed, he bowed too. His eyes played with hers. He received the chalice. He cradled and then fondled it gently in his open hand as he watched her retreat.

Herodias cleared her throat and made a fuss of repositioning herself on the bed.

Herod stepped back in front of Jesus. With great show he lifted the gold chalice to his lips, took a sip, and swirled it around his mouth. Then he coughed it full force over the front of the Messiah's robe.

"It's water!" he said, cackling. "It's water," he repeated as he coughed again to clear his throat. He found great humor in this and began to laugh uncontrollably.

Herodias joined in. Jonathon chuckled. I smiled just enough to be polite.

"I haven't drunk water in so long"—he broke off into more laughter—"I forgot what the stinking stuff tastes like."

He fought to bring himself back in control. Forgetting himself, his robe fell open, exposing all. This set him off cackling wildly again.

He turned from us.

I saw a repeated pattern of four brown stains along the back of the purple robe. Recognition was immediate. These were bloodstains—blood from the severed hand of a beggar boy.

I sucked in a sharp breath, as though punched in the stomach.

The demented cackle continued.

The Messiah stood in silence—a quiet silence that despite all, came to fill, even to dominate the room. Strangely, he was master here.

The Fox was unable to face him. King Herod was unable to face the donkey king, to look him in the eye.

I understood perfectly what was happening. I too had tasted of this unease in the Messiah's presence. Back in the temple I had put feet to my own fear.

Having laughed himself to lunacy, Herod gasped for air. Then with his composure suddenly regained, he wheeled around and held the chalice up to the face of the Christos, the Messiah. With his eyes pinched shut and his voice almost breaking, he hissed, "Now, change it to wine!"

The Messiah looked past him. He uttered not a word.

Herod, with eyes still shut, gasped three times, and as if counting, on three he hurled the contents of the chalice in Jesus's face.

Looking up, he cackled, "It's water! It's only water!"

There was genuine relief in his voice. He had feared it might be wine. And so he set loose again with a further bout of hideous laughter.

Now for a moment I dared look at Jesus's dripping face. I saw a noble serenity there that Herod, that small, shrewd monster, would never know.

The tetrarch saw it too, and it was driving him insane. He made no pretense of covering his nakedness now. He pranced about laughing, a raw fool on display.

Glancing at Jonathon, I could tell he too found no humor here. His troubled eyes spoke of growing discomfort, if not alarm, at the king's antics. Where this was heading defied prediction. Clearing his throat, he began. "Your Majesty, there are certain charges the high priest has brought."

"Charges. Ah yes, charges." He moaned as though aroused from a drunken stupor. "What are these charges?"

"I have them here," I answered and once more bowed and held the rolled parchments out to him.

He ignored them. Then in his nakedness he approached, put his mouth to my ear, and screamed, "Read them!"

He snickered and coughed, and he began to tremble violently until he collapsed into his throne.

With my left ear ringing, I opened the roll and began, "From His Excellency the governor . . ."

"From His Excellency the governor," he mimicked. "Hang the governor!" he screamed as his face contorted like one possessed. "There are charges. What are the charges?" He held his hands up above his head, with his fingers fully spread, as though he would try to capture the parts of his head should it explode.

Completely flustered, I blurted out, "He's charged with being the king of the Jews."

The reaction was instant.

Herod's head snapped back. It whacked the back of the throne with such force that it cracked the wooden backboard.

His body convulsed once more and he slumped forward onto his knees on the floor.

His eyes rolled back in his head.

His face contorted.

Then from a kneeling position, a demonic voice—a voice not his own—erupted from deep within Herod's being. "He is the king of the Jews! The Christ! The holy one of God!"

A low, guttural hissing sound followed.

The demonic manifestation was now complete. His body rocked and convulsed. Rocked and convulsed. Every muscle rippled and twitched. He had become what he was—a tautly coiled human cobra, even now spitting venom.

For the first time the Messiah looked to him.

"Be still," he whispered.

It was a whisper so quiet that I would have missed it had I not seen his lips move.

But his words brought an instantaneous reaction in Herod—Jesus's opposite. The pretender to the Jewish throne fell forward in obeisance to the true king. His body convulsed once more and then became still.

Still as death.

Long moments passed.

He stirred.

Then the tetrarch lifted his head and in his own calm, flat voice stated, "He is the king of the Jews."

He struggled awkwardly to his feet.

Taking the bloodied purple robe off his back, naked and whimpering, he approached the Messiah. He tied its sleeves around the neck of the people's king, so that the stained fabric hung cape-like over his shoulders and down his back. But all the while the Fox was careful not to look into his rival's face.

With his head hanging and in utter despair, Herod turned from the passive Christ. "Cestas," he called.

It was a weak call, barely audible.

I signaled my man at the door. He retrieved the bodyguard. By this time the tetrarch had dropped to all fours and was now sitting with his back to the king.

The bewildered Cestas approached.

"Bring the crown. The braided crown you're making. Put it"—he sobbed piteously—"put it on . . . put it on the king."

Cestas left hurriedly.

The Messiah stood in silence. His gaze was steady. Still, he looked beyond this.

Herod pulled his legs up against his chest. In his nakedness he rocked from side to side for eternal moments.

Cestas returned with a braided crown—a crown of thorns—in his hand. He appeared truly dumbfounded. He had no idea what he was to do with it.

Jonathon intervened. He gestured to Jesus and then nodded in his direction.

Cestas stepped before the king and firmly pressed his hand-fashioned crown down upon the regal brow. The sadist found a purpose for his carefully crafted creation.

Here was a fitting crown for a donkey king.

Cestas sneered, and then he began the same cackling laugh I had heard earlier from Herod.

As if on cue the tetrarch joined in the demented cackling.

"Now take him. Take him from me," Herod whimpered in a different voice from all the others I had heard from him. He did not even dare to look back following his rival's coronation.

On seeing their moment about to pass, the high priest's appointed delegates broke loose with a torrent of accusations against the Messiah. Rebellion. Heresy. Sedition. Sabbath breaking. All manner of false teaching. Threatening to destroy the temple. Blasphemy! The litany poured out till it reached a rabid crescendo.

The whimpering Fox showed no interest, no interest whatever. Still naked, seated and sobbing, with the back of his limp hand, he waved for us to leave.

A drop of blood trickled down the Messiah's thorn-pierced temple.

I put my hand to the Christ's elbow. Together we turned to the door. I was last to leave.

As I pulled the door shut, the naked Herod was on all fours. He was over at the bed licking the hand of a doting Herodias. With her free hand she soothingly stroked his balding head.

25

Seven fifty in the morning, Friday, April 7

JESUS HAD SURVIVED Herod. This was no small feat, in my estimation.

In reality he had totally dominated Herod. Without speaking a word, he had thrown him into a state of raving lunacy. Without raising his voice above a whisper, he had stilled the raging voice of hell. Without moving a hand, he had reduced this pretentious monarch to a pathetic fool, groveling and naked.

I was both impressed and confounded by what I had witnessed. His power baffled me. It was from another realm. Of that I was convinced.

He was the master of the events around him, not the victim. One couldn't help but feel that this was a drama of his own choosing, and we—all of us—were somehow players in it. We were players moving at his discretion, and at any moment he could step out of this drama, if he saw fit. Undoubtedly, the unfolding script for this play was written well in advance, and he was following it—following it to a destination he had chosen.

For the first time I began to actively hope for his release. I wanted free of this.

As once again I helped him on the stairs, I took courage and glanced into his eyes. If eyes are the windows to the soul, then this was a very different soul. It appeared to me that the wellspring of eternity was in residence there.

I felt so very small.

For those twelve steps down, our roles were reversed. I felt I was the weaker brother.

The same pikemen who had escorted us into the fortress were waiting to escort us back out. As our party stepped into view, the expectant mob on the street erupted with the cry, *"Crucify him! Crucify him!"*

They were vociferous.

"Crucify him! Crucify him!"

Leading the chant was an immaculately robed man. Unlike the masses, he faced the crowd and urged them on—the portly commander of his bloodthirsty cohorts. "Crucify him! Crucify him!" he bawled with his arms raised.

"Crucify him! Crucify him!" the crowd echoed.

As he swung around, I caught sight of his face. It was Timaeus. There was bloody determination in his eye. This was a battle he and his fellow merchants intended to win. A human sea of hatred urged him on.

The pikemen's magic had lost some of its charm. The men on the street moved when confronted with the point of a spear, but there was a belligerence there I hadn't noticed an hour ago.

"Crucify him! Crucify him!"

Some began to hurl dust in the air. I feared stones would come next.

We rounded the turret.

"Crucify him! Crucify him!"

They pressed in behind us as we advanced. Seething shouts lashed the air.

"Crucify him! Crucify him!"

I felt genuine relief when we reached the safety of our line of pikemen on the Praetorium steps. What a different response to this man from what I saw Sunday!

Jonathon and the guards with him rejoined Caiaphas and Annas on the third step. The high priest's appointed delegates were soon in animated conversation with their master. I moved past them with my purple-robed prisoner to where Flavio waited with three other centurions on the fourth step. They were standing to the right of the empty judgment seat.

"So what is the verdict?" Flavio discreetly asked.

"There is no verdict," I said.

"No verdict?" Flavio sounded surprised. "Did Herod hear the case?"

"Yes, he heard it." There was a vagueness to my voice that betrayed the baffling nature of what I had witnessed. Quick pat answers said so little.

"Did he find him guilty?" Flavio persisted as though he had not heard my earlier answer.

"No." I paused in thought. "He just sent him back."

"Well then, he should be free to go." He gestured in the direction of the Messiah.

Strangely, this had not occurred to me. I think I was so mesmerized by what had transpired in the guest apartment that I failed to link Herod's dismissal of the charges with Pilate's earlier acquittal of Jesus on the same charges. It logically followed that he should be freed.

"Go ahead and report to the governor." Flavio motioned in the direction of the Praetorium entrance. "Tell him what happened before Herod. Renaldo here can accompany you."

Then putting my hand to the nail pouch on my belt, I said, "I guess there will only be three men on Golgotha after all."

Flavio wrinkled his brow and then nodded in agreement with this assessment. But a quick glance out to the crowd hinted that he thought this was a verdict that would not go down well on this street.

I turned to the three soldiers accompanying me and gave them their new orders. "Report to Claudius. Have him get Barabbas and his two friends ready for execution. Have them brought out front here. We should be free to set out shortly."

Then turning to the Christ, I motioned for him to follow me. Renaldo took over as prisoner escort.

Once again I glanced up before passing through the Praetorium entrance. Once again the first lady was watching from her window.

Pontius Pilate was seated with the province's chief revenue officer when we entered. He glanced up from his ledgers and beckoned us forward. Addressing me, he asked, "What word do you bring from the tetrarch?"

I bowed. "Your Excellency, the tetrarch has heard the charges against this man—the charges prepared by the high priest. He has examined him and, my lord, he has sent him back to you."

Pilate sighed.

"Did he provide a written judgment?" His eyes flitted to the roll of parchment still in my hand.

"No, Your Excellency."

He frowned.

"He simply dismissed us," I added in an attempt to clarify.

Pilate put his hand to his chin and made a smacking sound with his lips. "Dismissed is dismissed," he said perfunctorily.

Then he fixed his attention on the Messiah. For the first time he noticed the crown of thorns and the robe. He arose. He came around the table where he sat and approached us. He examined the bloodied brow, the penetrating thorns.

"A fine bit of work!" He shook his head in disgust.

Then he touched the fabric of the purple robe, his interest piqued. He stepped behind the Messiah and immediately spotted the rust brown stains. He rubbed the crusted stain between his fingers. Recognizing its source, he snorted in revulsion. Here was the purple wrapping for Herod's wee presentation at the banquet just three days ago. The governor grimaced and once more shook his head.

"A fine bit of work!" The words dropped heavy with sarcasm.

My eyes shifted to Renaldo. I could hear the unspoken questions churning through his mind. A flicker of his eye told me we would talk of this later.

"A fine bit of work!" Pilate again repeated his words. He paused in reflection, and then he seemed to shake himself back to the present reality.

"Dismissed is dismissed," he reiterated as he came back in front of the Messiah. "We'll inform the high priest of your acquittal," he announced to Jesus.

Then he called for two of his attendants to take up their positions by the judgment seat on the steps out front. He intended to deliver this decision with the proper decorum warranted under Roman law. He moved to the window and surveyed the crowd on the street. The numbers had not grown. Marius and his pikemen had seen to that. But the assembled throng had grown more unruly.

By closing off the street and hedging in this partisan crowd, the army had ensured that there would be no clash between the opposing camps—the Messiah's followers and the high priest's temple faction. But this same move also served to provoke a strident hostility in this confined faction. It was hostility that stiffened incrementally with the passage of time.

The Badger shrugged and then sighed deeply. Instinctively he knew this would be a challenge. He turned back to us and brusquely declared, "Gentlemen, follow me."

He strode to the large double doors and then paused to see if all of us were ready to follow him at the moment he gave the signal to the door-keepers. As he turned for this final check, a messenger called out.

"Your Excellency, I have here a message for you from the first lady."

Clearly annoyed by this interruption, he threw up his hands and snapped, "What is it?"

The young man unrolled a small parchment and read, *"Don't have anything to do with that innocent man, for I have suffered a great deal today in a dream because of him."*

Having accomplished his assignment, the messenger bowed and handed this brief missive to the governor.

Pilate took it, sniffed as though amused, and then he cast questioning eyes on the Messiah.

I couldn't help but remember Renaldo's words from earlier in the week. "He has a certain way with women," he had said. If the harlots came to follow him, why not the governor's wife?

This time my eyes signaled my friend for a later conversation.

Pilate turned, readjusted the cuff on his sleeve, and nodded to the doormen. The eagle-emblazoned doors swung open. The sentinels snapped to attention. Once more, their right arms rose in salute. A hush fell upon the throng.

The governor strode out, head held high. We dutifully followed in his wake.

Upon taking his seat, he unrolled the note from his wife and read it for himself. I tried to read his face for a clue of what action he might take, but no clear course was written there.

We positioned ourselves before him just as before.

Jesus stood before me. His abused body was present, but I perceived his focus was elsewhere.

Pilate beckoned for Caiaphas and Annas to approach. He cleared his throat and with mustered authority he began. *"You brought me this man as one who was inciting the people to rebellion. I have examined him in your presence and have found no basis for your charges against him. Neither has Herod, for he sent him back to us; as you can see, he has done nothing to deserve death."*

With these words a murmur arose from the crowd.

As if taking this discontent as his cue, Pilate added, *"Therefore, I will punish him and then release him."*

I'm not sure these were his intended words, or if they were the words thrust upon him by the hostile throng. They were words intended to appease. But rather than appease, they had the opposite effect.

Caiaphas reacted. He put both hands to his face and clutched his graying beard. It seemed he would pull the whole mass of it out by its roots.

Annas stamped his foot and twisted his aged frame as though smitten with mortal agony.

A howl of protest erupted from beyond our line of pikemen on the first step. No, this pronouncement did not sit well. There was cold resistance. Had the prophet been released at that moment, this mob would have torn him to pieces.

Then fate seemed to intervene. I noticed Pilate's eyes move to a spot off to the far right, a spot near the turret. I glanced that way. It was Claudius and his contingent arriving with the three men destined for Golgotha.

Seeing Barabbas in chains, the Badger tried a new tack. Rising from his seat and stretching out an open hand to the Christ, he repeated, *"I find no basis for a charge against him."*

There was sincerity in his voice but a conniving manipulation at work in his mind.

He continued. *"But it is your custom for me to release to you one prisoner at the time of the Passover. Do you want me to release 'the king of the Jews'?"*

Again he gestured to the purple-robed figure.

The high priest's response was instant and vehement. *"No, not him!"* He raised his arm and pointed to the terrorist. *"We want Barabbas."*

"Barabbas! Barabbas!" The cry went up from the street.

The Badger smacked his lips. This was not the response he had wanted. But now, at this precise moment he determined that he would play with this crowd. He would play them to reach his own desired end. He loved this sport. He had seen Emperor Tiberius do the same with the crowds in Rome.

The Christ stood alone. He stood silent. He fixed his eyes beyond this. He had his own destination in mind.

Pilate strode over to me. His step was purposeful, resolute. "Have him flogged," he said with a decisive nod. "Then bring him back here."

He turned from me and once more retreated to his inner sanctum behind the eagle-emblazoned doors.

His wife's parchment note was left behind. It balanced precariously on the edge of the judgment seat. A sudden gust of cool wind caught it. It skittered and flew across the stone steps. Then it was caught up.

In an instant it was gone.

26

Eight fifteen in the morning, Friday, April 7

WEDGE FORMATION IS the best way to advance through a hostile crowd. Under Flavio's direct orders we formed up accordingly on the stairs, with added manpower assigned at his discretion. He viewed the mood of this mob with growing alarm.

The Christ was placed at the heart of this bristling wedge. He was there for his own protection. Renaldo and I accompanied him on either side.

Claudius and his contingent remained on the broad stairs with the three condemned men. The ultimate fate of Barabbas still hung in the balance, with the Christ as the counterweight.

As we set out, I couldn't help but reflect on what a change this week had brought for my kingly prisoner. On Sunday he had entered as the heroic savior riding the crest of a human wave of unsullied joy. I had feared the very power of Rome would be trampled under the feet of his horde of followers. Now, five days later, he was leaning on my arm, under Rome's protection from a mob of his own people—a seething mob thirsting for his blood. He needed our protection on the way to the whipping post. There was a dreadful irony in all this, an irony as cruel and twisted as the piercing thorns that crowned his head.

Once again the shouts of "Crucify him! Crucify him!" went up. Once again Timaeus raged against him. His puffy face was red with exertion. He kept just beyond the advancing spears of the pikemen—a huffing heckler bent on revenge.

Upon entering the fortress, I was thankful for the extra manpower. Flavio had exercised a rare bit of sober wisdom.

The whipping post stood at the very center of the fortress courtyard. This silent wooden sentinel reminded the errant or lazy soldier of the cruel consequence that might well await him. Insolence and insubordination found their remedy there.

The city's residents only rarely met such a fate. They had more to fear from the temple guards and the ritual stonings that were routinely carried out to enforce the dictates of religious law. Only when the offense was aimed directly at Rome would the offender be brought here. Already this morning Barabbas and his cohorts had endured the lash in preparation for the cross. Now, so too would the Messiah.

Oddly, the only bit of greenery within the fortress walls was to be found here at the whipping post. The courtyard itself was hard-packed, dun-colored clay, but a dandelion sallied forth from a crevice at the base of the whipping post. Its gaudy yellow flowers spoke eloquently of spring. Here it thrived while boldly mocking its drab surroundings.

I called for the men to administer the scourging. Every legion has its share of men who draw perverse pleasure in inflicting pain on others. Within our ranks were some of these. Today, two such men had been assigned to administer floggings, Lucius and Gaius. Wearing Herod's gaudy robe and the crown of thorns fashioned by Cestas, Jesus stood before them. His attire served as an invitation for abuse.

"Ah, the king of the Jews!" Lucius exclaimed. The news about the Christ had spread fast. His clothing confirmed the rumors of kingly aspirations. Lucius seized a corner of the purple robe. "We have a royal treat for you." He bowed low, and then as he straightened, he let fly with a vicious backhand slap to the face.

The Messiah reeled with the force of it.

"We have far more for you, Your Highness!" Gaius smirked. He seized him by the beard and gave a twisting yank, forcing the Messiah to his knees. Simultaneously, the soldier's knee smashed into Jesus's chin. The snapping slam of teeth to teeth testified to the force of the blow.

I intervened. "Look, you two. I need a man I can take back to the governor, not a mutilated corpse."

"Ah, Marcus," Lucius answered with a broad grin, "we'll give you your man. We were just havin' some fun. Weren't we?" He laughed as he glanced at Gaius. "It's not every day we get to flog a king."

"Flog him then. Don't kill him, or you'll be next on the post."

They nodded. A surly silence followed.

Gaius removed Herod's robe and handed it to me. Then they stripped him naked—naked except for his crown. They shoved his face to the post. Lucius shackled the king's upstretched arms to an iron ring near the top of the weathered cedar post. Meanwhile Gaius stooped to bind his feet to the base. Then suddenly he raised his head and exclaimed, "He smells like a bloomin' king."

It was the scent of perfume I had noted earlier.

They stepped back to admire their work. They chuckled at his nakedness. "Looks the same as any beggar's butt," Lucius groused.

"Yeah, but he smells like a bloomin' king!" Gaius shot back. He was quite astonished by this aromatic discovery. His nostrils flared as he inhaled several whiffs for the amusement of his fellow soldiers.

I examined both flagrums, the multi-thonged whips used to administer the scourging. I had pulled them from the large bucket of salt brine where they were temporarily stored. The lead balls and metal studs on the strips of leather determined the brutality of each blow. Forty lashes with the most vicious whip could shred a man's back. In Germania I witnessed a young man's death by whipping. The flailing had exposed his kidneys.

The Messiah had already been brutalized during his night with Caiaphas and the temple guard. A measure of restraint was warranted. I consulted Renaldo. Then I drew my dagger, and to the dismay of Gaius and Lucius, I cut the lead stud from four of the multiple leather thongs. There were plenty left to do their damage.

"Kings and beggars need a break sometime," I said as I handed each man his implements.

I gave a quick nod, and the flogging began.

"One.

"Two."

Lucius worked from one side, Gaius from the other.

"Three.

"Four."

They began at the shoulders.

"Five.

"Six."

Each thwack of the whip opened multiple wounds.

"Seven.

"Eight."

Their rhythm was established now. They were moving lower on his back. The pikemen cheered them on.

"Nine.

"Ten."

The blood began to flow freely.

"Eleven.

"Twelve."

His body quivered with the shock of each blow. But he was silent. Silent and gasping.

"Thirteen.

"Fourteen."

I moved to one side, trying to get a look at his face. His thorn-crowned brow was pressed to the post.

"Fifteen.

"Sixteen."

He was mouthing a word with each blow. What was it?

"Seventeen.

"Eighteen."

It came with a gasp. Barely audible.

"Father.

"Father."

At twenty I called a halt. They had traversed the whole of his body, from shoulders to feet. It was a bloody path. I examined the wounds—more damage than I expected.

His breath came in huge gulps. His eyelids flickered. He remained conscious. At least he remained conscious.

I stepped over to Gaius. I cut another three studs from his whip. Then I did the same for Lucius.

"Harder! Harder!" came a shout from above and behind me. It was Cestas—Cestas going wild on the balcony of the guest chamber. He couldn't wait for the lashing to resume. Like a giddy child, he bounced up and down and hollered for more.

I gave an upward nod to Lucius and then began calling out the stroke count again.

"Twenty-one.

"Twenty-two."

They started over at the shoulders.

"Twenty-three.

"Twenty-four."

Once more the frenzied cheers went up.

"Twenty-five.

"Twenty-six."

Each man aimed to outdo the other; each blow was more savage than the last.

"Twenty-seven.

"Twenty-eight."

He did not cry out, unlike many men I have seen. He was silent beneath the cracking whip, uncommonly silent.

"Twenty-nine.

"Thirty."

Stroke by flailing stroke they moved once more across his bloodied frame. A quivering, rutted mess. That's what was left by the time we reached forty. I stood near him—watched his breathing. It was fast but shallow, very shallow by the time we finished.

Lucius fell to his knees. Sweating. Gasping. Exhausted from exertion.

Gaius did the same. "That was floggin' good!" he exclaimed as he arose and clapped his partner on the back. "Floggin' good!"

Here they were laughing—laughing like two brothers in that tight but brittle fellowship that is formed by inflicting pain. The fellowship of the torturer.

I beckoned to a young soldier.

"Get me a bowl of figs." I motioned in the direction of the officers' mess. It was time for a bit of breakfast.

After that performance we weren't going anywhere fast. Jesus needed time to recover. I watched his eyelids flicker, saw his bare ribs heave.

The dandelion at the base of the post was drenched in blood.

The young soldier returned with a heaping bowl of figs.

I was hungry. And angry. More angry than hungry. Barabbas would walk free. I knew it. The Badger would bow to the crowd. I saw it in his eyes.

The Messiah? Where was the power? It must have evaporated like a desert pond, left him like a harlot's lover. Stripped naked, he was a man after all. Just a man. Wasn't he?

Renaldo recognized my brooding. While I ate my figs, he made small talk. He knew better than to probe. I felt now was not the time to tell him that the robe folded over my arm was stained by the blood of the beggar boy staying at his house.

The men filled the air with coarse humor and ribald jabs aimed at the man on the whipping post. On another day with another man, I might well have joined in. Why are men that way? Why do we wear cruelty like a second skin? Why do we revel in abusing others—draw comfort in it, like a pig in a wallow?

"Is there another one?" Gaius asked. He would cheerfully flog the morning away if we would supply the victims. When I shook my head, he grabbed the bucket of brine and dumped it over the Christ.

Jesus writhed and gasped—writhed and gasped.

Lucius freed the shackles from his wrists. Gaius untied his feet. Renaldo and I stood on either side of him for support, expecting he would collapse. His hands fell to his side. His head dropped limp. But after a few moments, he turned slowly, tentatively, on unsteady feet.

"Have some figs, my good man," I offered. "Have some water and some figs."

I motioned for a bucket of fresh water to be brought.

His clothes were returned to him. His hands trembled as he tied his loincloth about him.

He drank deeply from the pewter ladle I handed to him. When he dipped the ladle in the bucket for a second drink, Lucius grabbed it from his hand. He rapped the king sharply across the side of the head with it.

"Your Majesty"—he bowed low in mock adoration—"I did the work here. I'll have a drink now!"

A fresh trickle of blood flowed down near Jesus's left ear from where the ladle hit the stabbing thorns.

Jesus needed strength, I reasoned, strength to walk back and face the Badger. It wouldn't do to have him fainting on the way.

As he struggled into his outer garment, I pressed a dried fig to his lips. He received it like some sacred gift. Through a fog of pain, his eyes smiled back at me.

He might just as well have shot me with an arrow. I was wounded. Wounded by a glance.

Why did he bother me so?

Strangely, there was power in his weakness, more power than I dared imagine.

Seeing the king back in his commoner's clothes, Gaius cried out, "The robe! Where's his purple robe?"

Suddenly I was uncomfortable with the filthy purple article draped over my arm. I handed it to Renaldo. He made a grand show of flipping it fully open and then tying the sleeves once more around the Messiah's neck. He stepped back and bowed courteously.

Not to be outdone, Gaius fell to his knees in mock obeisance.

"Hail, king of the Jews!" he called out.

Now the platoon of pikemen joined in. One by one they knelt before the thorn-crowned monarch and hailed him as the Jewish king.

I ordered his hands bound once more. Someone produced a hickory stick that was shoved between his tightly bound fingers. Here was the royal scepter. A fresh round of bowing and hailing ensued. Lucius bowed deeply and then seized the crude hickory scepter and delivered a sharp blow to Jesus's head. Several other soldiers followed suit. For these men, months of pent-up frustration found a vent.

He was silent. Always silent.

Soon he grew unsteady on his feet.

When Cestas on his second-level perch began to shout and bounce about once more, I came to my senses. I called a halt to the abuse. After all, why should we entertain Herod's bloody butcher?

I should have stopped this brutal mockery far sooner. I felt less than a man because of it. I had my own anger to blame for it. My brooding had permitted this to happen.

With a backhanded slap to Renaldo's forearm, I snapped, "Have them form up!"

He began barking orders. In moments our pikemen were back in wedge formation. Once again I flanked the Christ at the core of the wedge.

"Forward ho!" Renaldo bawled. As we set out, he retook his position to the left of Jesus.

Once again Timaeus was waiting for us when we hit the street. While keeping just ahead of the lead pikeman in the wedge, he maintained a steady, full-throated scream.

"Crucify him! Crucify him!"

Again his confreres took up the chant.

"Crucify him! Crucify him!"

How Timaeus managed to keep just beyond the point of the lead spear defied logic. While bellowing himself hoarse, he retreated backward in the crowd, glancing to neither the right nor left. It was a stunt few fools would dare to repeat.

A few paces from the steps leading up to the Praetorium, his luck ran out. One instant I saw him clutching his chest; the next instant he was down. Felled by a spear, I presumed. The lead pikeman stepped on him. The other pikemen stepped by him. When finally we reached him, he was white-faced, gasping, twitching—a corpse in the making.

There wasn't a mark on him, though. His heart gave way, or so I thought.

Thus lying prone on the cold cobblestones, I stepped slightly to the left so his body would pass between me and my prisoner. The hem of Jesus's robe brushed lightly over his pallid face.

Timaeus emerged from beneath the Messiah's purple robe transformed, like one awakened from a dream. Not knowing where he was, he shook himself and arose. He arose and was silent. Arose and went home. At least that's what I assume he did. I never saw him again.

This was strange. Such a strange happening!

It happened so fast. But I saw it all. I saw the physical change—a miraculous transformation in the body of this fallen man. I saw it clearly.

I felt small once again, very small beside this man in the middle, very small helping him up the Praetorium steps, very small while waiting.

Waiting for Pontius Pilate.

27

Eight thirty-five in the morning, Friday, April 7

FLAVIO QUICKLY BROUGHT me back to present realities.

"It looks like our boys got the job done," he said as his eyes surveyed the brutalized Christ.

"Yes," I responded dryly. "Lucius and Gaius had a bit of fun."

"I guess we better find out what the governor wants done with him now," Flavio said.

The commotion that our arrival had created among the throng fronting the palace had not brought Pilate through the eagle-emblazoned doors, so some further action was warranted. Flavio turned and addressed Renaldo. "Report to the governor that you have returned with the prisoner." As Renaldo strode off, Flavio turned back to me and added, "You can wait at the door with your man till we know the governor's will."

They'd accomplished their purpose, so I dismissed the pikemen from our wedge formation. They rejoined their comrades on the first step, while I assisted Jesus to the top of the broad steps. We positioned ourselves near the door and waited for Renaldo to return with further instructions.

From this higher elevation I had a commanding view of the confined and seething masses on the street. Their patience was wearing thin. They had assembled for one purpose: to spill the blood of the man beside me. His life hung in the balance, but he seemed somehow distant from this circumstance, as though he was standing on an entirely different plane.

Perhaps he was.

Claudius and the soldiers with him waited off to the right on the second step. Beside them stood an anxious Barabbas and the other two condemned men. His fellow terrorists had a rather wilted appearance. Their heads hung low. Only Barabbas had a reason for hope. After all, it was he who was the favorite of the crowd on the street.

Annas, Caiaphas, and Jonathon fretfully consulted on the third step.

Flavio stood on the fourth step conferring with another centurion he had pressed into service. Next to the tribune stood the empty judgment seat. From thence the Badger would speak. One man would die; the other would walk free.

The Badger! I tilted my head back in thought. I once saw a dog attack a cornered badger. It was a battle royal. The dog barked and yapped. But the moment the canine would lower his head to sink his fangs into the smaller beast, the badger would lunge forward, hissing, his sharp claws flailing. The dog would retreat, and the same process would again be set in motion. Eventually the dog was distracted for an instant. In that moment the badger started digging. He disappeared in a hail of flying dirt.

This too was a battle royal. We would soon see how this Badger would respond.

Momentarily, one of the double palace doors opened, and Renaldo emerged. He beckoned for me to enter with my purple-clad prisoner. Upon entering, we moved to the same position we had assumed during the earlier interrogation. Pilate stepped back from the window where he had been scanning the street scene. Seeing me first, he asked, "Ah, centurion, how is our man—our man of truth?"

"See for yourself, Your Excellency," I answered with a courteous bow and an openhanded gesture in the direction of my prisoner.

Once again Pilate made a full circuit around the Messiah. He examined the spot where the ladle hit, saw the fresh welts inflicted by the hickory scepter, and took note of a broken front tooth.

Not satisfied with merely a facial view, the Badger barked, "Strip him."

I stepped forward and untied the purple robe. I handed it to Renaldo and then loosened Jesus's own garment. The blood from the flogging had begun to soak through the fabric on his back. Some of it had congealed. Tearing it loose brought a gasp from the people's king, and this was followed by a fresh crimson flow.

I dropped his bloodstained white robe on the floor.

"Hmm." Pilate grimaced and moved around for a better view. He smacked his lips and then looked away like one caught up in thought. "Tie Herod's robe back on him." He gestured to Renaldo, who quickly obliged.

The thorn-crowned Christ now stood in only his bloodied breechcloth with the purple robe draped cape-like over his shoulders.

The Badger looked him over as though Jesus were a courtier trying on the latest Roman fashion. Again Pilate circled him to catch the full effect. Satisfied with what he saw, he nodded approvingly and then grandly announced, "Our king! Our Jewish king!"

Pilate gestured to Jesus and bowed. He followed that up with a clever smirk. But throughout this time I noted that he didn't dare look Jesus in the eye, not even once. I suppose he knew, even as I knew, that looking truth in the face could bring a jolt of soul-searing distress.

Now having settled the issue of the prisoner's attire, with a quick, beckoning motion the Badger called for us to follow him out to the judgment seat. When we reached the doors once again, he paused. "Just as before, I will go first," he perfunctorily announced.

The doors swung open again. Sentinels saluted. As we stepped out this time, there was a surprising chill in the air. A bank of low-hanging clouds along the western horizon had replaced the brilliant morning sun. Once again rain seemed possible.

The hushed crowd watched as the governor descended to the fourth step, but before he took his seat, he motioned toward me as I advanced with my limping prisoner. Referring to Jesus, the governor announced, *"Look, I am bringing him out to you to let you know that I find no basis for a charge against him."*

Then as the Christ took his position in full view before this partisan crowd, Pilate stepped over to the bruised and bleeding captive and declared, *"Here is the man!"*

He was indeed a sight to behold.

Face swollen and drenched with spittle. The skin on his back and legs shredded and oozing blood. The mocking, filthy robe. The agonizing crown.

Here was royal splendor, stripped naked and standing on its head. Splendor enough for a donkey king.

If the Badger's intended response was pity for this man, none was forthcoming.

"Crucify! Crucify!" Caiaphas rasped.

His temple guards took up the chant. "Crucify! Crucify!"

Soon the entire crowd joined the chorus. "Crucify! Crucify!"

Their voices echoed off the palace, the fortress, and the rock-hewn temple beyond.

"Crucify!"

After a few moments, silence returned, and Pilate defiantly hissed, *"You take him and crucify him."* There was a flash of anger in his voice. *"As for me, I find no basis for a charge against him."*

Here was the nub of the issue. In the heat of the moment, the truth was blurted out. The Badger was unwilling to act as the high priest's butcher. Let the Weasel slaughter his own Passover lamb.

Caiaphas shrugged his stooped shoulders and scowled. His exasperation seemed complete.

The wily Annas intervened. *"We have a law,"* he said as he eyed the Messiah, *"and according to that law he must die, because he claimed to be the Son of God."*

The superstitious governor reacted to this statement with alarm. He shot a glance heavenward, then over to the tortured king. Perhaps there was something to his wife's discarded warning? Perhaps there was something to the rumors that had circulated? The rumors of miracles. Maybe this was more than an ordinary man? At the very least, his curiosity was piqued.

The Badger let out an audible sigh. He was clearly frustrated by this delay, but nevertheless he would investigate the matter. His pity-arousing tactic had fallen flat. Perhaps another approach was warranted. He turned and motioned for me to bring the prisoner back in for a further round of interrogation.

We had barely reached the spot where the king's outer garment still lay on the floor of the judgment hall when Pilate abruptly wheeled around and demanded, *"Where do you come from?"*

No answer came.

When the pause grew beyond enduring, Pilate snapped, *"Do you refuse to speak to me?"*

In that moment I drew some consolation from knowing that even the governor found this man baffling. The interrogator was flabbergasted.

Pilate went on. *"Don't you realize I have power either to free you"*—he paused to let the gravity of his words sink in—*"or to crucify you?"*

"You would have no power over me," Jesus said, *"if it were not given to you from above. Therefore the one who handed me over to you is guilty of a greater sin."*

Pilate paused to carefully consider these words. In an odd way he must have drawn comfort from them. I am sure he fancied the notion that his own authority ultimately came from the God of heaven. He may have reasoned, better from there than from that prancing, self-proclaimed Roman god, the Emperor Tiberius Caesar.

Then there was the second part of Jesus's statement—the part about the greater sin. The greater sin rested with Caiaphas; after all, it was he who had Jesus arrested. It was he who brought him before the judgment seat of Rome. Wasn't he the guilty party in this brutal travesty? Of course he was.

If guilt didn't rest in the accused, it must rest in the accuser, and the Weasel was the accuser. His was the greater sin.

As for his own responsibility, I am sure Pilate would rather not think about that.

Jesus's words provided the feint and dodge the Badger was looking for. The greater sin lay with the temple authorities. Let them carry the weight of it. If they would not accept the Messiah's release, then by the gods he would insist they carry the guilt for his death.

Still I could see that Pilate would fight to have Jesus released. He admired the man. This Galilean prophet had the courage, the guts, to stand up to the high priest—the common enemy in the governor's realm. At the very least the prophet deserved a modicum of support.

Pilate knew that Caiaphas had acted out of jealousy. He was jealous that the whole Jewish world was racing after this prophet. Caiaphas, the man of position, could not bear to watch the success of Jesus, the people's choice as leader. His entry on Sunday had left no doubt as to who was the most popular. Caiaphas was determined Jesus would pay for his audacity.

Suddenly the decision was reached.

"I will have you released," Pilate summarily announced. "You will wait here," he said, addressing the Jewish king. "Why provoke that crowd out there?"

Then turning to Renaldo, he said, "Put his own clothes back on him." The governor signaled his intent by giving a light kick to the bloody garment on the floor.

"Marcus, follow me," Pilate called as he headed for the door.

I was relieved, genuinely relieved. The ordeal was over. The decision was made. Barabbas would die. The innocent man would walk free.

Once more we trooped out to the Stone Pavement, the local term for the six steps on which these proceedings occurred. With Jesus safely inside, there was no jeering to greet my ears. Jesus could walk free after the high priest's hostile followers dispersed.

As we approached, the Weasel lifted his head from conferring with Jonathon. A thin smile crossed the corners of his grizzled mustache.

Without taking his seat, the governor cleared his throat to begin his address to this belligerent assembly. "As I stated earlier, I do not find the prisoner guilty of anything deserving death. Neither has Herod. I have questioned him repeatedly. I have had him scourged. Even now I find no fault in him. Therefore, I will have him released."

The Weasel's shrill response was instant. *"If you let this man go, you are no friend of Caesar. Anyone who claims to be a king opposes Caesar."*

The words pierced like a double-edged sword. The Badger had a choice. He could fall on it or retreat.

He retreated.

In that instant I could see Pilate knew the game was up. Here was the final squeeze. The governor's head dropped. Having dressed and paraded Jesus about like a king, he would now need to judge him as a king.

After a moment he turned to me. With grim forbearance in his voice, he said, "Bring out the prisoner."

With those words I knew Jesus's fate was sealed.

The Jewish king greeted me with an expression of sublime resignation, as though he were expecting me. Yes, he appeared to be expecting this outcome. He had preached of a kingdom. And for the folly of this kingdom message, he would die.

One last time I helped him as he hobbled down the steps.

Pilate was already seated, ready to pronounce judgment. A thin smile was now on his face. The cunning Badger would make the most of his final moves. When Jesus was in position, he began. Once more he motioned in the direction of the Christ, and to all assembled he announced, *"Here is your king."*

"Take him away!" came the instant response. *"Take him away! Crucify him!"*

There was vehement insistence coming from the crowd. Some began to hurl dust in the air. This was verging on a riot, a point that was surely obvious to the governor, yet he played them on.

"Shall I crucify your king?" Pilate called back to the throng.

"We have no king but Caesar," the Weasel spat back.

The Badger's eyebrows shot up.

The governor smiled and nodded. It was a smile of triumphant satisfaction. We have no king but Caesar. The Badger mulled over these words. I knew he had waited years for these words. After all he had endured in this place, wasn't it well worth hearing this confession from the high priest's mouth?

Ironically, the governor had Jesus to thank for the high priest's sudden conversion and submission to imperial Rome. This declaration would never have come forth from the Weasel's lips, except to secure the conviction of the good Galilean. Caiaphas was willing to stoop before

Rome in order to spill the blood of this prophet. Here was the true measure of his hatred for the Northern Messiah.

Pilate knew all this, and he drew a good measure of perverse satisfaction from it. He understood his foe.

He called for his personal attendant to bring a basin of water. Now he would lay the blame where the bloody blame belonged. With the attendant holding the basin before him, Pilate made a great show of washing his hands before the crowd, and with insistence in his voice, he declared, *"I am innocent of the blood of this man."*

Here was the feint, the great pretend.

Next came the dodge.

With water still dripping from his hands, he looked out over the crowd and declared, *"You yourselves see to it."*

He spoke as though he had abdicated—bore no responsibility for the blood that now trickled down Jesus's back. He absolved himself of that and of all that would soon flow on Golgotha.

This Badger could throw a bit of dirt.

It was fitting for Annas the aged priest to respond. It was he who answered for the people. With his finger pointed at Jesus and his gaze fixed on him, he replied, *"His blood be on us."* Then he paused as though looking down through the generations of time. *"And on our children,"* he added with a cold, sardonic stare.

Out on the street the people answered, "Yes!" They nodded their agreement with this verdict.

28

Eight fifty in the morning, Friday, April 7

"You yourselves see to it."

Pilate's words still reverberated in my ears, setting them on fire.

"You yourselves see to it."

They were fine words for him to say.

"You take him and crucify him."

I heard him say that earlier to the high priest. Fine words indeed!

Pontius Pilate wasn't the executioner. He could wash his hands and walk off into the palace. The provincial ledger books awaited his attention.

Joseph Caiaphas wasn't the executioner. He could crow over his victory, and crow he did as he returned triumphant to preside over his resplendent temple domain.

Herod? Herod Antipas could get back to what Herod did best, chasing and bedding women.

No, the mighty could blithely pronounce judgment and then walk off. But it fell to me and my men to execute this, their rendering of profane justice.

Justice? What justice was this?

I walked over to where Claudius stood with the beaming, exultant Barabbas. "You're a free man, Barabbas," I announced, stating the obvious.

"God be praised!" he shouted with hands uplifted. "God be praised!"

Why a just God would want this leprous dog out roaming free defied all earthly logic. This filthy dog's joy made my blood boil!

But then the completely unexpected happened. Barabbas turned to his comrades, and suddenly his head dropped. He had led them to this fate. Now he would walk away while they bore the burden of the cross. I saw the weight of it all suddenly come crashing down on him. In an instant he caught the despair etched on Thaddaeus's face.

It staggered him.

Barabbas, the free man, pinched his eyes shut and began to tremble uncontrollably. He turned away from his brothers, his two fellow terrorists, and sank to his knees.

The weight of his responsibility was too much for him. He was free. But now it was guilt that seized him—unbearable guilt.

"Get out of here," I yelled to the kneeling figure. "Get out before I run you through."

He was a sack of wheat rooted to the stone pavement.

I let fly with a kick to his fat rump to add force to my words. My hand rested on the pommel of my sword. It took real effort to keep it there.

"Move!" If he hadn't moved, I would have made good my threat.

Slowly he picked himself up and lumbered off—a sobbing, blubbering idiot, seized with remorse.

Surely, I thought, an accident could be arranged in the dark of the night for such a man. The common Roman soldier knows a few things about justice, even if the Roman governor doesn't. At a later date we could see to him—to this bit of unfinished business. Right now we had another bloody job to do.

Flavio caught my eye, then beckoned me over. "I'm heading back to the fortress now," he said. "I'll have a dozen cavalrymen meet you at the Fish Gate. There may be a big crowd out for this one," he said, referring to the public crucifixion. "If you need help, send a dispatch."

Without waiting for a reply, he walked off.

In the meantime, Claudius had three crossbeams brought out of the fortress, one for each man. The condemned would carry these patibulums to their death. In length they were the span of a man's arms fully extended. I inspected these roughhewn, squared timbers. They were notched in the center to fit into the similarly notched uprights standing at the ready on Golgotha. Since crucifixions were quite common, why go to the trouble of removing the upright poles from their secure position on the hill? Besides, their public display—even in the singular, empty state—served our purpose well. They acted as a deterrent for the hostile, the tempted, and the wayward. On more than one occasion, I had heard Jewish mothers warn their young sons, "Bad men end up there."

The crossbeams were reused time after time, until rot set in or the wood became hopelessly splintered due to repeated nailing—hence the need for this inspection. The first two cedar beams were showing signs of long service.

"I think these will do for today," Claudius said. "But we should get these two replaced for the next trip to the Skull."

I nodded absentmindedly in response and motioned for Thaddaeus to pick up his beam. The man we called Animal spewed curses as he shouldered his cross. The third beam was heavier and more recently put into service. It went to Jesus, the Messiah king.

As Jesus stepped over to receive it, a messenger arrived. He was clutching the crumpled purple robe in his left hand. He addressed me. "Sir, the governor sent this garment. He said it belongs to the prisoner."

I took the filthy thing from him and flung it over to Claudius. "Tie it on him," I said in disgust.

The Christ seemed to receive it willingly. But it came on him like a weight—the weight of the world. It was his now and every stain on it. And now that he was royally dressed, the patibulum was placed upon him. The notch in the beam fit neatly over his bloodied shoulder. He staggered and swayed under it.

The condemned were ready to proceed.

Setting this death procession in array took only a few brief moments. I had an ample supply of men to call on. With the final sentencing of the Christ, a more relaxed atmosphere prevailed. Part of the angry crowd began to disperse. I was now free to call on my men who had been used for crowd control. I reassigned the same pikemen who had served us earlier. They would advance before us in wedge formation. Then twenty foot soldiers were arrayed on either flank of the procession, and finally an additional half dozen pikemen brought up the rear.

I specifically assigned two soldiers to guard each criminal. At the back, Claudius oversaw two soldiers with his prisoner, Thaddaeus. Then came the two guards with the Animal. Jesus led the way, with two more guards escorting him on either side. I walked behind him. If there would be any trouble from the public, I knew it would erupt around him.

"Forward!" I shouted.

The men lurched into motion.

Jesus moved on unsteady feet. Each step was summoned with effort.

We were heading north, out through the Fish Gate. We were retracing the same route that Herod had followed on his gloriously ignoble entry on Tuesday. The very thought of him made me grimace and reflexively clench my fist in rage.

Bloody Fox! He had brought this on. In my mind he was the reason I was leading the Healer out to the Skull.

I reached down for my nail pouch. The worn leather held its grim treasure. They were there. Five-inch spikes. Hard iron. Ready for use. Ready to pierce bone and flesh.

And before me the victim struggled beneath his burden. Wrong victim. Dead-wrong victim. Hell's choice for a victim.

But then, where is heaven's justice in this world?

I caught sight of Renaldo as we marched past the Antonia Fortress. Strangely, it was seeing him that served to remind me that the notices had not been picked up. The notices were to be posted over the head of each crucified man. Each flat wooden board announced to the world what crime had been committed—what brought the malefactor to this wretched state.

I hastily beckoned for Renaldo to approach.

"I forgot the crucifixion notices." I gestured my frustration with the upraised palm of my hand. "They're with the jailer in the southeast turret. You'll need to get Pilate to rewrite the notice that was meant for Barabbas."

With a shake of my head and a huff, I added, "I don't know what he'll write for this man." I motioned in the direction of the stumbling Messiah and shrugged, "I guess it's Pilate's problem."

"Don't worry, Marcus. I'll look after it," Renaldo said. "I'll have one of my men deliver the two notices that are ready. And when the other one is ready, I'll bring it out myself."

He shot a glance at my thorn-crowned prisoner. Then he pressed his lips tightly together, shook his head, and turned from me. It was his way of signaling his displeasure with this turn of events. He too would have preferred seeing the backside of Barabbas heading off to the Skull.

Barabbas! He was the reason I was on this assignment. I detest crucifixions, but for him I had made an exception. I needed to be here to oversee this bloody ending. I owed it to the dead, to Andreas and Hermes. Hell, I owed it to the living, the men alongside me now.

But the murdering dog walked free. Free!

I was left fuming—in a killing mood.

The wrong man trudged slowly, each step conceived and born in pain. He was mocked continually by the angry mob surging along both sides of the street. But why had the free man buckled? Why had Barabbas folded?

His fall before Thaddaeus just minutes earlier reminded me of the siege of a wood pole stockade back in Germania. Twenty men and I pushed forward, straining every muscle. Suddenly the wall gave way, and we all pitched forward and collapsed right along with it. The arrows showered down.

That's how he fell, how Barabbas came down. He resisted Rome, pushed against Rome, until Rome backed off. Then he fell flat on his face. Only the arrows were missing.

Or were they?

The response that a pardon can bring is well beyond understanding. But then bloodguilt has a way of fashioning its own sharp arrows.

We were advancing slowly, far too slowly. The guard to the left of Jesus barked at him, "Move your feet, Jewish dog!" He followed this up with a slap to the shoulder. It was a light enough slap, but it caught the king off-balance, sending him sprawling in the dirt.

Chest heaving, Jesus struggled to get to his feet, but the crossbeam was clearly too heavy for him. After an initial attempt to rise, he sank down again.

"Halt!" I shouted up the column to the advancing pikemen. Then with a backhanded jab to the guard's shoulder, I demanded, "Pick up the beam."

He obeyed with a reluctant scowl aimed at the Christ.

Jesus rose.

I silently motioned with a jerk of my head for the beam to be passed back to the king. He shouldered it once more and advanced again on struggling feet. I could tell the effort was valiant, but from the labored breathing I knew he had very little left to give. I was beginning to wonder if he would make it to the hill.

"Forward!"

We were soon in the market section where the evicted temple merchants had set up shop. Many of them were still there. It seemed that none missed this opportunity to jeer and heap abuse upon the man they viewed as their nemesis. I half expected Timaeus to appear among them and lead the verbal assault. But he was nowhere to be seen.

Timaeus had disappeared. Disappeared like Barabbas.

Timaeus too had fallen. His vitriol had been silenced—silenced by a pardon—a healing pardon.

The Christ stumbled again. He spilled forward like the tipping of a stone water jar.

"Halt!" I commanded once more.

Both guards shouted obscenities at him. But then they glanced my way and moved to lift the crushing beam off his bleeding back.

He rose slowly. Street dust stuck to his sweat-drenched face and beard. A bit of yellow straw had been speared by one of the thorns in his crown. He sucked in each breath as though he were drowning. With effort he straightened and then slumped forward again, unable to hold himself erect or assume his burden.

He drew in three more gulps of air and straightened once more. Now he was ready, and the beam was shifted back to him.

"Forward!"

The Fish Gate was now within sight. He pressed onward with whatever vigor he could summon.

The crowd changed now. Here for the first time we encountered his supporters. Women. Wailing women in full anguished lament over his fate. They fell to their knees on either side of the narrow street.

Pleading! Hands outstretched. Disheveled. Begging for his release.

A pathetic sight.

Not a few were kicked or pushed aside by the soldiers on either flank. And they were incessantly heckled by the high priest's mob.

Now we were near the spot where Cestas had sliced off the beggar boy's hand. Lucas, young Lucas!

The images rolled in. They were relentless. There was no blocking them. I found myself clutching tight my wrist, just as he had done.

Suddenly Jesus fell again. He had reached his limit. His collapse was complete.

I stood over him, the fallen wreck. It was clear that further progress at a reasonable pace would require a change in tactics.

"Halt!" I bellowed above the wailing voices.

Off to the right, behind the weeping women, I spotted a tall young man. He appeared to be making his way into the city. Here he was, a fish swimming against the current. I stepped his way, aimed my index finger at his dark-skinned face, and demanded, "You! Carry his cross." With my other hand I stabbed my thumb in the direction of the fallen king.

Startled by my approach, the man took a half step back. His eyes darted to the two boys half-hidden behind him.

His sons.

I dropped my right hand. It came to rest on the pommel of my sword. A gesture well noted by this momentary conscript. His eyes took in the whole scene.

I pumped my thumb once more in the direction of the fallen cross carrier.

The tall man stepped forward, but the boys desperately clung to the back of his robe. Terror marked their faces. Surely they dreaded the worst.

"Papa! Papa!"

He nodded his willingness to comply, but then stooped before his sons to whisper some words of assurance.

The youngest boy would have none of it. "Papa!" he bawled as tears streamed freely down his face.

A twitch of my eyebrow signaled the soldier next to me to intervene. He drew his sword and then put a hand to my conscript's shoulder. Seeing the situation take on a deadly urgency, the conscript turned from his children to assume his service.

My soldiers became a wall between him and his sons.

He was a fine choice: tall, broad-shouldered, and muscular. He shouldered the crossbeam with ease.

The boys were another matter. They reminded me of my sons. They trailed along the whole way to Golgotha, crying piteously, gnawing an ever-deepening hole in my conscience.

"I'll be fine, Alexander," he shouted across to them. "I'll be fine, Rufus! I'll be fine."

They clung to each other but seemed little comforted by their father's words.

With his burden lifted, Jesus rose to his knees. Then with gasping breaths he addressed the kneeling women just beyond the military cordon. *"Daughters of Jerusalem, do not weep for me; weep for yourselves and for your children."*

In fact, the two boys were weeping. The women sobbed as he spoke.

But his words grew dark. *"The time will come when you will say, 'Blessed are the childless women, the wombs that never bore and the breasts that never nursed!'"*

Slowly struggling to his feet, he continued in ominous tones. *"Then they will say to the mountains, 'Fall on us!' and to the hills, 'Cover us!' For if people do these things when the tree is green, what will happen when it is dry?"*

When he had spoken his piece, I motioned him on.

"Forward!"

Soon we were through the Fish Gate and were joined by the promised escorts on horseback. It was a mixed throng that surged around us in the more open space. Mostly it was made up of Jesus's enemies, the men who endured his trial. Now they would gloat over his demise. They would see this through to the bitter end.

His disciples, the men I had seen around him earlier in the week, were strangely absent. All the better from my perspective. No hostile confrontation. No need for reinforcements. Perhaps they knew better than to mess with the Roman army.

Only the women were here vainly pleading his case.

He limped on. Jesus slowly limped on. He was free of the burden of the crossbeam but not the burden of the robe.

On his own power he limped right on up the round stone hill.

29

Nine thirty in the morning, Friday, April 7

THREE UPRIGHT TIMBERS stood alone on the barren hill. My tall conscript lowered his burden before the middle timber. His job was done.

"Papa! Papa!" the youngest boy, Alexander, cried once more. Then he rushed to where his dad stood within the military column's inner circle. This time my soldiers did nothing to restrain him. The father caught the young boy up in his strong arms, then dropped down to hug his older son, Rufus.

Their ordeal was over. This tall man would walk off the barren hill. The other man would not.

A party of five young soldiers stepped forward—the crucifixion detail, led by the head jailer. They had been patiently waiting on the Skull for our arrival. They saluted. Their leader swaggered forward with one hand planted firmly on his hip.

"Greetings, Marcus," Octavio began. "We brought a ladder and the props." He motioned to these with a toss of his head. "Oh, and we brought the drink." He gestured to a wooden bucket containing a crude copper dipper. It stood off to his right in the shadow of the central cross. "The notices"—he hesitated—"there's only two of them."

"Yes, I know that," I snapped. "I looked after it already." Gruff irritation leaped from my throat. "It should be here soon."

Then a quizzical look came on the jailer's face. He took a step forward and inspected the thorn-crowned prisoner. He had never seen this man. "Where's Barabbas?"

"Free." I spat out the word. "Free as a summer sparrow."

Octavio caught the extent of my frustration. He gestured with upraised hands, wanting some explanation.

"A governor's pardon. A stinkin' Passover pardon," I answered with bitter anger dripping from my lips.

My eyes dropped, dropped to the foot of the central cross. "Instead of him, we have the king of the Jews here." And with that I kicked at a bit of loose rock and sent it skittering down the back side of the knoll.

"King of the Jews?" Octavio asked. Once more he eyed the purple-robed prisoner and then gave a derisive snort.

With a quick turn from the jailer's reception party, I barked and waved my orders to my own men. With a sweeping motion I signaled for the cavalrymen to take up their positions surrounding the hill. "Thaddaeus to the right." I indicated with a wave of my arm. "Animal to the left."

Jesus was where he needed to be. His central position needed no comment.

A crowd of a few hundred men gathered just off the knoll. Kneeling women gathered in tight little knots a good distance off. They were on what we call the Mother's Hill. Knowing their role, the pikemen instinctively moved to secure the perimeter of the Skull.

The religious men, the merchants, and the riffraff had come for a bloody spectacle, and a bloody spectacle they would get.

Let the show begin.

The guards moved their victims to the appropriate upright. Only now did the two other unfortunates drop their crossbeams. Thaddaeus immediately fell to his knees. He began to quiver and shake—a strong man reduced to a groveling, whimpering mess.

The Christ stood silent.

"No! . . . Noo!" The fear-filled Thaddaeus began a low, desperate wailing, panting between each utterance. "No! . . . Noo!"

The guard to his left began to kick at him viciously.

"Shut up, dog! Shut up!" he shouted at the bent figure.

A few quick strides brought me to his side.

"Soldier!" I yelled in his ear. "Get the notice up there." I signaled with a jerk of my thumb. It was my way of getting him out of the immediate situation. When he stepped aside, I turned to Thaddaeus.

"Thaddaeus!" My voice cut through the swarm of activity that engulfed the hill. "Stand to your feet."

Whether he recognized my voice from our previous meeting last evening, or he simply recognized the authority behind my voice, I could not tell, but it brought the desired response. He stopped his mournful wailing and slowly brought himself to an upright position.

"I brought the myrrh. Like I promised." I looked into his despairing eyes. "I brought the myrrh."

Relief spread across his tortured face. Here was a straw of hope to distract the hapless while he drowned in this sea of doom.

"Bring the drink!" I said with a summoning wave of my cupped hand.

One of Octavio's men saw to it. I took the bucket from him. It was just over half full. The dark liquid beckoned. I retrieved a copper dipperful. The acrid smell of wine vinegar punched holes in my brain. I took a sip. The myrrh was in there all right. The bitter after-kick numbed my throat.

"It's good. A good strong batch," I said with a backhanded wipe of my mouth.

I passed the half-filled dipper to Thaddaeus.

He downed it all in three voracious gulps.

I took it back from him and turned to refill it once more. Behind me the ladder went up. Soon the condemned man's notice would be nailed in place.

Now as Thaddaeus reached for the dipper, I pulled it back. "First," I said, cocking my head to one side, "take off your clothes."

His face dropped. He knew full well what this meant. Would he comply? He sucked in a breath and then plunged ahead, pulling off his outer garment.

I handed him the swill. He downed the second dipperful with the same raw enthusiasm.

As he drank, I motioned with a jerk of my head and a twitch of my eyebrow for the crucifixion crew to stand ready. The crossbeam was laid behind him. Then four men gathered behind the prisoner on either side.

"Another?" I asked as he lowered the dipper.

He nodded, and just a hint of a smile crossed his handsome face.

I stooped once more to fill the dipper, to supply his need for another drink of this potent brew. As I handed it to him, three hammer blows rang out. The notice was now pinned to the top of the cross.

He drank more slowly now. His movements were more determined, as if some great effort was required. Perhaps he sensed what was coming, and the dread of it made him slow. Perhaps the effects of the drug were hitting home.

I could not see his eyes. They were hidden by the uptilted dipper. But my eyes signaled to the men on his right and left. They were fully prepared.

After a long pause he brought the dipper down. I took it from his hand. He had a far-off look.

I smiled at him, then gave a sharp, signaling nod with my head.

In that instant eight men seized him.

"Aaaaaahh!"

Two men on each limb.

He was dragged back.

Slammed down onto the crossbeam.

"Aaaaaahh!"

His scream pierced through my hollow soul.

Octavio swooped down, hammer in hand.

A spike was pressed into the base of his palm.

Xchuuuung!

Hammer to spike.

"Aaaaaaaaahhh!"

His scream seared the morning air.

His back arched upward till I thought it would snap.

Xchuuuung!

Xchuuuung!

Xchuuuung!

Three strong blows drove it home.

One nail in.

Two huge strides brought Octavio around to the other pinned arm. Two men were kneeling on the condemned man's forearm, pressing it to the rough beam.

His arched spine collapsed.

The victim's breath came in enormous gasps.

The point of the spike was jabbed into the base of his second palm.

The hammer rose.

Xchuuuung!

"Aaaaaaaaahhh!"

Fresh scream.

Arched back.

Xchuuuung!

Xchuuuung!

Xchuuuung!

Two nails in.

His arched back collapsed.

His breath came in monstrous gulps, then changed to short, quick bursts. His face was ashen. Beaded sweat ran in rivers down his brow.

Octavio smiled my way.

"Well done," was my response.

I stooped down and pulled the breechcloth, the last shred of clothing, off Thaddaeus. Then I tossed it over the shoulder of the nearest soldier.

He would die naked—naked and despised, like all the victims of the Roman cross.

"Hoist him up!" I yelled.

Instantly, four men responded by lifting the beam and dragging the nail-pinned victim to a point directly below the upright.

His face was contorted. Weak, agonized groans escaped from his lips. He could do no more. Pain overwhelmed.

Two forked wooden props were shoved beneath either arm of the crossbeam. Two of Octavio's men were on each prop. At this point Octavio took full charge of this rather difficult maneuver.

The ladder was moved to the back of the upright. One man hastily climbed it to a point just above the notch in the upright that would receive the crossbeam. He had a short but sturdy length of rope draped over his shoulder.

At this point Thaddaeus was held in a standing position. The crossbeam was supported equally from the front by the men on the forked pole props and from the back by the four men holding the beam in place.

Octavio motioned with a raised hand.

The men behind the beam responded by lifting it above their heads.

Thaddaeus gasped as his arms were forced above his head. His heels left the ground. With hands pinned and bleeding profusely, he was forced onto his toes.

The prop men adjusted their implements to this new, higher position.

At just the right moment Octavio called out, "Ready . . . one . . . two . . . three . . . now!"

The pole props were pushed upward. The pinned victim was launched skyward. A fresh scream erupted.

His back slammed against the upright, and he was dragged higher by the upward thrust of the pole props.

The notch in the crossbeam found its mate in the upright.

With lightning hands the ladder man secured the crossbeam by means of the rope. He wrapped it around the point where the two beams crossed and then drew it tight.

The victim dangled. Dangled naked. Naked before the crowd. Naked between heaven and earth.

Blood poured from the piercing, ripping wounds.

Two men grabbed his loose, hanging legs.

Octavio stepped forward, hammer in one hand, a six-inch foot spike in the other.

Soldiers' hands pressed the victim's feet together, pressed them firm against the upright.

Octavio checked the spot, the contact point between flesh and wood.

Xchuuuung!

Iron hammer onto iron spike.

Xchuuuung!

Iron spike into flesh.

Xchuuuung!

Iron spike into bone.

Xchuuuung!

Iron spike into wood.

Xchuuuung!

The human scream reached heaven.

Then silence. Hushed silence enveloped the crowd.

Three spikes in.

Two men left to do.

I aimed a grim nod at Octavio and then added a slap to the shoulder for a job well done.

But the Christ stood silent—silent through all this.

Beyond him, near the far upright, a scuffle broke out. The man we called Animal had sensed his own fate. He lashed out in abhorrent panic.

I walked by the quiet Christ. The crucifixion crew followed. The guards pinned Animal to the ground. The swill bucket stood nearby.

"Has he had his drink?" I called out.

"Drank most of it."

"Then let's do him."

He was dragged screaming onto the crossbeam. Strong hands did the rest. Blow for blow, scream for scream, arching back for arching back, the same thing happened.

One in.

Two in.

"Hoist him up."

Naked scream.

Xchuuuung!

Xchuuuung!

Xchuuuung!

Xchuuuung!

Three in.

One man left to do.

A smattering of applause broke out among the spectators. But they had come for more than just this. The main attraction was up next.

With Animal crucified, Octavio stepped back from his handiwork, hammer in hand, blood dripping from his fingers. "Now, that's how it's done!" he grandly announced. "That's how it's done! The next man's yours, Marcus." With an upraised hammer he gestured in the direction of the Christ. "He's all yours."

I fell strangely silent. I had spent the whole week waiting for this moment. But this was not Barabbas. This was the wrong man. This was Jesus of Nazareth. The guilty man's substitute.

Jesus . . .

Close encounters with him had always filled me with apprehension. But surely his powers, whatever their source, were diminished. Why else would he be in this vulnerable, weakened state?

The notice board had still not arrived, nor can I see any sign that Renaldo was on his way. The work had gone well. Quick. We had established a certain rhythm. Why stop now?

I picked up the nearly empty bucket and walked over to the Christ, uncertain yet what course I would take. "It's your turn, good man," I announced while extending the bucket his way.

He made no response, showed no interest. But he knew the routine. As the crew gathered around, he untied the purple robe at his neck and let it drop to the ground. In movements made awkward by pain, he began to pull the tunic over his head.

Midway through this procedure, Octavio seized the tunic and yanked it free. Then, to my surprise, he picked up the purple robe and tied it back on the prophet from Galilee.

"A king needs a robe—a robe to go with his crown," he grandly announced.

I tipped the bucket to one side to get enough swill to fill the dipper. I offered it to Jesus. He took a sip, worked the liquid around in his mouth, discerned the true nature of this bitter potion, and then spit it out. It left a dark stain on the dull gray rock near his feet.

"It will dull the pain," I said emphatically.

He raised his eyes. They locked with mine. I saw in him the same look, the same determination I saw on the first day I set eyes on him, the day he rode the donkey into this city. I could still see he had a destination in mind. Some mystical purpose he somehow felt compelled to fulfill.

I dropped my gaze. He must be a fool. In his condition, in this situation, he must be a fool. A fool who unnerved me, but a fool nonetheless.

Once more I offered the drink.

With lips pressed tight, he shook his head.

He was a fool. An arrogant fool! A fool who thinks he's tough—who can handle this—who can take it straight.

We would see who's tough. I would show him who's tough!

Let the big show begin.

"Now, boys!" I called out to the crew.

Still wearing the purple robe, he was snatched like a young child and slammed down onto the crossbeam.

A cheer went up.

My right hand seized the hammer from Octavio. My left fumbled, then dove into, the nail pouch.

I dropped my knee onto his fingers.

Stabbed the sharpened point of the spike into the base of the palm.

Raised the hammer.

Xchuuuung!

An enormous cheer went up from the crowd.

Blood spurted across my thigh.

Xchuuuung!

Xchuuuung!

Xchuuuung!

One in.

The Christ was silent. Still . . .

Octavio urged me on. "That's it, Marcus!"

I sprang to my feet, remembering the full rush of battle. Then scrambled to the other arm.

From just off the hill, in the throng, a chant began and established itself. "More. More. More. More."

Knee on fingers.

"More!"

Spike jabbed in.

"More!"

Hammer raised.

"More!"

Xchuuuung!

"More!"

Xchuuuung!

"More!"

Xchuuuung!

Two in.

The Christ was silent.

Still . . . He was still beneath the piercing blows.

I rose, panting. Heart pounding. Bloodied hand dripping. Seeing a stainfree area farther up my hairy arm, I wiped it across my sweat-drenched brow.

Octavio saluted me with a smile and a thumbs-up signal.

The crowd roared their approval.

This time it was Octavio who yelled, "Hoist him up."

The Christ was dragged gasping—desperately gasping—to an upright position before the death mast.

Now they could see him, and the crowd went wild with frenzied excitement. Cheering. Clapping. Hooting. Bloodlust took hold.

The props were applied to the arms of the crossbeam.

A new chant went up.

"Raise him up!"

"Raise him up!"

"Raise him up!"

Octavio signaled, and the men in back lifted the beam on which the Christ was pinned above their heads.

Then we all saw it—saw the obvious. He was still clothed. The purple robe billowed out as it was caught by a sudden cold gust of wind. The sight of it brought all my frenzied demons to the fore.

I stepped before him, looked into his agonized face, and said, "You won't be needing this . . . king of the Jews."

Then to the cheers of my men, I spit into his face. I added my spittle to all the rest that had dried and was clinging to his beard.

I untied the royal robe and dropped it in a heap to my right. Finally, with a wicked smile, and to cheers all around, I snatched his breechcloth from off his loins.

I tossed it to Octavio. He held it up. A trophy!

We laughed. We all laughed.

It was a laugh not our own.

I recognized it. It was Herod's laugh.

When he had regained some composure, the head jailer started the final count.

"Ready . . . one . . . two . . . three . . . now!"

To chants of "Raise him up, raise him up," the Christ, the Messiah, the king, was lifted up—up before the world.

His head twisted from side to side in writhing agony. His whip-sliced back slammed against the upright as he was dragged higher.

Then with a flesh-tearing lurch, the notch in the horizontal beam found its match in the vertical. The rope was flung around, then drawn tight, securing the two cross members as one.

The silent Christ hung. He hung naked and bleeding before a jeering world.

Only the last spike remained. Awkwardly, I fumbled for it.

But a creeping unease overshadowed me. I glanced over my shoulder. Claudius stood alone, off to the side. Silent . . . He was ghastly pale and silent, transfixed by the sight before him.

I handed the last nail and the hammer back to Octavio and said, "You do it." He snorted his surprise, but then set quickly to his task.

The blows rang out. They echoed off the distant city wall . . . off the temple Pinnacle . . . off the Mother's Hill . . . off the cavernous abyss within me.

Then silence.

A great collective gasp was heard from below the hill.

The trophy had been mounted. The high priest's trophy had been mounted. The clever Weasel's victory was assured.

30

Ten in the morning, Friday, April 7

WITHIN ME I knew there was something primeval about this position, the position on the cross. This is a man's first nightmare, his worst nightmare. Here he hangs, naked, ripped open, nailed open, unable to cover himself. He is unprotected. He cannot hide; he cannot run. In shame and nakedness his tormentors lift him up. His sin is posted above his head. Body and soul are pried open, and he hangs fully exposed. He is exposed before heaven and the world—the world that has rejected him—the heaven that he has offended.

Nothing can be worse. It breaks the strongest men.

But he was silent. The Christ was silent. He was still—quiet—beneath the flesh-piercing blows. I had never seen or heard the like of it.

It troubled me.

Now that he was pinned and mounted, he summoned his strength and raised his voice for all to hear.

"Father," he gasped, *"forgive them . . . They don't know . . . what . . . they are doing."*

Then silence, troubling silence.

I dismissed his words. I knew what I was doing.

Claudius doubled over as though punched in the stomach. He staggered off the back of the Skull and began vomiting.

He's green, I thought, green and soft, yet to be hardened by the sights and sounds of the battlefield. He reminded me of how I was when I first arrived in Germania. A few more of these trips up the Skull, and the toughness would come.

A squabble broke out over the Messiah's clothes. Who gets what? I intervened and said, "The purple robe goes to Octavio's crew."

I wanted nothing to do with the abominable thing.

"Yeah," Octavio said. "But I got my stinkin' reward!" He laughed as he looped the king's breechcloth around an open spot on his belt. "Your men can have the other clothes."

One of my crucifixion crew, a young fellow named Philip, said, *"Let's not rip it apart. We will gamble to see who gets it."* And with that he produced a pair of dice, and after a few tosses, it was decided. In point of fact, the Messiah's clothes changed hands several times that day, as bored soldiers in small, huddled groups entertained themselves with the roll of the dice. After a few moments, Octavio's crucifixion workers borrowed the same dice and used the same method to determine the ownership of the accursed purple robe.

"I think I'll take my crew, and we'll be off now," Octavio said above a howling wind. "You can handle the rest?"

"Yeah, we'll be fine." Then checking the sky, I added, "Maybe a little wet, but we'll be fine."

As Octavio's men walked off the hill, a low, rumbling thunder pursued them. The sky was ominous. But it was the wind that toyed with us. It clawed at our clothes, reaching down from dark, swirling clouds. It picked up sand and grit, then spit it in our faces. It chased away the spectators. It seemed to come at us from every angle, buffeting us until it made the crosses creak and sway.

Then came the rain, big, dark splotches of it, dark as the Christ's own vinegar spit. But that's all there was, dark splotches exploding on the rock surface of the Skull. There weren't enough drops to darken the whole of the rock, just enough to spot it, stain it.

Then it stopped. The sun came out to tease us, and the Christ's hecklers returned.

One of the more audacious, well-clad men approached. He aimed his finger up at the Christ and yelled, *"Ha!"* He wagged his head. *"So you're the one who claimed you could tear down the temple and build it in three days."*

Venomous sarcasm dripped from his lips. *"Come down from the cross, if you are the Son of God!"*

"Yeah," another chimed in, "come on down, Son of God!"

A frocked man from the high priest's coterie gave a snort of contempt and then started in at him. *"He saved others, but he can't save himself!"* Then he puffed himself up, and with his hand raised in gesture to this, the high priest's Passover lamb, he called out, *"He's the king of Israel! Let him come down now from the cross, and we will believe in him."*

He laughed, but he was not finished.

"He trusts in God. Let God rescue him now if he wants him." He snickered again and went on, *"For he said, 'I am the Son of God.'"*

These words troubled me. The Son of God? Who was his father anyway?

Then my men took up the taunt.

"Hey, this dog thinks he's the Son of God. The Son of God? Did ya hear that?" Philip motioned to his comrades. "They called him the Son of God?"

"Well, his daddy ain't treatin' him too good."

"Hey, Jewish dog," Philip addressed the Christ. "Maybe ya oughta get a new papa. He must be some mad at you." He shook his head in mock dismay, "He ain't treatin' ya right. No." He shook his head again. "I'd walk right out on him."

"'Cept you can't walk."

They all laughed, thought this was great fun, a fine bit of grim humor. They went on in the same vein for quite some time until Renaldo finally arrived with the notice board.

"Sorry I'm late. It took longer than I thought," he said as he dismounted. "First Pilate was busy, and then it took a while to find someone to do the Hebrew inscription."

He handed it to me. It read, JESUS OF NAZARETH, KING OF THE JEWS. The top line was in Latin and clearly had the marks of the governor's own writing style. This was followed by the Greek translation and then finally by the Hebrew.

"King of the Jews," I said. "I was wondering what he would write."

"He wrote the truth," Renaldo said dryly. "He'd make a far better king than Herod."

I sniffed and nodded my amen to that. Then I turned from him and called out to Claudius, "Are you well enough to nail up this notice?"

"Sure," he instantly said. He rose from where he sat on a small boulder.

But he didn't look all that sure. The ladder was erected once more at the back of the cross, and with two men holding it, Claudius ascended with the sign tucked under his arm. He fumbled awkwardly for a nail. I could see fear on his face, and it was more than just the fear of falling. He feared what he saw on the front of the cross. But then the hammer rang out once more, and the job was done.

The notice set off a new round of mocking from the soldiers. One man fell in obeisance before the monarch on the cross. He was the first of many; others followed in his steps. Mock supplication followed for all manner of asinine trivialities. It was a pathetic sight that went on for hours until it wearied me, and I called an end to this sham.

I motioned for Renaldo to follow me off the back of the hill. There we could have a more private conversation. He led his horse past the ring of encircling cavalrymen.

"That was some storm," I said with a look skyward at the bank of retreating clouds.

"What storm?" he asked.

"The storm that nearly blew us off the Skull. It nearly blew the crosses down."

He seemed genuinely surprised at this. "I didn't notice it," he said and then changed the subject. "So you've had no trouble from his followers?"

"Not a single dog has barked, not one." Then I motioned with my head toward the Mother's Hill. "Of course, there are the women, but they'll keep their distance."

"Where did they all go? Where did his cheering thousands go?" Renaldo referred to the splendid entry on the first day of the week.

"I guess they went home. Don't you know? They're hiding under their beds. They know better than to mess with us. We're the bloody Roman army," I said.

He gave a grim smile, but then added, "If there is any trouble, signal the watchman at the Fish Gate, and we'll have more cavalry out here at double speed."

"I'm sure we'll be fine," I said. "But all the same, I'll make sure everyone here keeps their eyes open."

"So, what do you make of this, Marcus?" But before I could answer, he went on. "I guess you were right about the high priest. You said he would go after the prophet, and he did."

"Yeah, and he got him." There was bitterness on my tongue. "Got him exactly where he wanted him." I pointed to the cross. "The pompous Weasel wins again! And Barabbas the killer, Barabbas the terrorist, walks free!"

I was livid. I was ready to start in on the dark-eyed Badger but thought better of it.

Renaldo sighed. I could tell he wasn't sure how to respond. For my part, I was just glad he was here, so I could let some of this out. I didn't want to explode in front of my own men.

"Look, Marcus. We are the middlemen. We do what we're told. And plenty of times, we do it with one hand over our nose and the other hand over our mouth. You told me that once. And by mothers' breasts, I swear you're right. Marcus, you're right! We know too much, but can do too little. The big boys always decide. But they don't know which end of the mule they're lookin' at. And they're too fatheaded proud to ask." He paused and looked off in the distance. "And for us, I suppose life will always be that way."

"Yeah, it will always be like that," I echoed. "But it doesn't make doing the wrong thing on their bloody behalf any easier."

I kicked a loose bit of rock and sent it skittering off into the weeds.

"So this is the wrong thing?" Renaldo made a sweeping motion up the hill to encompass the crosses.

"Is it the right thing? Is it right to strip a good man, a healer, a miracle worker, and nail him to a cross?" I paused for his response, but none came. "And you! You should know the answer. You've got the proof living at your house. That boy is proof we've got the wrong man up there," I fumed. "Hell is laughing—laughing all the way to heaven's heights."

After a long and surly pause, I shook my head and added, "Stinkin' Barabbas is proof enough we got the wrong man up there."

He was quiet for a time. He knew I was right.

My argument wasn't with him, anyway. It was with those higher up. They produced this situation, rendered this judgment, sent me on this mission. I was just the dutiful soldier obeying their bloody, filth-covered orders.

"Look, Marcus," Renaldo began. "You're right, absolutely right. But that isn't going to change anything now."

"I know." I sighed. It was a sigh of grim resignation. "I know."

After a moment spent staring at the ground, I began again. "You know, when it comes to leaders, political leaders in this world, it's not the cream that rises to the top. It's the crud. The stinkin', scummy crud!"

"You're right again, Marcus. You're right again."

I slowly shook my head. I said my piece; I changed the topic. I looked up at him and asked, "How is the boy? How's Lucas?"

"Better. Much better. He'll pull through all right."

"Good. At least we won't lose him," I said, while taking another kick at some loose rock.

Then he moved toward his horse and said, "I should go. Tomorrow is the Sabbath. We can talk then."

I nodded, and he was off.

I walked back up the hill and into a storm of trouble. Angry voices were all around.

"What do you mean by pinning that up there?" It was Jonathon, the head of the temple guard. He, along with some high priestly official, had pushed past the pikemen at the base of the hill, and now they were castigating one of my men.

"We were following orders," the soldier answered, holding his ground.

"This is a travesty. A total travesty!" Jonathon stormed. "It will have to be changed." His voice rang out with authoritative insistence.

Then my archrival caught sight of me.

"I should have known you were behind this, Marcus." He pointed an accusing finger.

"Behind what?"

"Don't play innocent with me," he shot back. "The sign. The notice!" He gesticulated angrily. "You had it nailed up there."

"Yes, I had it nailed up there," I said.

"Have you read it? Or can't you read?"

"Yes, I read it. And yes, I can read." And to prove my point I faced the cross and read it out to him. "JESUS OF NAZARETH, KING OF THE JEWS." I read it out in Latin and then in Greek. I followed this up with some guttural grunts and snorts in mock imitation of Hebrew. This set my men off in hoots of laughter, while the two temple officers glowered in a state of red-faced agitation.

After a long, self-calming pause, Jonathon said, "It isn't funny. None of this is funny." He waved a finger in my face. "Hundreds of people come down this road"—he stretched out a long arm to trace the path—"the imperial road, and they walk right past this." He thrust his hand skyward. "This declaration that—that fool—that naked fool is the king of the Jews. It's an affront to the whole Jewish nation."

He was shaking with rage.

"What nation?" I shot back. My voice rose. "I didn't write that notice. The governor wrote that notice. If you want it changed, see him." Then I looked him square in the eye. "I don't take orders from temple scum.

"Now, you're standing on my hill." I jabbed a finger in a downward gesture. "Get off my hill!" I yelled in his face.

Behind me I heard swords being drawn. My men would back me up.

He huffed a mighty huff. "I will see Pilate," he said. And with that, he and his fancy-robed friend turned and walked off.

"You just do that, big man!" I called after him.

I waited all day for some new, revised notice board to arrive, but none came. I knew it wouldn't come. The Badger had already bowed once to the Weasel, and a man hung dying because of it. Pilate would never bow twice in one day, not over some words on a board.

This defense of the public notice set off a new round of ridicule. One of my men walked over to the dying Christ and yelled up at him, "Did you see that, Jesus? We stood up for you. You're still king of the Jews.

We believe in you, Jesus." He raised his fist in a show of mock support. "You're king of the hill, king of the whole bloody hill!"

Now another soldier joined in the game. "He's a funny king, though," he said with a glance to his friend. "A very funny king! I've never seen a king on a cross. Have you seen a king on a cross?" he asked with a slap to his partner's arm. Then looking up at the Christ, he hollered, *"If you are the king of the Jews, save yourself!"*

"Save yourself, Jesus," Thaddaeus called out.

Then Animal called to him, *"Aren't you the Messiah?"* There was cold derision in his voice. *"Save yourself and us!"*

But Thaddaeus, to his credit, would not let this lie. Yelling past the Christ to his partner in crime, he said, *"Don't you fear God?"* He paused to breathe. *"Aren't you getting the same punishment as this man?"* He pushed down on his pinned feet so he could pull in a gulp of air. *"We got what was coming to us."* Fresh push for air. *"But he didn't do anything wrong."*

Then he turned his face to the Christ. *"Jesus,"* he gulped. *"Remember me"*—he pushed up on spiked feet—*"when you come into your kingdom."*

He dropped back with the effort of his words. His lungs were filling with fluid. The characteristic pattern of launch, gulp, collapse, wheeze was now established. It was the rhythmic pattern of a man on a cross. They would each die, one by one, when they were too weak to launch up and forward to catch their dying breath.

Jesus responded. Each phrase was marked by chest-heaving gulps for air after a painful upward thrust on spike-pinned feet. He turned to the repentant thief.

"Truly I tell you . . .

"Today you will be . . . with me . . .

"In paradise."

I turned away and looked skyward. The wind had shifted. Now it was coming from the north. A fresh bank of clouds was moving in from that direction. In just a few moments it had covered the noonday sun. It was strange weather, more than a little unusual.

It chilled me.

A large clay jar was brought out from the fortress. A skin of wine was emptied into it. Here was a small reward for my men, a reward for an abominable job done well. Some flatbread and a few pressed dates were distributed.

Now there was movement on the Mother's Hill. A middle-aged couple came down. Their heads were hanging. They clung to each other, supported each other, every step an anguish. They made their way before the encircling pikemen.

I knew who they were—knew why they had come. Here were the broken parents, broken beyond this world's repair. I met them at the base of the hill, told them they had some time.

They advanced up the Skull. She fell, fell whimpering before her son. Thaddaeus.

Boisterous soldiers fell silent and then walked off, right off the hill. The family was alone with their grief.

Having witnessed this grim but welcoming reception, another party stepped off the Mother's Hill and advanced to Golgotha. This was a group of five. The women clung to one another in couples. They were shepherded by a tall young man. His fresh face and scant beard bore witness to his youth. I recognized him. He had been with Jesus, had stood closest to him.

He introduced himself. He said his name was John. I received his party—ushered them by the outer ring of soldiers.

They were bowed by the sight. They clung to one another afresh, repulsed by the horror of what met their eyes.

After a few moments the young man came before two of the huddled older women. He stooped to speak with one of the women—the Christ's mother, I assumed. Then with his arm about her shoulder, John advanced up the rock mound.

Jesus saw them.

He struggled.

"Woman . . . behold your son!"

There was a double-edged meaning here, almost too painful for words. At first I thought he was simply referring to himself—to his own wretched state. And perhaps on one level he was.

His body sagged. But then he thrust himself up and forward for another breath, and with his next words his meaning became clear. To the young man, to his disciple, he said, *"Behold your mother!"*

He had committed his mother into this disciple's care.

She fell to her knees. She trembled, unable to speak. Only wretched sobbing was heard from within the circle of the hill.

In due time I led both families off. They left willingly. This was too much to bear, too much to watch.

From his cross Animal watched the Mother's Hill. But no one came. That's when he broke—broke like a clay pot dropped onto the hard rock of the Skull.

He sobbed. He moaned.

His tears flowed like rivers into his dark, young beard.

But no mother came. No one came at all.

The wind picked up. The sky grew dark. Then it grew darker yet. The horses began to neigh and paw the ground. In the distance a dog barked. It was a bark that changed to a howl but ended in a whimper. I looked about. I could see it on every face. It was fear. Raw fear. This was not the dark of cloud or storm. This was the sun covering, hiding its face from what it saw upon the earth.

A total darkness descended, as black as any night.

There was a discord here—a discord utter and complete. If heaven and earth had come into some perfect union—some perfect harmony—on the day Jesus arrived in this city, it was in blaring dissonance now. Blaring dissonance echoed off the empty chambers of my soul.

It was a deafening darkness.

The mocking crowds fell silent. The highway traffic stopped. All was still.

Silent.

Only the three men were heard. Heard in the darkness. Three men working to maintain this perverted thing called life.

Working.

Pushing up.

Up to catch a breath.

Retreating.

Exhaling.

Mounting up.

Ever-heightening pain.

Catching a breath.

Retreating.

Here is the obscenity of crucifixion. Naked men are unwillingly mated to two wooden beams. They must thrust the whole of their bodies upward in excruciating pain, ever-increasing pain to catch their next breath—until all strength is drained away. Then death steals in.

This is the shame of the cross. Here is the depravity—a profane sacrilege inflicted upon the human body.

The ghastly rhythm of it was driving me mad.

Then in soul-wrenching anguish, his voice erupted. *"Eli, Eli, lema sabachthani?"*

"What does that mean?" I cried out into the darkness.

From beyond the military cordon came the answer. *"My God, my God, why have you forsaken me?"*

He had broken. The Christ hung broken. The cross had broken him. He too was human.

We were all together now, a great crowd caught up in this drama. There was no us and them. We were together. We were caught between heaven and hell in this dark, surreal atmosphere.

It was dreadful.

Someone frantically yelled, "It's Elijah! *He's calling Elijah.*"

Exhaling.

Mounting up.

Ever-heightening pain.

Catching a breath.

Retreating.

From on the Mother's Hill, a wail went up. It was steady, constant, a wave of woe flowing over the dark scene.

Exhaling.

Mounting up.

Ever-heightening pain.

Catching a breath.

Retreating.

"Will Elijah come?" someone asked. "Will he come?" Many of the hostile were even now on bended knees. The cavalrymen dismounted.

Exhaling.

Mounting up.

Ever-heightening pain.

Catching a breath.

Retreating.

"I thirst!" the king called out.

Claudius leaped to his feet. There was a jar of wine off to one side. The soldiers had been drinking freely from this. He ran over to it and got a sponge. He dropped the sponge into the jar of wine and then skewered it with a long reed. This he held up to dampen the lips of the donkey king.

But some yelled out, *"Wait! Let's see if Elijah will come and save him."*

Exhale.

Mounting up.

Ever-heightening pain.

Catch a breath.

Retreat.

The rarified air crackled with anticipation.

Exhaling.

Mounting up.

Ever-heightening pain.

Catching a breath.

Retreating.

Can the Creator—the God of heaven and earth—save him now?

Exhaling.

Mounting up.

Ever-heightening pain.

Catching a breath.

Retreating.

"It is finished!" he cried.

But there was no anguish in his voice. There was the ring of victory to it, as if he had caught with that last breath a glimpse—a glimpse of his kingdom. A glorious kingdom! He had gained the summit. Now with vigor renewed, he pushed up and forward one last time.

Exhaling.

Mounting up.

Ever-heightening pain.

Catching a breath.

Retreating.

"Father . . .

"Into your hands . . .

"I commit . . .

"My Spirit."

His head dropped. It was over.

As his chin hit his chest, the earth began to rumble. Low thrumming. Building . . . building . . .

The rock Skull began to move beneath my feet. And with it, my soul.

I fell to the ground.

The crosses began to vibrate and rock with the power of the quake. His head bobbed from side to side.

But he was dead.

He was dead!

Everyone was with me on bended knees.

Heaven had rendered its dark judgment. The sun had hidden its face. The very earth had answered back. The verdict was in.

I caught two huge breaths of air, and then for the whole world to hear, I cried out, *"He really was the Son of God."*

He was the Son of God.

The sun broke through.

A rooster crowed.

31

Three thirty in the afternoon, Friday, April 7

I ROSE TO my feet. We all rose to our feet, like men aroused from a nightmare. But the nightmare was not over. It hung before us, a cruel reminder of what our hands had done.

The light had come, but what it showed left me in desolate misery. Strangely, it was I who felt naked. It was I who was exposed. I stood exposed before his bloodied, naked corpse. His brutalized body was a mirror erected before my very soul. And what I saw of myself there brought no comfort, no comfort at all.

I felt that the weight of his patibulum now rested on my shoulders. And what a crushing weight it was! I had brought him here, and now that he was dead, the full weight of who he was and what he bore came down upon my own head. It was no wonder that I bowed.

An oppressive heaviness settled over me.

A good portion of the crowd that had assembled below Golgotha now disappeared. They went slinking off. Even in death the Christ had managed to silence his enemies and rattle his critics to the core.

With most of the crowd dispersed, my troop requirements were also reduced. I sent twenty of my foot soldiers back to their regular assignments on the wall. Six of the cavalrymen were ordered back to the stables, but I also asked that my own horse be brought back. I sensed that I needed the lift my mount would bring. I still retained ample manpower to finish this job on the Skull.

On the hill, only Animal and Thaddaeus remained. They hung in perpetual motion, fighting for each breath on pierced limbs. There was a good deal of strength left in them. Unlike the Christ, they had suffered only the whip, not the brutality of the multithonged and studded flagrum, nor had they been beaten and abused by the temple guards. Their ordeal could go on long into the night, perhaps even for days.

Quite unexpectedly, Marius arrived. There were a half dozen soldiers with him.

He saluted. "I've just been sent by Pilate," he informed me. "A Jewish delegation requested that the bodies be removed before the Sabbath. That's why I'm here"—he pursed his lips—"to finish the job."

I looked to his men, then to the crosses. "Go ahead," I said with a grim jerk of my head.

The lead man among them, a heavyset fellow, pulled a hefty sledgehammer from the holster on his hip. He strode over to the quivering Animal. With one hand he gripped a position just below the dying man's knee. With the other he raised the hammer and delivered a smashing blow directly to the shinbone.

A piercing scream followed.

Then he handed the sledge to his comrade and held firm the other knee while his friend delivered the next tibia-shattering blow.

Animal moaned. His body slumped. Now he could only rise for air by drawing himself up on spike-pinned hands, a near impossible task. Death would come to visit soon.

They moved over to the Christ. He hung motionless.

"He's dead!" I called out. "He's already dead."

The lead man gave a shrug and a snort, and moved on to Thaddaeus.

I turned my back to them. I stared off to the city, to Jerusalem. But my ears heard the thudding crack. The rending screams.

"O Jerusalem!" I whispered to myself.

Then another thudding crack.

"Jerusalem!"

The final whimper.

My mind flew back to when we left the city, when Jesus spoke to the wailing women. He said something about the wood being green. Now what was it?

"Hey, centurion. Are you sure he's dead?" the lead man called out to me. He cut right through my sound-blocking thoughts.

I turned. They were back before the Jewish king.

"Yeah, I'm sure," I called back, irritation ringing clearly in my voice.

"Let's make sure," he said, addressing no one in particular.

"Hey, pikeman!" he called out to a fellow standing idle at the base of the Skull. "Lend me your spear."

The pikeman promptly complied.

The lead man took this, but he didn't use it as I had expected. Rather than delivering a decisive quick thrust, he used it like a probe. He placed the tip just below the left side of the Messiah's rib cage. Then he began a slow push angled upward.

He pierced the skin.

A trickle of blood.

Probed higher.

A sudden burst of water!

It splashed down upon the rocks at the base of the cross.

"The lungs!" he called out.

They were water filled all right.

"Now for the heart," he called again.

He thrust higher. More water trickled out. It ran down the full length of the spear shaft. Then suddenly, a second flood. This one thick and red.

"He's dead." He stated the obvious as he withdrew the gore-covered head of the spear.

I turned to Marius. "You've got quite the crew," I said.

"Yeah. They're old hands at this."

"Look, Marius," I began slowly. "I've been thinking that I should report what I have seen here today to Pilate."

"You've had some trouble?"

"I guess you could call it that," I answered, not wishing to go into the details of all that I had witnessed.

He gave a nonchalant shrug. "Sure, go ahead. You have been here all day," he said with a sigh. "Take a break. We'll stay."

"I'll be back before sundown," I promised.

"And don't forget, Marcus. You need to complete the execution registry. It's with Flavio. You may as well do it on your way in."

"Oh, yes," I said. "I'll do that first."

I turned from him and walked off the hill. At the base of it, I looked back, saw the crosses etched against the sky. My head dropped.

That's when I saw it. There was still blood on my hands. Dried blood.

It was the blood of the Son of God!

32

Five in the afternoon, Friday, April 7

A BRISK RUBBING of my hands removed the dried blood, the visible stains.

The shadows were already getting long. But then, the very fact that there were shadows bothered me. It was as though normal had returned. After storm and cloud, and black of night in midafternoon, we were back to a typical sunny, spring day.

But the ground had shifted within. There had been a double quake. Within me, normal could not be found. Seeing Jesus crucified had completely overturned my inner world. What troubled me most was that I now knew who he was—who he really was. But I knew it too late.

I was nearly halfway to the city gate when I was met by my groomsman coming out with my horse. It was convenient timing. I rode the rest of the way back in. But it was a different ride. I rode lower in the saddle. It seemed I had to look up to find ground level. I couldn't help but think that a donkey might provide a better view.

There was activity to the left of the Fish Gate. A long, narrow fissure had opened up. It traced a jagged course from the base of the wall right to the top of the parapet. Earthquake damage. Several men were out inspecting this. Renaldo was among them, but I did not stop.

In the city itself I saw only one instance of damage. Some roof tiles had slid off an old building. They lay in a broken heap to one side of the street.

I went directly to the fortress, and after hitching my horse to a post, I took the stairs up to Flavio's briefing room. I brushed by the sentinels at the door.

Something was different. I didn't see anyone; the room looked empty. Then I noticed it. It was the god shelf; it had collapsed.

Something stirred. It was Flavio. He was on the floor behind the great cedar table, picking up the pieces of the magnificent Apollo. He looked as shattered as his bronze god.

"He's broken!" he lamented as he heard me approach. "Broken beyond repair."

And it was true. The cast bronze idol lay smashed like an old clay pot. Flavio had gathered the pieces together, but assembling them was beyond anyone's skill.

"Help me up, Marcus."

He reached up a hand to me. I fidgeted nervously before extending both of my recently bloodied hands.

His head swayed from side to side. Clearly he was drunk. With what seemed like a great effort on his part, I managed to get him to his feet.

"You're a good man, Marcus." He slurred his words. "A good man."

I helped him to a seat.

He looked back at the broken heap, and then he repeated himself. "He's broken! Broken beyond repair."

He shook his graying head. Then he put his elbows on the table, and with his head in his hands, he began to cry. "I'm broken too, Marcus. I'm broken too." Tears streamed down his face. "Broken," he said, sobbing. "Broken beyond repair."

I sighed. I did not know what to make of this drunken confession.

"You need some sleep, sir. You need a good night's sleep." Then noting the slanting rays coming through the window, I added, "It's getting late."

He sniffled a few times as he seemed to consider this. When he made no response, I called out, "Servant!"

He arrived promptly.

"The general here needs some help to his sleeping quarters," I said.

He gave a knowing smile and nod.

"Shall we go, sir?" He held out an arm to the broken man.

We both worked to get Flavio to his feet, and then he tottered off clutching his servant's arm. At the door he stopped and turned. He called back. "Did I tell you, Marcus? You're a good man." He raised his free hand, and waved an uplifted index finger. "You're a brave man—a good man."

He left. But I was unconvinced. I was brave and good! Good for what? What courage does it take to nail an innocent man to a cross? What good is there in killing a healer of children? After the events of the day, and my involvement in them, I didn't fit the description of a man who is brave or good.

Fortunately, I was able to find the execution registry without any difficulty. I entered the date and three names: Thaddaeus Crispus, twenty-two; Jesus of Nazareth, thirty-three; and Animal, twenty-eight. He never gave us his proper name, and I only guessed at his age.

There was also a spot to enter who claimed the body. I completed this for Thaddaeus. His parents expressed great concern about this matter. As I escorted them off the hill, they told me over and over that they would wait as long as needed to collect his remains.

Jesus was another matter. John, the young man who accompanied the Messiah's mother, told me arrangements were being made. But he didn't know the details. They were all far from home. Undoubtedly, finding a burial plot in a strange city on a few hours' notice presented its own set of challenges.

I left that spot empty. I could complete that section tomorrow when I had the information.

Animal was the big question mark. But if no one came, we did have our own solution for him.

I left my horse standing where it was, rounded the turret of the imposing fortress, and then walked on through the great eagle doors. I hoped to give the governor some account of what had transpired on Golgotha. I entered the same large room where the Christ had been interrogated that very morning.

The governor was seated behind his great oak desk. He was discussing some point of law with someone from Herod's delegation. His voice grew impatient. Finally, after some perfunctory remarks, he looked beyond the man before him and called out, "Next!"

But I was not next.

A tall, tassel-robed man had entered before me. His religious garb and overall deportment bespoke money and position. He stepped forward, bowed, and then began. "Your Excellency, I have come to request the body of Jesus of Nazareth."

"And you are?" Pilate asked.

"My apology, Your Excellency." He bowed once more. "My name is Joseph of Arimathea, a member of the Sanhedrin."

"Humph!" the governor snorted. "You had him put to death. And now you want his body?"

The Badger obviously found this a strange turn of events. He looked at his hands and then nervously rubbed them together.

"I did not consent to his death, sir." Joseph swallowed. "I stood opposed."

"You opposed Caiaphas?" Pilate responded with surprise. "I suggest you watch your back, holy man."

Joseph appeared to take note of this remark, but then added, "We were not all of the same mind concerning the prophet."

Pilate paused to consider this, but when he made no response, Joseph continued. "I have just come from the hill of execution. The prophet is dead. His brother, James, asked me to request the body from you."

"He's dead!" Pilate feigned surprise. "Dead already?" He rubbed his hands once more.

"So I have been told," Joseph said.

Pilate looked my way and, with a beckoning motion, called me forward. "Is the Christ, the Jewish king, dead?" he asked.

I found his choice of words most interesting, revealing.

"Yes, Your Excellency." I nodded. "It is as you say."

"Hmm!" He rubbed a hand across his chin, then furrowed his brow. He glanced at his hands again. He looked pensive, perhaps even worried. Then with a deep sigh, he addressed the holy man. "Follow the centurion here. He will give you the body."

With that said, the governor motioned for us to leave, and even as we did, he too got up and left the judgment hall.

33

Six in the evening, Friday, April 7

"MY NAME IS Marcus Longinus," I said with a slight nod of my head.

"Joseph," he said. "Joseph of Arimathea." Then he signaled to another well-dressed, tassel-robed man waiting outside the eagle-emblazoned doors. "This is Nicodemus, a fellow member of the Jewish high council, the Sanhedrin."

This man had an anxious look. I gave another nod, and then I addressed them both. "Look. I'm sure you want this done before sunset." I gestured skyward. "That gives us less than an hour. My horse is just inside the fortress. I will ride ahead and get things ready."

"That would be wonderful," Nicodemus said as though a great weight had been lifted off his stooped shoulders.

"The tomb where we will lay him is just a stone's throw from Golgotha," Joseph added.

"Good. I'll be off then," I said.

It was the Sabbath that had them worried. "Of course this would have to happen before a Sabbath," I fumed to myself as I headed to the fortress. No work could be done after sundown, and they wanted him buried by then.

I soon had my horse moving at a light trot.

I was angry. The whole of this day made me angry. I had no opportunity to say anything to Pilate. Everything was out of my hands. Everything seemed to conspire to place me in a role I did not want to play. I hated this drama—this nightmare. I hated my part in it. I was as much pinned to my role as those agonized men were pinned to their crosses. And it was a role that was making me sick—sick of heart, sick of soul.

I arrived at Golgotha only to find it in a state of disarray. No. It was more like a scene of primeval chaos—a small outpost of hell on the face of the earth.

The clusters of distraught women had abandoned their spot on the Mother's Hill. They had come closer and were wailing mournfully as sunset drew near. Their high-pitched, discordant voices floated over the scene.

Not a single soldier was to be found on the hill itself. They were dispersed around the base in raucous groups. Some were clearly drunk, and the rest appeared to be well on their way. Marius must have sent for another skin of wine, or maybe two or three. The only exception to this was Claudius. He sat like a stoic, off by himself.

A shaggy mongrel had slipped through these less than vigilant ranks and was now lapping up the blood at the foot of the central cross. Three or four more dogs were skulking around the back of the hill, waiting for their chance to come near.

Swarms of flies had settled in for a macabre feast. The piercing wounds of the dead were black with them.

"Claudius!" I called out, barely controlling my fury. "Where's Marius?"

He got to his feet and sheepishly said, "He said he was going off to relieve himself, and he hasn't come back."

"Pfff!" A fierce puff of air exploded from my lips. "He relieved himself all right, relieved himself of all responsibility."

I slipped off my horse's back, grabbed a loose pebble, and fired it at the shaggy stray. It caught the mongrel on the rear haunches. He spun around, let out several sharp yelps, and then vanished from the hill.

This action caught the attention of most of the clustered soldiers. They rose to their feet, as two or three men among them alerted the others of my arrival. But one particular group was totally oblivious. They were squatted in a circle, engrossed in a game of chance. Philip was the most boisterous among them. The young fool would gamble away his brain, if he had one.

A quick, sharp lesson was in order. I stepped over to them.

I seized the squatted soldier by the back of his armored collar, yanked him full force onto his back, dropped my knee onto his chest, put my dagger to his exposed throat, and then screamed in his face, "You're dead! Dead, soldier! Three times dead!"

I released him and rose.

"Where's your battle readiness?" I yelled at him once more and then glared at the other men.

"Get to your feet." I delivered a kick to the fallen man's ribs. "We've got work to do." My voice crackled with anger. I scanned their stunned faces. "Get those rotting corpses off the crosses." I gestured with both arms raised.

They leaped into motion.

But as Philip turned to follow the others, I caught my example by the arm. I pushed my finger into his face. "You'll see me on Sunday," I snarled. "Sunday morning."

A flogging might well be in order, I thought, or perhaps the latrines could be emptied.

My actions achieved the desired result. They began with Thaddaeus. Using a heavy pry bar and a block of wood as a fulcrum, they pulled out the six-inch spike embedded in his feet. The ladder was thrown up once more at the rear of the cross. The rope that bound the two pieces together was removed. The pole props were again applied to the horizontal crossbeam. The man on the ladder pushed the patibulum free of the notch in the upright. Then the corpse was lowered.

The condemned man's father laid out a linen burial sheet. The body, patibulum and all, were placed upon it. Then the pry bar was used again to remove the five-inch nails that pinned the hands. Once this was done, the crossbeam was rolled off the sheet.

The weeping father lovingly wrapped the burial sheet around his son, and then, aided by what appeared to be his three younger sons, they carried Thaddaeus's body away.

In the interim Nicodemus and Joseph arrived. They worked in feverish haste below the central cross. They spread out a similar linen sheet and then sprinkled it with myrrh and aloes.

The removal of the Christ began.

His mother drew near with a clutch of weeping women.

The bottom edge of the sun touched the horizon.

Nicodemus straightened his back, and thus seeing the sun, he raised both hands to heaven in supplication. "May the great Name forgive us!" He shook his head mournfully. He knew they could not possibly make it to the tomb before the sun set. But having come this far, they were determined to press on. They would throw themselves upon the mercies of God.

I knew this was no small concession for a religious Jew of his rank and station. It was, in fact, a measure of his high esteem for the crucified Christ. Being of the priestly class, he was prohibited from touching the body of the dead. But here he was, on the hill of execution, hovering near the lifeless corpse.

Jesus was laid upon the burial cloth.

His healing hands were pried free from the cruel clutch of the cross.

Joseph stood on one side of the body, Nicodemus on the other. Then Joseph instructed two of the young men in their party, "Now, bring down his arms."

One of the young men, possibly John, grabbed one of the Christ's death-stiffened arms and laid it by his side. From the opposite side a young man did the same to the other.

Now his mother knelt over him. She wrestled the thorn crown off his bruised head. Then, one last time, she kissed his face.

She turned away and wept like only a mother can weep. Aren't a mother's deepest sobs saved for sons?

The young men wrapped his face with a white linen cloth and then enfolded his entire body in the death shroud.

The sun sank below the horizon.

"It's over here," Joseph directed. And with that, the young men picked up the body and followed Joseph off the back of the hill.

"Move on to the next one," I called out to the whole troop. Only Animal remained. Then with an aside to Claudius, I said, "I'll be right back."

I wanted to confirm the location of this tomb. Something inside me hinted that I would be questioned about this matter. I tagged along behind the burial party, and it was just as Joseph of Arimathea had said. It was a stone's throw away, on the back side of the next rock hill.

And quite the tomb it was. It was newly constructed. In fact, I had seen excavation going on in that location for as long as I could remember, and now this rather grand project was done and ready for its first occupant. It contained a large chamber, cut into the white dolomite. A huge circular stone, as tall as a man, had been chiseled and shaped to cover the entrance.

It was a tomb for the wealthy, fit for a king, at least for a donkey king.

I did not dare linger. I was not about to relieve myself as Marius had done. Even so, by the time I returned, the third corpse was down and darkness was closing in on us like a great shroud.

Claudius approached me and, gesturing to the corpse, said, "There's no family. What do we do with him?"

Of course, there probably was a family, but the young rebel had been disowned by his parents, by all his relatives. Quite likely this was something that had happened a good long while before today. Now here was the ultimate outcome, the final fate.

"That's not our problem," came my curt reply. "He and Barabbas dumped Andreas on the street. We'll dump him in the bushes." There was a measure of grim satisfaction in my voice. "Pull him off the hill, down to those bushes over there." I motioned with my left hand. "The dogs will do the rest. And what the dogs don't get will be left for the birds. The birds and the worms."

I rode back into the city alone, downcast and alone, into the gathering darkness. I returned my horse to the stables at the hippodrome and then walked home in solemn gloom. Just before I reached the villa gate, my foot brushed against something soft. I stopped and then stooped.

It was the sparrows' nest.

The purple-skinned hatchlings lay dead on the cobblestones.

34

Seven in the morning, Saturday, April 8

IT WAS A horrible night. Horrible!

I could not sleep. The events of the day kept flooding over my mind—a constant bloody torrent. During the daylight hours you can steel yourself against another man's suffering. But at night your hard shell dissolves from around you, and you are left in just your own skin again. Then their suffering soaks into your flesh, and it becomes your own.

There seemed to be no end to it—no end to this torment. I willed myself to sleep. But I could not find that door of escape. It eluded me. Instead I was pursued relentlessly by the dreadful events of the day. The hammer blows kept ringing in my head. And now their pain was mine.

All night my mind was on Golgotha.

Why me? Why Jesus? Why by some cruel twist of heaven's fate did I find myself with him upon the hill of execution?

When I closed my eyes, his face appeared before me. His gentle eyes stared down on me, boring a hole into my very soul. Blood oozed down from the stabbing crown of thorns. It pooled and dried along his eyebrows. And his pain? His pain was my own.

Once in the night Zelda put her arm around me and drew close.

I pulled away. I could not be comforted. I could not be loved, and neither could I give love. She could not reach me. I was well beyond all this.

Why did I spit in Jesus's face? Why did all hell erupt from within me? I hated being forced into this role, the role of the killer, the executioner. Just as in Germania, I was compelled—forced by circumstances into a role that I despised. But when my moment came, with my men gathered around, I played it to the hilt. The brute lurking at the bottom of the chasm within me took full control. Today on Golgotha the horror and rage of Germania had found a fresh vent.

But this was no barbarian village. This was no blond-haired girl; this was the Son of God.

The Son of God . . .

The words of my confession reverberated through my throbbing mind, over and over, until I thought my head would split.

Finally, toward dawn, a dream came—a dream as horrid as the state of my own soul.

Now I was on the cross. The flies buzzed and droned all around my naked, heaving frame.

They licked the sweat from my face, drank my trickling blood, mated on my flesh, laid their eggs in my piercing wounds.

And I? I could do nothing. Nothing!

My nail-pinned hands could not brush them away. I had no puff of air in reserve, so I could only blow them from my face. I had no means whatever to resist their fickle, buzzing dance of torture. I was helpless and beyond all help.

Three times I dozed. Three times I fell into this unfathomable hell. Each episode was more vivid than the last, until finally my will to sleep crumbled. Then I fought against the very notion of sleep. I got up more weary than when I had laid my head upon the pillow.

It was late, much later than I usually rise. But then it was Saturday, the Sabbath. This day had no urgency to it. The day of rest. Here was a Jewish custom that in normal times I quite enjoyed. May it come to the whole of our world.

Technically it was not a day of rest for the Roman military, but practically it was, since all commerce in the city was shut down. We reduced our operations proportionately. We maintained a mere skeleton crew on the city walls. The gates were closed. Quiet reigned.

But while Zelda and the boys still slept, I resolved to visit Pilate and speak my mind. I pulled on my multilayered linen cuirass, strapped on my sword, and slipped out of the bedroom door.

Noisy sparrows chattered about the villa courtyard. I placed my hands on the familiar handrail and looked over all that was my home. I could see no earthquake damage. But yet there was damage. There was no peace here. But this damage, this problem, was not in my home. It was in my heart, in my soul, and on my mind, so oppressively heavy on my mind.

It was the prophet, the Galilean, the Jewish king, the Son of God! The man with a thousand titles. It was he who had upset my world. He turned it upside down, threw all of it into chaos. I blamed him.

Or should I blame Pilate? The Badger knew more than he let on. He knew this was wrong. But he caved in like a brick-roofed hovel. Why did this man have no spine? Why did he let Caiaphas lead him around like a bull on a nose ring?

For the second time I would try to talk to him. I would tell him what I saw. How I saw the prophet heal. How he brought the dead Timaeus back to life. How the very sun refused to shine, refused to see what we had done to him. How the earth quaked and the cross shook when he died. I would tell him. I would tell it all to him. I would tell him who the prophet was. The Son of God!

Maybe that would bring me some peace.

But then, I suspect Pilate already knew—knew in his heart that this was no ordinary man. He had heard all the miraculous stories and then read the warning message from his wife. He had seen the same darkness and been shaken by the same quake that rattled me.

Still, I would go. Let the Badger rage. Let him hang me on a cross if he so desired. In my tortured mind I was there already. The real thing might not be so much worse than this, this hellish torment.

I went down the stairs. I ate some of the cook's thick porridge with a few of the early-rising men. I savored it like a last meal. And then I set out, not knowing what response might await me at the other end of my journey.

The streets were largely quiet. A few men sat out in the morning sun. Not a child was to be seen.

For the second consecutive morning, I walked up the six broad steps of the stone pavement. I stood before the carved eagle doors. But to my great surprise, someone was already there before me. Three clerics were waiting in their gold-ornamented garb. One of them I recognized. It was Annas. The other men were high-ranking Pharisees, members of the Sanhedrin.

What could possibly bring them to the governor's palace door on the Sabbath, the Passover Sabbath nonetheless?

On hearing me approach, Annas turned and greeted me. "Ah, a centurion! What a pleasant surprise." He nodded, and then he raised a finger my way and said, "We may have need of you."

There was a curious twinkle in the old man's eye.

"I am here to see the governor," I said.

"As are we," one of the Pharisees confirmed, stating what was patently obvious.

"Have you spoken to anyone?" I asked.

"His chamberlain," Annas replied. "He said he would be right back, but we have waited here for quite some time now." He heaved a weary sigh.

To this I made no reply. Stony silence descended. No natural link existed between us, nor was one desired by either party.

In due course the governor's chamberlain arrived. He showed a measure of surprise at seeing me with this group. But then he bowed courteously to Annas and said, "His Excellency will see you now."

Annas beckoned me to follow, and so I entered. The chamberlain undoubtedly thought I was a late-arriving addition to this delegation.

Pilate was seated even as I saw him yesterday. He wore a rather haggard look, as though he had slept on the bloodstained rocks of Golgotha. He motioned for the temple delegation to step forward. I waited at the back of the room in a repetition of the governor's late-day interview with Joseph of Arimathea.

Annas bowed and began. *"Sir, we remember that while he was still alive that deceiver said, 'After three days I will rise again.'"*

A strange tingle ran through me as he said this.

Pilate rubbed his hands.

Annas continued. *"So give the order for the tomb to be made secure until the third day. Otherwise, his disciples may come and steal the body and tell the people that he has been raised from the dead."* Then he concluded by lifting a bony finger and saying, *"This last deception will be worse than the first."*

On hearing this, Pilate sighed deeply, then beckoned me forward. There was worry in his eyes. "The centurion here, Marcus Longinus, is fully acquainted with the case of the Galilean prophet. He oversaw his crucifixion." Then he addressed me directly. "Is that not so?"

I nodded. "Yes, sir. It is as you say."

With that he raised his hands and motioned both parties together. Then, speaking directly to all of us, he said, *"Take a guard. Go, make the tomb as secure as you know how."* Rubbing his guilt-stained hands once more, the Badger got up and skulked off.

Annas was jubilant. With eagerness in his voice, he turned to address me. "How soon can you have your troops at the tomb?"

"We should be there in about an hour."

"Excellent! These two gentlemen will meet you there. They will ensure that all is in order. Understood?"

"Yes. Understood," I said. Then I addressed the Pharisees. "Do you know which tomb? Do you know where it is?"

Annas answered for them. "Ah, they know it well." He gave a contemptuous snort. "The traitor's tomb, Joseph of Arimathea!"

"I will bring my men and meet you there then." I gave a slight bow with my head.

The chamberlain saw us to the door, and then I was off, back to my home.

I shook my head several times in disbelief as I trudged back. Every time I tried to extricate myself from this Messiah pit, this kingdom of God affair, this abysmal hole, I would find myself sucked in even deeper. And now it had happened again. Was there no escape?

Would I ever be allowed to speak my mind before Pilate?

I decided to see Renaldo first, so rather than turn into my gate, I went directly to his. There was no sign of Renaldo or Keeper, his big, friendly dog, but there were a dozen soldiers in the courtyard. Some of them were about to leave for the fortress. Competitive games had been planned for today—races and feats of strength between Flavio's hometown team, and Caius and his men.

"I may have some work for you men," I called out to these soldiers. "So don't leave just yet."

Upon hearing my voice, Renaldo emerged from a side room. "What is it, Marcus?" he asked.

"Oh, I need some men to guard the prophet's tomb." It was impossible to hide my frustration.

"Why?" Renaldo reacted with a perplexed shake of his head.

"Well, it seems that the high priest and his crew are worried that either Jesus will arise from the dead or his disciples will come and steal his body."

"That's bizarre." Renaldo shook his head again. "Just bizarre. Where did they get that notion?"

"From the prophet himself. Apparently he predicted it."

Renaldo bowed his head slightly, and then brought his hand to his forehead in what appeared to be a desperate attempt to mentally digest it all.

"Look, Renaldo. I don't have time to try and explain this." My exasperation was clearly showing. "And I don't really know if I even can. Right now I need sixteen men to take to the tomb for the first shift. I need them there within the hour. I thought if we combined your men here with my men next door, we could make up this first contingent."

"First contingent?"

"First contingent—first shift. They want it guarded day and night for the next three days."

"Fine." He threw up his hands angrily. "We'll prance around and do the Weasel's bidding. Did Pilate approve this?"

"Yes, sir." I bowed low in a show of mock subservience. "He's back licking the holy man's stinking feet once again! He started yesterday during the Messiah's trial," I said bitterly, "and now, who knows when he'll stop."

"I can only shake my head," Renaldo answered as he did just that.

Then after a pause, with grim resignation in his voice, he said, "Let's get on with it. I suppose we have to do it."

He turned and bellowed at the twelve waiting men, "All of you head next door."

After a bit of haggling and to-and-fro banter, we settled on eight men from each troop who would accompany me to the tomb. The rest of the soldiers were released to go to the fortress in preparation for the games that were to begin at noon.

I lined up the men four abreast, and we marched to the tomb in rhythmic military style. We would do this right. On the surface I protested being drawn into this—the high priest's plan of preemptive precaution—but within me, I was filled with dark apprehension. These measures had merit. This guarding of the tomb might well be warranted.

I did not fear his disciples. There had been no sign of them, no sign of armed uprising. No, it was the prophet himself that I feared.

This notion of him rising from the dead did not strike me as all that far-fetched. On the surface the Christ's prediction seemed impossible—utterly impossible—totally preposterous. But then in life he had been a total master of the impossible. The example of the blind Bartimaeus sprang to mind. This Messiah had tossed off miracles like he was tossing off the covers from his bed. Could he now toss off the shroud of death?

There was something far larger at work here. This was more than the raving of a lunatic. Why else would the sun refuse to shine as he hung dying? Why else would the earth shudder with his last breath? No, he was the Son of God. My very own words came back to haunt me. Anything was possible; nothing could be ruled out!

I remembered the worried look I saw on Pilate's face just this morning when Annas had raised this matter. Without exchanging a word, I knew we were of the same mind on this. He too thought a resurrection could occur. Why else his prompt response?

Oh yes, and then there was the rubbing of the hands. Guilt stains are not so easily removed. I should know. After all these years the blond-haired girl still visits me quite regularly on those soul-tormenting nights.

Only the high priest's men seemed sure of themselves, cocky in their victory, but not cocky enough to throw all caution to the wind. Why else post a guard? But winds can change, and all this might yet blow up in their faces.

They were there. The two pompous Pharisees were already there at the tomb. There was a change of garb, though. They were no longer in their Sabbath-day finery, not for a visit to this king's tomb. They would burn these clothes when they returned to the city.

"Greetings," I said rather stiffly.

They ignored this remark. One of them began. "This is all your men?"

"All that I'll be bringing," I said.

"Humph!" He sniffed, obviously disappointed with the number. "Well. This tomb will need to be sealed," he said as he put his hand to the huge rock door.

"Why sealed?" I asked.

"Because I don't trust your men," he shot back.

Now it was my turn to go, "Humph!"

"If a bit of silver crosses their palms, they'll remove that body." He motioned toward the tomb's contents lying behind the rock door. "No. It will have to be sealed. We will have it no other way."

I frowned, but by way of defense I said, "I trust my men. Nevertheless," I conceded, "for your sake, we'll seal it."

"Now let's see if he's there," the other Pharisee said as he motioned again to the round rock door.

"He's there. I saw them put him in here last night." I spoke with growing impatience.

"We will see if he is there," he repeated with marked insistence in his voice.

I sighed, then called two of my larger, more muscular men by name. "Roll back the stone."

They responded eagerly enough. The whole platoon had listened intently to our conversation. Now they were being drawn into the action. One man crouched low and applied his back and shoulder to the polished rim of the boulder. He would push up and forward with the full strength of his legs. The second man placed his hands above the first man's head and braced himself for a tremendous push in a forward direction.

I counted out the numbers. "One, two, three. Push!"

To cheers of encouragement from the other soldiers, the huge rock slowly ground into motion. It rolled ever so slowly in its cut rock track. After a Herculean effort, the opening lay fully exposed. The light shone in. My two men collapsed in a jubilant heap.

"Well done," I called out to them.

The Pharisees stepped inside, and I followed. There were several rock shelves cut in the sidewalls. All of them were empty. It was, after all, a new tomb. But in a central position near the back was a raised rock platform, the place of honor. On this the Christ lay. The Pharisees cautiously drew near. One of them turned and beckoned me to approach.

"Unwrap him," he instructed.

I stiffened. "I will not unwrap him." I glared defiantly.

"Then have your men unwrap him," he demanded.

"I will not have my men unwrap him," I answered with growing anger. "If you want him unwrapped, do it yourselves!"

This produced an impasse. For a moment no one moved. The whole scenario bothered me. We crossed an invisible line when we rolled back the stone. We crossed another line when we entered. I was not about to cross the third line. We were now verging on the desecration of the dead. I would not yield on this point. I found it shocking that these men, these holy men, who abhorred the presence of the dead, would insist on carrying this matter so far. And without question, they were acting on the explicit instructions of the hoary-headed Weasel.

Some holy man!

"Look," I argued. "This is Jesus of Nazareth, if that's your concern. I saw him taken off the cross"—I motioned in the vague direction of Golgotha—"wrapped in that shroud." I pointed to it. "He was carried into this tomb. This is his body." I put stress on each word.

"Will you swear to that?"

I raised my right hand. "By the emperor's throne, by the sacred temple, by all that is holy, I will swear." I spoke with mounting anger.

This assertion appeared to satisfy them.

We walked out of the tomb, and I chose two fresh men to roll the stone back.

Then once more I addressed the high priest's men. "I didn't bring any plaster, or water, or a pot to mix it in. I will need to send someone to get these."

This news was greeted with a disdainful sigh, but they insisted they would wait by the tomb until the job was done.

I sent two men off to retrieve the required tools and material, and in due course they returned. We mixed the fine-powdered plaster with water in an ample-sized iron pot. Using a stonemason's trowel I scooped the wet, gray plaster over the narrow crevice that separated the rock door from the rock face of the hill. Soon an airtight plaster seal was in place around the giant circular rock door. At two points, one on either side, I affixed the governor's own stamp into the yet pliable plaster.

Any tampering would break this seal and obliterate the imperial stamp.

At last they were satisfied. Caiaphas himself would have approved of this seal. But then, why was I working for him?

It was midafternoon when we were finally done. I posted my men on guard and headed back to the city.

Some Sabbath! Some day of rest!

But I was done sealing the dead.

35

Five in the afternoon, Saturday, April 8

THE BOYS BOUNCED around me like playful puppies as at last I walked through the gates of home.

"We made a kite," Julius said, and with that he rushed off to retrieve it.

"You were gone all day," the youngest boy complained as he grabbed my hand and started swinging from it.

"Yeah, I was gone. I had work to do." I sighed and rubbed my free hand across the back of my neck.

"Look at this!" Julius trumpeted, and then he went careening about the courtyard with the kite tail streaming out behind him. "Let's go fly it, Papa!"

"I think it's too late." I answered slowly. I found the nearest bench off to the side and collapsed onto it.

My words took the wind from both their sails.

"Can't we go, Papa? We waited all day."

"I just can't do it today," I said with genuine regret. But then, to soften the blow, I said, "Let me see that kite. It looks great."

Julius handed it to me with some reluctance.

"So you did this?"

"Mom helped," he admitted.

"She helped a lot," Andrew corrected him.

"Your mom is really good at this kind of stuff."

"You're better," Andrew said, "but you weren't here."

With that mild rebuke, my depleted patience ran out. "Boys, go away!

Just go away!" My voice rose, and I motioned them out of my sight. "I just need some time to myself."

They retreated in crushed despondence.

It was not very long before Zelda came. She was wearing one of her best dresses. Her long hair was freshly brushed, and I quickly caught the scent of her perfume.

"You look exhausted, Marcus," she said.

"I am."

"Let me get you some wine," she said.

"Have the servant girl get it. Come and sit down." I slid over. "Come sit by me for a while."

"She's not here, Marcus. Remember, it's the Sabbath."

"Ha! The Sabbath," I muttered. "Some Sabbath!"

"So where were you all day?" She sat down and then continued. "I kept telling the boys you would be home soon, but you never came."

"Pfff!" I glowered. "I was working for the Weasel. The bloody Weasel!"

She was taken aback, unfamiliar with this derogatory term.

"The high priest. Caiaphas. The holy stone thrower." I erupted. "That butcher has the morals of a grave robber!"

I threw my head back and rubbed my fingers over my hair. A week's worth of exasperation gripped me.

"How come you're working for him?" Zelda asked. She was truly confused by all this. I usually said very little about my work.

"It's a long story." I felt myself tensing up. "I—I don't even want to go into it." I hesitated. "Just get me the wine." I motioned with a backhanded wave. I slumped forward with my elbows on my knees and my chin cradled in my hands.

She got up and touched her hand to my hair, like some kind of blessing, and then was off. In a few minutes she was back with a wine-filled chalice cradled in her hand.

I took a few sips.

Zelda stood awkwardly before me without speaking a word. I knew she had something to say.

"What is it?" I said.

"Junia and Renaldo invited all of us over for supper." She paused before adding, "I said we would come."

"Humph," I snorted from within my ongoing state of dejection.

Normally this would be welcome news. But nothing could shake me from the dark foreboding that had settled around me like a death shroud. Besides, I felt my whole life was being planned for me. Everything was out of my hands, whether at work or at home.

"If you have a nice bath, I'm sure you'll feel better."

I made no response.

"She made shlemkins. The boys are looking forward to it."

"Fine," I snapped. "We'll go." It was a reluctant concession. "But I'm not sure that I'm fit company for anyone."

She left me. I sat in bleak silence, then drained the chalice and headed for the bathhouse.

Within an hour we were ready to head over to our neighbors. Zelda was right. I did feel better after a bath and a change of clothes, and the boys had gotten over their earlier disappointment. I told them to bring their kite because Renaldo was a kite-building expert, or so I said.

We walked over together as a family. I told Julius to call out at the gate. Soon Rana greeted us with a graceful curtsey and ushered us in. She was the oldest of Renaldo's four daughters. In contrast to all the other days this week, the courtyard was deserted. By common consent our uninvited military guests were spending the night at the hippodrome.

The boys rushed over to the corner where Keeper usually sleeps, but the dog wasn't there. Renaldo called out to them, "He's gone. I let him out this morning, and he's still not back." Then as an aside to me he said, "He probably found a lady friend."

But young Andrew heard this comment and asked, "Do dogs get married, Papa?"

This brought a good bit of adult laughter. Then Renaldo motioned to me for an answer.

"Not exactly, but they like each other a lot."

More laughter.

"We can talk about it another time. Now, boys, why don't you show Renaldo your kite?"

The kite was presented and duly admired. In the meantime, Zelda went off with Junia to help with the meal.

"I know who would like a look at this," Renaldo told the boys. He returned the kite to Julius and, with a beckoning motion, said, "Come, follow me."

We mounted the stairs to the sleeping quarters, and there on the balcony sat the harlot's son on an old wooden chair. He had been watching us with eager eyes from the moment we arrived.

"This is Lucas." Renaldo began the introduction.

The boy smiled.

"He has had an accident." Renaldo spoke the words more slowly, by way of explanation. "But he's getting back his strength." He turned to him. "Aren't you, Lucas?"

"Yeah," he said. The boy turned, and as he did, he brought the bandaged stump into view.

I saw my sons' eyes widen. Julius stepped back. Andrew took my hand.

"It's getting better," the older boy said. "It doesn't hurt as much today."

But I could see marks of strain in the beggar boy's eyes.

"I'm getting a new hand," he said. "Jesus of Nazareth said he would give me a new one." He spoke the words with a matter-of-fact confidence.

Renaldo shot a glance my way.

"Ah, Lucas," I began, "when, ah . . . when did Jesus say this to you?"

"Last night. He told me last night. He came to my room."

"It was a dream?" I asked.

"No." He was emphatic. "I don't think so. He was real." Then he extended his formerly crippled leg, glanced down at it, and with conviction asserted, "He fixed my leg. He'll fix my hand."

"It was a dream," I said with a shake of my head. "You can't put your trust in a dream."

He turned away from me. His lips tightened. I thought he might start to cry.

He did not want to hear this. Neither did I want to say it. But why let some false hope linger? Why let the poison of disappointment take root? This was one dream that ought to be shattered before it had time to fully form. This boy had suffered enough. Why let false hope add to his torment?

The whole topic—the visit from Jesus—brought an eerie discomfort, a startling disconnect with what I knew to be reality.

Renaldo gave me one of his instant eye signals. The signal spoke of his approval of my words. He probably had told Lucas something similar. I did not want to tell the boy that the Northern prophet was dead. At times like this, such things are better left unsaid.

I gave Julius a nudge.

He held up the kite and said, "We brought this for you. We made it today."

Suddenly the kite had turned into a gift.

Lucas's whole face changed. He took it and held it with his one hand. He moved it in a swooping fashion as though it were in flight. But then a tear did trickle down. He tried to wipe it on the sleeve of his upper arm while he still held the kite in his hand.

"I've never had a kite. I couldn't run." He choked on the words. They were spoken with a rare combination of bittersweet joy. "But now I can run."

"Yes," Renaldo said, "in a few days you'll be running."

Rana called up from the courtyard below us, "Supper! Supper is ready!"

Renaldo helped him to his feet, and except for the stairs, Lucas walked the whole way to the dining hall on his own.

"I thought Claudius might come with you for supper," Renaldo said.

"Ah, I've got him out guarding the tomb tonight," I said.

"So how did it go today with the Weasel's men?" Renaldo asked.

"Pfff!" The breath exploded from my lips. I shook my head. "Let's just say they're happy. I'm dead. But they're happy."

There was enough bitterness in my voice to ruin my meal. And it did.

We all sat down together. I ate only a little and drank a little too much. Voices, conversation, children's laughter buzzed all around me. In my overtired state it had a lulling effect. But all too soon it reminded me of flies, lazy Sabbath day flies, buzzing, buzzing over a corpse.

I seemed to awake from this half stupor as Zelda put her arm to my shoulder. "Marcus, you're so quiet. Are you falling asleep?"

"I guess I am," I admitted.

"You poor man! They're working you too hard," she said with a quick kiss to my brow.

Then she turned to Junia. "I guess we should go. I hate to leave so soon after supper, but I don't want Marcus falling asleep on your table."

"Oh, he can sleep on our table—just not in our bed," Renaldo quipped.

Junia rose from beside me and called the boys from the next room, where they had gone to play. The mandatory compliments and thank-yous were exchanged as we all made our way out to the courtyard.

The night watchman had arrived, and he opened the gate for us. As he did, a large dark beast surged by us. It was Keeper.

Something white protruded from either side of his jaws. Even in the dim light I saw it.

Recognition was instant. It was the well-gnawed bones of a forearm. The hand with fingers intact dangled from one end.

"It's Keeper!" Andrew called out eagerly as the dog retreated to his corner with his ghoulish trophy.

The dog was so quick and the light so poor, no one had seen what I saw.

"Stop!" I screamed as the boy started running to greet Renaldo's family pet.

I lunged for him, caught him by the shoulder. "Stop! Stop when I say stop!"

My voice was breaking. I was shaking as I gripped him tight.

He started to cry.

"Why don't you listen!" I yelled. I shook him so that his teeth rattled.

The poor boy was terrified. He had never seen me in such an agitated state. My chest heaved with each breath. I was visibly shaking with ragged-edged rage.

When my hands released him, he ran bawling to his mother.

I rose from off my knees. "He's got a bone!" I snapped. "Don't bother a dog with a bone."

It was a feeble attempt to explain what appeared to be a bizarre overreaction to an innocent situation. No one knew why I had lost control, and I was not about to tell anyone. Both families stood in stunned silence, unsure how to respond to what they saw as an irrational outburst.

"Take the boys home, Zelda. Just take the boys home." I motioned.

They left with Andrew still crying. "I didn't mean to, Papa. I didn't mean to." His body convulsed with huge, aching sobs.

"Let's go back in, girls," Junia said. "There's cleanup to do."

Only Renaldo, the gatekeeper, and I remained in the courtyard. I stood with my head down.

"Are you all right?" Renaldo asked as he approached.

"No. I'm not all right," I confessed in a voice just above a whisper. I threw up my hands in exasperation. I bit down on my lip—shook my head. I walked over to the gate. With a jerk of my head, I called Renaldo to follow. When we were out on the empty street, I leaned my forehead against a brick in the outside wall. As Renaldo drew near, I began to whisper, a hoarse whisper, with my face into the wall. "I'm going crazy! I'm going crazy!"

He put a hand to my shoulder.

"That Messiah—that crucifixion! It's driving me crazy!" The words hissed out from me. They were more breathed than spoken. I clenched my fists and rolled my forehead over the jagged surface of the brick.

Long breath-catching, throat-stinging pause.

"Your dog, your filthy dog, came home with a dead man's arm tonight. Hand and all. Ugh!" I whimpered. I rolled my forehead over the brick again. "It's from Golgotha! The bloody Skull!"

I sank to the ground, turned my back to the wall, hung my heavy head between my knees.

Renaldo stooped before me. He was speechless.

Time passed.

"It's Animal. It's Animal," I whispered.

I don't know if he knew what I meant by this.

More time passed. More aching silence.

Then he spoke. "I'll kill him."

Pause.

"I'll kill the dog!" he said.

"No." I sighed. "No . . . Just clean it up." I rolled my head from side to side. "It's your dog. Just clean up after your dog." I looked up into his face. "Don't let your girls see it."

My head dropped like a stone again.

I said my piece, but there was no peace.

I braced myself against the wall, put my hand to Renaldo's shoulder, and pulled myself up.

I walked home.

I collapsed onto the courtyard bench. For about an hour I lay there alone, rolled up against the chilly night air. Then from the yard next door, I heard a yelp.

A singular, sharp yelp.

Then silence. Just cold silence.

36

Three in the morning, Sunday, April 9

THE SAME COLD snow. The same wooded valley in Germania.

The same stealthy, encircling approach. The same signal for attack.

In unison we rushed forward, swords drawn, bucklers held at the ready, swift but silent. Surprise was our sharpest weapon.

I rounded the corner of the first hut and all but collided with a child—a girl.

Thhuuck!

My sweeping blade caught her just below the ribs, slicing three-quarters through her slim torso.

Her blond head snapped back in shock.

Questioning blue eyes shot upward, looking me full in the face.

She spoke. For the first time in a hundred nights, she spoke.

"There is a solution." The words tumbled from her lips even as her body fell severed from this life.

I felt a hot, red gush cover my sword hand.

I leaped from the bed, sweat drenched, chest heaving, once more filled with dread and dark foreboding.

I rubbed my guilty hands in the moonlight. Collapsed by the window. Rocked back and forth in the darkness.

Here I was again, caught in another round of torment, with each nightmare more hideous than the last.

I wondered what she meant. I wondered why she spoke. Why did she speak tonight? She never spoke before. What solution could there be?

What cleansing for the constant, dripping stain within my hollow soul? What cleansing for my bloodied hands?

What solution?

After a time Zelda hauled herself out of bed. She knelt beside me.

I made no response.

She wrapped her arm around my shoulder.

Why did she still care? Why did she even care?

I scared her. My outbursts scared her. My nightmares left their own cut marks inside her gentle heart. Why come close to me again?

I hurt the boys. Today I hurt the boys. Would I lash out at her next?

Suddenly my life was careening out of control, like an arrow glancing off the rock-hard surface of the Skull. Next it would go slamming into hell. In the last week the demons long held in check had all been let out. And now they were laughing. Laughing! I could hear them laughing in the night. And their maniacal laugh echoed off the gaping chasm deep within me.

Zelda kissed the side of my head. Then she sighed deeply.

After a long while she spoke. "I'm pregnant."

Long pause.

"We're going to have another baby," she said as she rubbed her hand across her tummy. "It's three months, Marcus."

I was silent.

I sighed. My head dropped lower.

"What's wrong? What's wrong, Marcus? Whatever has come over you?" Her tone was not accusatory. These were words borne out of loving concern.

At last I lifted my head and spoke. "I'm scared, Zelda. I'm scared . . . I'm scared that I'll never see that baby. I'm scared that it will be stolen from us, just like Tara."

"I'm scared too," she admitted.

"I'm scared of what I'm turning into," I confessed with a slow and mournful shake of my head.

My head dropped again between my knees. I wrapped my arms around my knees and then squeezed my knees together. My head, my skull, was caught in this vicelike grip. My posture, my physical form, now reflected my spiritual reality.

Somehow she wrapped her arms around me. She kissed the top of my fallen head.

"I love you, Marcus. Don't ever leave me."

I sighed a sigh from so deep that it rattled around the very roots of the chasm.

After a time I got up and dropped myself into bed. I lay flat on my stomach, my head turned aside.

She put her arm over my shoulder and whispered in my ear, "You're a good man, Marcus. A very good man."

But then she didn't really know.

She didn't know what my hands had done . . . She didn't know me.

37

Five forty-five in the morning, Sunday, April 9

THE EARTHQUAKE JOLTED both of us awake.

It was a different kind of quake. Friday's quake was of the slow, rumbling, grinding type that rolls to a crescendo. This one was short and sharp. It felt as though for an instant the earth had disappeared from beneath us, and we were allowed to fall into the lurch left by this pocket of empty space.

The foundations shuddered; the walls shook. My helmet fell off the peg on which it hung. It clattered to the floor, bounced once, and made a crazy half roll over the floorboards.

It was sunrise. The first shafts of light streamed through our open window.

It was late, later than I usually rise. But then I desperately needed that bit of sleep. I scrambled to my feet. All the while I could hear voices on the street. The city was awake, and this seismic tremor was giving them plenty to talk about. Fortunately for the moment, there were no aftershocks, and I could see no obvious damage when I emerged onto the balcony in only a breechcloth.

The sparrows resumed their flitting here and there, but their chatter had been stilled. I moved quickly and pushed open the door to the boys' room. Both of them were sitting up in their beds. They too had been jolted out of sleep.

"Something happened, Papa!" Andrew said with fear in his small voice. He held out his arms to me for a hug.

I pulled him right out of bed and into my arms.

"Yes, something happened. It was an earthquake," I said as I moved over to Julius. I put an arm around him too and said, "Let's go downstairs, boys."

By this time Zelda was clothed and at the door. "We'll go down to the courtyard." I motioned with my head. "There might be another one."

We walked down together. I pulled two benches to the middle of the courtyard for us to sit on. Then I felt the morning cold.

"I forgot my clothes." With that said, I turned to go back upstairs.

"Be careful!" Zelda called after me.

I pulled my linen cuirass, my helmet, tunic, belt, and sword out onto the balcony. I felt safer dressing there, and my family was within view.

It was the strangest quake, singularly sharp and potent. But nothing preceded; nothing followed. Urgency was replaced by an uneasy calm.

As I strapped on my sword, the cook called up to me, asking if he should proceed with breakfast. I answered in the affirmative. With some apprehension, I followed him back into the house, and since the porridge had already been prepared, we simply scooped it into four bowls. Then he helped me carry these out to my family in the courtyard. We felt safer out there.

It was a strange way to start the day.

I had downed three big spoonfuls when someone started banging at the gate. There was clearly a commotion out there. The pounding was urgent. I set my bowl down on the bench and covered the ground to the gate with large, quick strides.

Where was that gatekeeper anyway?

But the bar would not release. The gateposts must have shifted in the quake, and now the bar was jammed. Finally I jarred it free with a painful upward thrust with my open palms. A dozen men surged in. The guards from the tomb. They were breathless. Sweat dripped from them. Some collapsed on the ground. Others were doubled over and gasping for air.

They must have run the whole way from the tomb. But it was more than exhaustion I saw written on their faces. I saw fear.

"What's happened?" I called out to no one in particular.

Philip caught his breath. "There was a light. It came down." He shook his head violently and then grabbed some more air, but he could not go on.

I moved to another man, who was stooped over, hands on his knees. I motioned for him to speak with quick, desperate jerks of my hands. But he shook his head.

I spotted Claudius. I grabbed him by the front collar of his cuirass and forced him upright. "What happened?" I demanded as I yelled in his face. "What happened?" My words were forced out through clenched teeth.

"The light . . . the light became a man." He swallowed. "When it touched the ground . . . the earth shook. It dropped out from under us."

His head slumped down.

I shook him. "What then?"

Nothing came.

From behind me, Philip resumed the account. "We all fell down. Fell flat."

I stepped toward him again.

He caught another gulp of air. "It was so bright—like lightning. I closed my eyes. I couldn't see. We couldn't look." He held up his hand as though he were shielding his eyes. "We lay there shaking."

And he still was shaking. I looked about. Others were nodding their heads.

"What else? Was there more?"

A third man came to his aid. "When I opened my eyes, this messenger from heaven—this angel—was on the stone. He was sitting on the stone."

"The tomb was open," Philip continued, and he fell to the ground. "A man walked out of it. The dead man walked out!" He wailed out these last words, as though he had seen a spirit—a ghost.

"You all saw this?"

Each man nodded assent.

"We all saw it," Claudius confirmed.

I brought my hand to my forehead and then expelled a huge breath of air. This was beyond understanding. It was clearly from beyond the realm of the normal. How do you handle heaven's messenger? How do you deal with the supernatural?

I looked over them again. "Some of you are missing. Where are the other men?"

"I don't know," Claudius said. "Some just ran off. I guess they were too scared." He shook his head as though he were waking from some dreaded nightmare.

I did a head count, confirmed there were twelve here, then told them to sit still. With a few quick questions, I determined who was missing.

But the men before me were in shock. They were as traumatized as any troops routed in battle. You could see it on their faces. This was no fabrication. Whatever they had witnessed had nearly scared the life right out of them.

I had no idea what to do. My family had watched all this—this double quake. They would have questions for me later. I turned to them now. Then I turned back to my men. I never felt more caught between two worlds.

Where did this all go from here? What did I do next?

I turned again to Zelda. I walked to my little two-bench island in the middle of the courtyard. "I'm leaving," I said. "I have some work to do."

After a round of hugs, I said to Zelda, "Have the cook serve these men some breakfast. I should be back in an hour or two."

"Be careful, Marcus."

I returned to my tomb-guarding platoon. I singled out Claudius. "You're coming with me." He slowly got to his feet. "We're going back to the tomb. We'll see exactly what happened."

As I spoke the word "tomb," he fell to his knees. "Don't take me back there!" he cried out as he slowly shook his head. "Don't take me back, sir!" Fear rippled through his voice.

I considered this for a moment and then said, "You are a man. Not a dog. Now stand on your feet."

He hesitated.

"Stand now, or I'll have you flogged tomorrow."

He obeyed.

"Philip. On your feet," I barked. "You are coming too. Here's your Sunday morning appointment. As for the rest of you, wait right here." I pointed to the ground on which they sat. "If our missing four show up, have them wait here with you. I should be back before too long."

Then the three of us set out. I walked at a brisk pace, and as I did, I listened for the two men's footsteps right behind me. They were keeping up.

Unlike Friday, the signs of earthquake damage were everywhere—cracked mortar, shifted stonework, broken tiles. And everywhere people were out of their homes. They were out on the streets, drawn out by fear, inspecting damage, talking in loud, excited voices.

Although I tried my best to hide it, I was terrified. I learned long ago that the best way to hide fear is with action. Sitting and thinking brings deadly paralysis, but moving, doing, advancing on your fear, brings relief. It's the only way I know to overcome it. But it was not the earthquake that unsettled me. That was only a minor concern. It was the cause of the quake that rattled me to the core.

It was the timing of the quake that was uncanny. On Friday it was at the point of death that the earth shuddered. This morning, did it jump at the start of life? Was that what jolted us out of bed?

Had the prophet's last prophecy come true?

I stopped suddenly. Both Philip and Claudius nearly collided with me. I swung around. "Tell me about this light."

"It was like lightning."

"It came down from the sky."

"It was like it turned into a man."

"What sort of man?" I asked.

They both turned their eyes away and squinted as though they were shielding themselves from the memory.

"Like a warrior," Claudius said, and then he started to slowly shake his head, just as he had done earlier, as though his mind could not handle what his eyes had taken in.

"Yes," Philip said. "An almighty warrior!"

"When did the earthquake hit?"

"When he touched the ground," they both said.

"When his feet touched the ground," Claudius clarified.

"You weren't dreaming this? You weren't asleep?"

"No!" There was angry annoyance in his voice. "No, sir! We weren't dreaming. We all saw this." His face was red with the intensity of his words, his voice raw with emotion. "Flog me if I'm lying, sir! Flog us both!" His eyes were pleading to be believed. Then his head dropped, and he began to roll it from side to side. Claudius was clearly at the breaking point.

"Come then," I said more gently. I put my hand to his arm. "I want to see what you saw."

We resumed our trek. We passed the steps of the governor's palace and the Antonia Fortress. The soldiers were scurrying about like ants that have had their anthill kicked in. Damage to the fortress gate was clearly visible; undoubtedly, there was more destruction that we could not see.

If the day had gone as planned, I would have been arriving at the fortress about this time to pick up another platoon of guards to replace the men who were now sequestered at my villa. I had already drawn up the list of soldiers yesterday afternoon. But if I correctly understood this morning's hair-raising report, the very purpose for this next shift of guards had gotten up out of his tomb and walked away.

It was unbelievable! Though my men's words appeared credible, though their physical response appeared credible, I had to see this to believe it! It was too fantastic, too otherworldly, too far beyond the natural realm!

But then, in life Jesus seemed to be that way. At times he appeared totally natural, even ordinary, but at other times there was nothing natural about him. The supernatural moved through him, and the power of God showed up.

Did it show up this morning? Did it move upon his corpse?

At the Fish Gate the cracks that had appeared due to Friday's quake had grown exponentially. In fact, the wooden members of the gate were in a mangled and twisted state. Some heavy stone blocks had fallen from the gatehouse. I feared for my life as I passed under it.

Now as we headed north, I thought of the other king, Herod Antipas. He had come this way, been carried through this gate, and passed by the cross uprights that were now coming into view on Golgotha. On Friday he had his rival nailed there. I could not help but wonder who was the real pretender, the pretender to the throne. In my heart I knew the answer. This morning had heaven pronounced its own verdict on the matter? In a few moments I would know the answer.

The uprights were there, just as we left them on the Skull. They looked somehow different in the morning light, perhaps less threatening, less ominous, more at peace with their surroundings. What a strange thought that was!

We were drawing very near now. I made a short detour around the Skull. As I stepped off the road, I turned to my two companions. "You changed nothing? You left everything as it was?" I asked.

"We did nothing," Philip said. "We dropped everything. All we did was flee after the angel came."

They were clearly apprehensive.

"I just don't want to see that angel again." Claudius shuddered as he spoke.

"Just stay behind me," I said. "If he's there and he's as scary as you say, we all have legs. You can use them again."

These words brought only a small measure of assurance. We had gone only a short distance when two men came running from the tomb. They ran right by, ignoring us completely. One of them I recognized. It was John, the Messiah's young disciple.

This did little to stanch our fears. My two followers were now on the verge of becoming panic-stricken.

"We will advance more slowly," I said. "But we will advance."

And we did. It would be fair to say I crept around the corner of the last hill. The tomb came into view, but my two soldiers were well back. Seeing no one there, I beckoned them forward and then advanced a few more steps.

It was as they said. The stone was rolled away. But it was not merely rolled to the side as I had expected. It had been pushed right up and out of its stone track, and it had toppled over a good distance from the tomb entrance.

I edged my way toward it. About two paces from the end of the stone track, there was a gouge in the shallow soil, where the round cover stone had landed and then rolled. This was a real headshaker. How had this happened? It must have been rolled back with such force that when it reached the end of the track, it bounced up and out. No wonder the men were scared! This was awesome. Forty men could not do this!

Suddenly I felt very small, small and afraid.

And this was the very stone we had sealed just a day earlier. A close examination showed that in a few spots there were still fragments of broken plaster on it.

I exhaled a huge puff of air. This discovery in itself was beyond all expectation. The force of the quake could not have done this. A quake of such magnitude would have collapsed the tomb itself, and not a building in the city would be standing. No, a direct force had hurled this boulder away from the tomb's entrance.

An almighty warrior from heaven's realm?

I rejoined my two men. Suddenly they gained a new level of respect in my eyes. Their fears had become my own. I found I was rolling my head from side to side just as I had seen Claudius do.

"You saw this happen?" I gestured to the fallen round rock and then put a finger to my lips. I was astounded.

"Actually," Philip admitted, "I didn't see him roll the stone. We all fell like dead men when the earthquake hit. But after, when I opened my eyes, the angel was sitting on it, and . . . and Jesus was walking out of the tomb." He fell to his knees and began to beat the ground as he said this last part. He was gripped afresh by the memory.

"Where were you when this happened?"

He raised his head and pointed to a spot a few paces away. "Right there."

"And you?" I looked at Claudius.

He pointed to another spot. "Just over here," he said. "That's my cloak. I left it when I ran."

There was, in fact, a good bit of flotsam scattered about: a few cloaks, a water jug, Philip's precious dice, even a helmet. Here were all the signs of panicked flight. They had left all and fled for their lives.

For me only one question remained. Was the open tomb truly empty?

"Get to your feet, Philip," I said. "You two stay here and watch while I go take a look inside."

I took three deep breaths and set out on my little journey. It was only about twenty paces to the tomb entrance. A distance made much longer by my fear. But the whole scene was bathed in the warmth of morning sunlight. I started slowly. About halfway to the entrance, a songbird broke forth in glorious melody. The sun's rays streamed into the rock tomb, lighting my way.

It was empty! The stone slab lay empty. Actually, it was not entirely so. The death shroud had been rolled up, and the face covering was neatly folded and lay off to one side. It appeared as though the awakened corpse took a moment to make his bed after getting up.

The Galilean prophet, the true king, had arisen and gone forth!

38

Nine in the morning, Sunday, April 9

WHEN I RETURNED, both Philip and Claudius were on their knees. It seemed fitting. They might well be overwhelmed with awe, but they might just as well pray for their lives. Whether they knew it or not, their lives were hanging in the balance. The consequences for deserting one's post, whatever the circumstances, could be severe indeed.

I motioned them to their feet. "We will have to report this to Caiaphas," I said.

"To Caiaphas?" Claudius expressed surprise.

"Yes, Caiaphas," I said. "We were doing this job for him." I brushed my index finger over the coarse stubble on my chin. "He could insist that you be put to death for desertion, dereliction of duty."

They were white-faced.

"I'll back you," I reassured them. "By God—by the God of heaven—I'll back every one of you!" I let out a deep sigh, then said, "Let's go."

Claudius took a few quick steps over to his cloak and then scooped it up.

"No!" I called out to him. "Drop it! Drop it right where it was. I want those religious bloodsuckers to see exactly what happened. We will leave everything as it is." I made a quick beckoning motion. "Let's just go."

As we walked, my mind raced. This was serious. Deadly serious. I knew that, without a doubt, the temple authorities would shift the blame for this event onto the backs of my men. After all, they were there when it happened. And they let the dead man get away! I was sure the high priest would insist that they pay the ultimate price.

But the evidence—the evidence as I saw it—all pointed to divine intervention. Their account of the events was convincing in and of itself, but the evidence at the tomb was even more compelling. Raw panic is hard to fake, material evidence even more so. The fallen position of the round cover stone spoke volumes to me. It did not get there by human hands. This fact would be patently evident to even a casual observer.

Then there was the body itself. It was gone. It had gotten up and left, according to the witnesses. An absurd proposition to any thinking person. It was absurd unless you saw this man Jesus in operation, unless you saw him heal the sick, saw him give sight to the blind, saw him transform the crippled, saw him restore the dead. It was all absurd! This was only the last absurdity in a long list of absurdities.

But then maybe his disciples did come and steal the body. There was ample time between the quake and my arrival at the tomb. After all, we did see John and his friend leave from here.

But body snatchers would do just that. They would snatch the body. They would grab it and go. They would not take off the death shroud and roll it up neatly. They would not fold up the face covering like a fine tablecloth and lay it to one side. That would be ridiculous, out of the question. No. John looked as shocked as I now was. He looked as perplexed and overawed as any man from my tomb-guarding platoon.

Then there were the prophet's own words, his own outlandish claim. I had not heard it, but his enemies had. He had predicted this. He had declared that after his death, he would arise. He even put a time limit on it. And today was the third day after his death.

I shook my head in amazement. "He is the Son of God," I muttered.

"Did you say something, sir?" Philip asked.

"Yes. I said, 'He is the Son of God.' Jesus is the Son of God."

"I heard you say that on Friday, sir," he said. "You said it when he died."

"Yes," I said. "I believed it on Friday, but I know it today."

"I believe it too," Philip said. "I believe it too."

"I know it." Claudius joined in now. "I knew it the moment the angel came." He shuddered with the remembrance of that instant. But then he nodded his head as though he were reflecting back over the week, and he slowly repeated, "I knew it. I knew it . . . In my heart, I knew it all along."

I had no cause to doubt his words.

We walked on in silence. Every sign of earthquake damage took on new meaning. The earth beneath us had jumped at the start of life!

As we approached the fortress, Claudius asked, "Sir, where are we going?"

"We need to report this to the authorities. First, I'm going to see the tribune, and he will pass the news on to the governor. Then we'll go back and pick up the other men. Then we will go and see Jonathon. He will relay the news to the high priest. Then, who knows?" I shrugged. "We'll see where they take it from there."

My attempt to see Flavio ended in failure. The door to the briefing room was closed. The two sentinels on duty had yet to set eyes on the man today. He was probably still broken, broken beyond repair.

As the three of us came down the stairs, Marius spotted me. He called out my name and beckoned me over. He had a rather confused look about him.

"Marcus, just a short while ago four of your men showed up here. They were looking for you." He gave himself a light blow to the forehead with the flat of his hand. "They were a mess. Crazy! They said something about a bright light, a stone, and a man coming out of a tomb?" He gestured wildly as he said all this. "They were terrified! Like they had seen a spirit! I—I, ah, didn't know what to make of it. I sent them on to the Golden Gate." He gave a questioning shrug. "I thought you might be there."

"Jesus of Nazareth has risen from the dead," I said plainly. "That's what this is all about. Flavio needs to know. The governor needs to know. My men saw this. That's why they're a wreck." I gave my head a quick shake as I absorbed the images of this account. "Now, Marius," I asked, "can you send a messenger to Pilate with the news?"

"What news?"

"Jesus of Nazareth has risen from the dead!" I repeated with some annoyance. "Just have the messenger tell Pilate that Jesus of Nazareth has risen from the dead. The governor will understand," I insisted.

Marius gave me a bewildered look.

I felt like I was speaking to the deaf and dumb.

"Just tell him," I insisted again.

As I turned from him, I heard him call a man over, and he began to give him my instructions verbatim. At least this time he did not relieve himself of his responsibility. One job was done.

We hurried to my home. This time Arius responded to our pounding at the gate. The ten remaining men were pretty much where I left them. They stood as I walked in. They were expecting me to speak, to report on what I found, and so I did.

"The stone was rolled away—violently thrown away," I corrected myself. "The tomb is empty. I found everything just as you men reported. The prophet rose from the dead. He left his graveclothes and walked out."

This news was greeted with a measure of relief. It was vindication. They had not imagined this terrifying nightmare at dawn. This was no group hallucination. It really happened to them. The proof was at the site itself. Their commanding officer had just confirmed what they knew to be true all along.

Yet, it was only a measure of relief. The full implications of this rising from the dead could not be absorbed, not in two hours, maybe not in a lifetime. But it was plain to see that these men needed no convincing in regard to the veracity of this event. It had been indelibly etched upon their psyches with a stylus of supernatural power.

"A message has been relayed to the governor," I said, "so he has some idea of what took place. I will try to give him a full account later. But in reality we were guarding that tomb on behalf of the high priest. Now we have to report this to him."

This news was greeted with a fitting measure of chagrin.

"Oh yes. The other four men showed up at the fortress, and they were sent on to the Golden Gate. So we'll try to meet them there."

This was good news. It brought smiles and nods to several faces.

"Now fall in behind me," I instructed. "We'll head over there now."

Within a short time, we were at the Golden Gate, the Messiah Gate. The gatekeeper was relieved to see me.

"Sir, four of our men arrived about an hour ago. They were completely distraught. They kept mumbling something about seeing a dead man walking and an angel. I couldn't make sense of it—couldn't understand a thing." He threw up his hands in frustration.

"Where are they now?" I asked.

"They went with Jonathon. He came by looking for you, all huffy like he usually is. Anyway, when he saw these men, he started asking them questions. Whatever they said seemed to make sense to him. Then all of a sudden he says to me, 'I'm taking these men to Caiaphas.'" The gatekeeper threw up his hands again in a questioning manner and then concluded by saying, "So he took them and left."

"Pfff!" The breath exploded from my lips.

"Did I do something wrong?" the gatekeeper earnestly asked.

"They should have stayed. You should have told them to stay. They're not Jonathon's men. He has no right to order them around."

He responded to this rebuke meekly. "I see."

"Oh well," I said with some frustration. "I need to see Jonathon anyway. I'll work it out with him."

Then I turned to the other twelve men who had followed me and said, "Just wait here. I should be right back."

I descended the stairs from the gate, gave a quick wave of greeting to Jonas at the tax booth, and then walked directly to the entrance proper of the temple compound. I knew I could always find a temple guard at this main entrance. There were, in fact, two on hand. I hailed one of them and said, "I have an urgent message for Jonathon and the high priest."

"Ah yes," came his response. "Jonathon has been expecting you. I will tell him you are here."

He disappeared for only a brief time, and when he returned, Jonathon, the head of the temple guard, was marching briskly before him.

"You son of a harlot! You Gentile jackass!" Jonathon waved his finger in my face. "You let them steal that body, didn't you? Now what do you mean by sending those four yellow dogs over here?"

"I didn't send those men here," I shot back. "And you have no business hustling them off. They're under my command, not yours."

"Come and get them, big man. You're on my hill now!" He pointed to the temple grounds and sneered.

"You touch so much as a hair on their heads, and I just might do that! I'm not scared of you, big boy."

Our eyes locked, and I stared him down.

"So where are the other yellow dogs? The four I've got said there were sixteen of them in all."

"They're up there." I turned and pointed to the top of the Messiah Gate. Some of the men were watching this highly animated discussion.

"Bring them down here. The high priest wants to have a word with them."

"He can have a word with them after he has a look at that tomb. And not until then. Those men aren't liars. The rocks don't lie. Take a look at that cover stone, and you won't talk so smart." I waved my finger in his face. "Something happened there that's bigger than sixteen men. It's bigger than you and your fancy temple." I bristled. "So the high priest can have his word when he has a look, but not until then."

"Humph!" He glared at me.

I stared right back and held my ground. We were at an impasse.

After a moment he said, "I will report to the high priest on our little discussion"—he brimmed with sarcasm—"and get back to you."

"I will be right over there at the gate with my men." I nodded.

He turned and left.

I climbed the stairs back up to my soldiers above the gate. When they asked me what they should do, I simply said, "Wait. Wait and see."

The time dragged on. To fill it, with the help of the gatekeeper, I did a thorough inspection of the gate from top to bottom. There appeared to be no damage at all. I was surprised after the damage I had seen first-hand at the Fish Gate. I dispatched a messenger to report on the state of this gate to Flavio. Maybe he was on duty now.

There was still no sign of Jonathon.

I sauntered over to Jonas at the tax booth. He motioned to his son and then stepped aside to join me.

I propped myself up against a stone section of the wall and began. "We didn't nail your man," I said, referring to Barabbas. "He was pardoned."

"I heard." He shook his head in disgust.

"Free the terrorists! Hang the healers!" I snorted. "It's a sad world we live in."

"We do what we can, Marcus. We do what we can." He glanced my way and added, "You did all you could."

"Yeah. You do it, and then you have those strutting idiots dump all over it!" My bitterness overflowed as I looked away.

"They'll have their day. This will all come back on them, Marcus. You'll see." Then with a nod of his head, he added, "Some of it already has."

I knew a story would follow. He drew me farther aside as we stepped just outside the gate. He continued in a hushed tone. "The Almighty has answered back."

"What do you mean?" I looked at him quizzically.

"The temple veil has torn in two," he said with a quick glance back to the Holy Place. "When the earthquake hit on Friday, it tore from top to bottom—like it was ripped by invisible hands."

I wrinkled my brow. "How do you know this?"

"My uncle."

"The temple guard?"

"The temple guard," he confirmed. "It's got them in a panic. They're all in a holy panic. They thought they were playing religious pretend games. But now reality has hit. The Lord has answered back!"

"I don't understand," I said. "What do you mean, he has answered back?"

"They have committed blasphemy—the ultimate blasphemy. And they know it. He has told them." He glanced heavenward as he said this. "He has shown them."

Jonas's skyward glance left no doubt as to who this heavenly "he" was.

"I don't understand," I repeated.

"It's a sign from God," he said with some impatience. "It's a sign that they have committed blasphemy. It's God ripping his clothes over what they have done—what they have done to his own son."

I wrinkled my brow again as I tried to grasp this.

"Now listen," he went on. "When this prophet, Jesus, was brought before the Sanhedrin on Thursday night, Caiaphas asked him if he was the Son of God. And Jesus confessed that he was. My uncle was there. He saw all this. Then Caiaphas"—he nudged me on the shoulder to make his point—"Caiaphas rips his robe from top to bottom and yells out that this is blasphemy. Well, on Friday"—he repeated himself for emphasis—"on Friday when Jesus died, God ripped his robe from top to bottom. Don't you get it?" He nudged me again. "Ripping the veil in front of the Holy of Holies was God's way of answering back. It was his way of saying, 'You got it wrong! You got it all wrong! He was my son!'"

"Ohh! Now I see."

"They are scared spitless." He spoke each word slowly and distinctly for emphasis. "Nothing like this has ever happened before." He slashed the air to make his point. "Nothing!"

"Well then, I've got a story for you!" I continued. "This morning when the earthquake hit, something else happened."

"What?" he asked, brimming with curiosity.

I raised my hand to my head in a sudden gesture of frustration. "I can't tell you now. I have to go with Jonathon."

The head of the temple guard was strutting toward me. He was accompanied by the same two Pharisees who oversaw the sealing of Jesus's tomb on the Sabbath.

39

Noon, Sunday, April 9

"WE'RE COMING FOR a look at the job your men botched," Jonathon said with a huff.

I chose to ignore this provocation. I looked past the two Pharisees and asked, "Where's the high priest?"

"Marcus"—Jonathon shook his head—"you surely don't expect the high priest to come out to inspect the tomb of a common criminal."

"A common criminal? I didn't know that the high priest was in the habit of sealing the tombs of common criminals. Oh yes, and does he usually post sixteen men to guard the graves of these common criminals? I think not!"

This brought a moment of tense silence.

One of the Pharisees ventured into this heated environment. "We have been sent by the high priest. Both of us have just come from meeting with him."

"Fine then," I said. "I'll get two of my men who were on duty at the time, and we'll set out. They're just up there." I motioned to the top of the gate and walked off to retrieve them.

Most of the twelve soldiers, my resurrection witnesses, were seated in a row in the shrinking shade of the parapet.

"Claudius, Philip," I called out, "you two are going off with me for another inspection of the tomb. The rest of you are free to go for a stroll along the wall or head back to the fortress. But be back here within an hour." I pointed to the sun. "Watch the time."

I rejoined the temple delegation with my two men in tow, and we set out. It was a speechless journey. We had nothing in common except a loathing for each other. We kept our thoughts to ourselves.

Yesterday still bothered me. I found it hard to believe that these strict fundamentalist Pharisees thought nothing of putting me to work all day on the Sabbath. They invaded a tomb, wanted me to disturb the dead, and treated me like a rebel for not obeying their unholy wishes. The incongruence was stunning to say the least. I suppose doing right, and being seen doing it, was what really mattered in their minds. Public display mattered. What was done on the sly, and more particularly, what was done on the sly with a Gentile, was of no consequence at all. Their holiness rang hollow. It was only decorative, even as their bulging phylacteries were only decorative.

By this time some of the fallen debris at the Fish Gate had been cleared away. When we left the imperial highway, we followed the same path that Claudius, Philip, and I had taken earlier that morning. We skirted past Golgotha and came around to the front of the tomb.

But there were people here now. The news of these strange events had spread like wildfire. Family members, followers, and the curious had come. They would troop out, take a timid look inside the tomb, and then return to the city. They would tell someone else, and of course, the hearers of this tale would have to come out to confirm that what they had heard was really so. A cycle had been set in motion.

But this was no joyous throng. The curious stood in small, huddled groups. They were a frightened and perplexed lot. Clearly they did not know what to make of this. It too had caught them by surprise.

I overheard one of the women suddenly exclaim, "He's alive. He is alive!" But the man beside her just shook his head. Whether it was in unbelief or bewilderment, I could not tell.

This was the scene into which we stepped. Our presence changed it. Officialdom had arrived; the common folk drew back.

Fortunately, almost everything had been left exactly as we found it in the early morning. I imagine the curious visitors found the random scattered debris as interesting as I did, and for the sake of the next visitors, they left it just as it was.

"Take a look at this stone," I said. "Now see where it hit the ground." I pointed to the dark gash it had caused.

"Centurion." One of the Pharisees addressed me brusquely. "We have our own eyes. We can see. We don't need you to interpret these events for us. Just stand aside."

I did. Murderous thoughts sprang quickly to mind, but I did stand aside. Eventually, I had a seat with my two men on a nearby rock. The three temple officials moved rather quickly about the site. I interpreted their haste as a mark of their unease with their findings.

Finally, they peered into the tomb. But they did not enter, not today. Others would see them. Fortunately, the death shroud and face covering were still in plain view—exactly where the risen corpse had left them.

I stepped toward them again. "Did you want to speak to my men?" I asked. "They can tell you what they saw."

"No," came the quick reply. "We can speak to them later."

The inspection was over. The verdict and the conclusions reached were unknown. And I dared not ask.

I signaled to Philip and Claudius. "Now you can pick up what you left behind when you fled."

They quickly scurried about doing just that. Soon they were overburdened, and I took a cloak and a water jug from them to ease the load. Only Philip's dice were missing. I showed no disappointment in this.

We trudged back to the city in the same divergent silence. The temple men were grim-faced—more grim-faced and joyless than usual. Their gloom put a certain spring into my step, even though I tried my best to hide it.

When we reached the Golden Gate, the gray-bearded Pharisee turned to face me. "We will report to Joseph Caiaphas, the high priest. He may wish to hear the testimony of your men. Will they be ready to appear before him?"

"I will make sure they are ready," I said.

"Good. In due time we may call on you."

"But my other four men?" I quickly asked.

"They are being well treated," he said. "They have been questioned. We will return them to you for punishment, after the other twelve appear."

I sighed. This was not an arrangement to my liking. But these men had abandoned their post and run off on their own. A taste of temple hospitality might be in order. I wanted to say that a day spent with glum-faced Pharisees should be punishment enough, but by this time the temple officials had turned and walked off.

The afternoon wore on, and as it did, a distinct unease set in. My twelve men were reassembled. They were ready to testify as to what they saw. They asked me for advice, but all I said was, "Just tell them what you saw. Tell them exactly what happened. No more and no less."

Some of the men were still clearly distressed, and this interminable wait heightened the sense of tension. Lack of communication only exacerbated the situation. By this time some response from Flavio or Pilate certainly should have been forthcoming. I felt cut off, like I had no support. Why weren't they getting back to me?

Renaldo, who usually showed up for some conversation during the day, was also absent. Undoubtedly he was overseeing repairs to the Fish Gate. The earthquake certainly could account for a good deal of this silence, but at this juncture some sign of life from higher up would have been most welcome.

Finally, I could wait no longer. I called for a scribe and a messenger. I dictated to the scribe: "Greetings, Flavio. The temple guard is holding four of my men. Twelve more are about to be questioned by the high priest regarding the appearance of an angel or spirit and the sudden rising of Jesus of Nazareth from the dead early this morning. I await any instructions you may have. Your servant, Marcus Longinus."

The messenger was dispatched with the message in hand, but before he set out, I said, "If Flavio is not available, for whatever reason, proceed directly to the Praetorium and present this message personally to the governor. Understood?"

"Understood, sir."

"Off with you then."

‡ ‡ ‡

No response came.

Finally, at midafternoon Jonathon and three of his men arrived at the Messiah Gate.

"The high priest will see your men now," he summarily announced.

I called my men to attention, and they descended the stairs of the gate as though they were entering the gloom of hell. Jonathon and the same two Pharisees took the lead. The twelve dutifully followed, and a temple guard and I brought up the rear.

As soon as we entered the temple compound, thirteen additional temple guards met us—one of their men, for each one of ours. We were ordered to turn over our swords. When I protested, I was told they would be returned to us later. We were then led off. We skirted the edges of the Gentile court for some distance and then were escorted into a rather dark and musty anteroom.

"You will wait here," Jonathon said as more armed guards entered.

What transpired in the next number of hours, I found to be both frightening and bizarre. I had expected we would all be led together before the high priest for questioning. But that was not what happened.

First we were not permitted to speak to one another. Our personal armed escorts saw to this. Jonathon would come into the room. He would select one of our men, and then he would walk out with the hapless witness. After what seemed like eternity, he would return with this same man and then choose someone else. By the time Jonathon led away the tenth man, darkness had descended and three oil lamps were brought in to provide a flicker of light. The unsteady flames did an eerie shadow dance across the walls.

And so on it went through all twelve men.

Finally my time came. I was led down a long corridor and into a sizable chamber. There may have been seventy long-robed, priestly officials present—the Sanhedrin. The hoary-headed high priest sat on an elaborate throne at the front. After giving my name and position, the questioning began. The interrogation was pointed, detailed, and thorough.

Questions were permitted from anyone in the assembly. I kept my answers brief and to the point.

After a time, the worried Weasel spoke. "We may call you again," he said, and then he dismissed me with a backhanded wave.

Jonathon led me back to the antechamber, where we all continued to wait.

In due course two of my men were taken out for a second interrogation. Everyone's patience was now wearing thin. Time dragged on in gloomy silence. Evening hunger pangs added their own edge to the mood within this holding cell. Possibly another full hour passed, and at last we were all ushered down to the same large council chamber.

This time it was a very different scene. The room was mostly empty. There was no sign of the high priest. We were shown to our seats, and then my four missing men were brought in. Despite the temple guards' best efforts, cheers, waves, and smiles erupted. They all appeared to be in good health, and among us a general sense of camaraderie pervaded.

Surely our ordeal would soon be over.

And it was. A table was brought in, and two long-beards seated themselves behind it. A hefty brown jute sack was placed on it. Jonathon and the two tomb-sealing Pharisees stood before us. Jonathon cleared his throat to get our attention, but it was one of the graybeards who spoke.

"A decision has been reached in this matter. You will each be paid a full year's wages. The table is set up, as you can see." He made a sweeping motion toward it. "You will line up before it."

Everyone sat in stunned silence. He certainly had our attention.

Then with the same hand, he made a sweeping motion over all of us. *"You are to say, 'His disciples came during the night and stole him away while we were asleep.' If this report gets to the governor, we will satisfy him and keep you out of trouble."*

Then he gave us all a sly nod and the devil's very own smile.

The lineup formed quickly. The money was dispensed promptly, but with ample judicious prudence.

Our swords were returned.

And we went out into the night.

40

Nine at night, Sunday, April 9

THE MONEY BOTHERED me. They paid me five times the amount given to the common soldier. But at first it wasn't the money itself that bothered me, or the amount. If they were stupid enough to offer it, we were all smart enough to take it.

What bothered me was the bold-faced lie. Here was the classic bribe. We were being asked to spread this lie, and to make it worse, we were being asked to do this by religious men, by these teachers of the law, these Pharisees. That's what really bothered me.

Yesterday, the haughty graybeard claimed my men would yield to a bribe from the Christ's disciples. But here, a day later, it was he who was handing out the bribe money. It was an astounding reversal. Their hypocrisy knew no bounds. It never failed to surprise. Yet they were blind to their own stinking corruption. They were insulated by conspicuous fat, a hoard of wealth, and the robes of power. They loved pointing out the faults of others, while they wallowed freely in their own moral filth.

How effective this money would be remained an open question. My soldiers all knew the truth. For that matter, so did the high priest and the whole Sanhedrin. Why else offer the bribe? Jesus did rise from the dead. In a day or two, every soldier in the barracks would know the real story. These things always get out. There would be an official line, which would be conveniently trotted out to appease the right sort of people, and an informal, unofficial line, which, of course, is where the real truth lay. Most thinking people can sort these things out, and in the end, I had confidence that the truth would prevail. It always does.

I neatly stacked the silver coins into the same pouch that only two days earlier contained the crucifixion spikes. The coins were heavy. The bribery money hung like a lead weight on the belt about my waist—a lead weight tied to a drowning man.

Dark, oppressive thoughts pulled down on me as I climbed the moonlit stairs to the top of the Golden Gate. It really was the Messiah Gate. Now I realized that truth afresh. The Messiah rode through it, triumphant, just a week ago today.

"Who goes there?" a nervous night watchman called out.

"Marcus Longinus."

"Oh!" He expressed his surprise. "Sir, I didn't know it was you."

"You're awake," I answered wearily, "and you're doing your job. That's good enough for me."

I took a few strides along the wall and then cast my gaze over the parapet and down toward the Kidron Valley. The familiar view was bathed in moonlight. The path Jesus had taken was clearly visible. The light-colored roadway stones took on the soft glow of the moon.

Then in my troubled mind, the scene played back. The donkey king was riding again. The cheering thousands sang his praises. "Hosanna in the highest heaven! Hosanna to the Son of David! Blessed is he who comes in the name of the Lord!" The palm branches waved. The Messiah advanced. At the proper moment our eyes met, and I heard the words afresh: "I have a future for you."

"I have a future for you?" I breathed out the words in a whisper. What did he mean by that?

Why did I hear him speak?

I slowly shook my head. It was a mystery to me. It was all a mystery to me. Why did he speak in mysteries? Why did he haunt me so?

Was I stupid? Why didn't I understand?

I shook my head again. I thought about going back home—the logical thing to do. But there was no peace there. No peace at all. I had turned inward and felt cold toward Zelda. If she knew me, knew what I had done, she could never love me. She should never love me.

I didn't even have the peace that comes with sleep. The blond-haired girl would surely come again. Or worse yet the flies, the crucifixion flies, the torturing flies of hell!

No, for me there was no peace, and there was no rest.

But she spoke. Last night the blond-haired girl spoke. While her warm blood flooded over my hands, she said, "There is a solution."

Here was another mystery. What solution?

Death was the only answer I knew. Is that what she meant?

I surveyed the valley again. It was quiet down there, quiet and dark. The dark silence beckoned.

I ambled back to the watchman. "I'm going down." I motioned in the direction of the stairs. "Raise the gate and let me out."

"I'll watch for you when you come back," he called after me.

But I didn't answer. I was not at all sure if I would be coming back.

He raised the great iron grid enough so I could slip under. I walked ahead a few paces and waved back up at him. Chains rattled as he dropped it down again, and I resumed my walk down to the Kidron.

It wasn't long before I could hear the brook. It babbled peacefully, but then I was reminded of the bloody flood that joined this tranquil flow only a short distance downstream. The temple outflow. Water and lamb's blood. First came water, then came blood, just like the spear that pierced his side. Like the spear that pierced his side—over and over that thought echoed through the dark chambers of my mind.

Why did Jesus haunt me so? Why did I drive in his spikes? Why not some other man? Now I was weighed down with the burden of his death—a death that I brought on.

And what a burden it was! Heaped on what I already bore, this was crushing, as crushing as the round tombstone that gouged the hillside soil. Guilt was crushing me. The gouge was too deep—the ponderous weight too heavy.

He was the Son of God. But that profession brought no peace. It was a naked sword aimed at my heart. Surely I would fall on it. Or, now that he was alive, Jesus would drive me into it. Or he would hunt me down. Divine vengeance would surely follow. That was the essence of what Jonas, the tax collector, said today. At the time I fully agreed with him.

But I was implicated right along with Caiaphas and Pilate. They gave the orders; I carried them out.

How could I hope to escape this judgment?

I could rage against Caiaphas and Pilate and Herod too. But when my moment came, I spit in Jesus's face. I too played my part in this perverted drama. I played it with all the pent-up blood-lusting force of hell. It was a force that had been turned loose in Germania, and as the hammer blows rang out on Golgotha, it had come writhing to the surface once again.

I hung my head. I stooped by the brook. I washed my hands in its cool water. No relief. The stained soul is not so quickly cleansed.

I got up and wandered on. Very soon the olive groves of Gethsemane invited me in. It was a better place to die. The earth here felt cooler on my feet, the shadows darker, the dewy scents of spring fresher.

By a rock outcropping I dropped to my knees. I unbuckled my sword and then withdrew it from its sheath. I laid it carefully by my side. At the right moment I would take it up.

All about, dark silence reigned.

My head throbbed. My heart pounded. Stinging tears welled up.

"Why is there no peace? God in heaven . . . Why is there no peace?"

There was silence, only dark silence.

I unfastened my cuirass, laid it over to my left.

"God in heaven . . . Why is there no peace?"

Of course no answer came.

I slid the coin-filled pouch from off my belt. I stashed it in the folds of the cuirass. Perhaps the bribe money would be turned over to Zelda, or so I hoped.

Then in my tormented mind the early-morning scenario played through its gruesome images. A Jew, perhaps a young lad, would discover the bloodied corpse. He would call his father. Upon seeing the crested helmet and cuirass of a Roman officer, he would alert the guards at the Messiah Gate. Renaldo would be summoned. In due course, the blood money would be found where I laid it within the cuirass.

I expected Renaldo to do the honorable thing. Zelda would be well provided for.

I looked skyward as the anguished words escaped my lips again. "Why? Why is there no peace?"

I fell forward, face to the ground.

"Great God in heaven . . . Why is there no peace? Why is there no answer?"

Only deafening silence roared through my empty soul.

I lifted my head again and called out into the blackness, "Why don't you hear?" With pleading hands lifted high, in desolate anger I cried again, "Why don't you hear? Why don't you listen?"

As I did this, my hands came into view. In that moment I knew the answer. It was my hands. Of course, it was my hands. It was what my hands had done. That's why the great God was silent. That's why my Tara was dead. That's why there was no peace. Blood was on my hands. The blood of a blond-haired girl. And now. Now, the blood of his son!

There was no hope for me, and there was no peace.

In a blur of anguish, I pulled off my tunic. I took up the sword. I fixed the pommel into a depression in the soil. I placed the point of the blade just below the left side of my rib cage. A quick downward thrust of my body would drive it home. I knew exactly how this was done, through the lungs to the heart.

Peace would come. I would find it my way.

As I steadied the blade with the fingers of my left hand, the demons cackled. Their demented laugh echoed off the blackness deep within.

Now only death could bring me peace.

"Tara, I will join you," I whispered.

"Zelda, forgive me," I gasped.

"Boys. Julius . . . Andrew . . . forgive me!"

And now with heaving sighs, I sobbed, "Great God in heaven, forgive me. Forgive me! Forgive me for what I have done to your son!"

"I have." The voice came loud and clear.

It startled me! It startled me so that I dropped the sword.

"I already have." It came again, so distinct, so deep and strong, it took my breath away.

I turned to the left and right. But I saw no one.

I staggered to my feet and wheeled around, but still there was no one. No one there at all.

But I heard him. I heard him as clearly as I heard his voice when he entered the city. It was the same voice, gentle but strong—incredibly strong.

A deep and frightening sense of awe overtook me. I was not alone. He had heard me!

I fell to my knees again, and then his first words on the cross came echoing to my mind: "Father . . . forgive them . . . They don't know . . . what . . . they are doing."

"They don't know what they are doing," I echoed right back. "I didn't know what I was doing. Father God, I didn't know what I was doing! I didn't know."

I fell back, flat onto my back. Then as my mind grasped his words, his strong but gentle words, an incredible sense of warmth flowed right through me.

"But I'm forgiven! I'm forgiven." As I spoke the words, a rush of pure joy flowed right through my soul. It was a surge so strong I thought my head might explode. "I'm forgiven. I'm forgiven!"

Now I tried to lift my hands in thanks. But they were pinned back, right back onto the ground on which I lay.

It was the cross position. I lay open before him in the cross position. Open and naked in soul, as naked in soul as he had been naked in body.

I was exposed.

Everything was there. Every bit of my past. Every thought. Every intent. Every joy and every sorrow.

My eyes closed. I could not force them open.

In the still darkness he touched me. In the cool of this tree garden, the naked shame of Eden was reversed.

I heard him approach, his footfall on the dewy grass. The Christ knelt near me, by my right hand.

While I lay pinned open—while I lay silent—he pressed his nail-scarred hand onto my hand. Four times he did this. Four blows of love.

First the right.

Then he got up, and he moved around to my left. There he did the same. He put his knee upon my fingers. He pressed the base of his palm onto my hand.

Four more open-handed blows. Four blows like I had done.

Though he was silent, in my mind I heard the hammer ring.

Xchuuuung!

Xchuuuung!

Xchuuuung!

Xchuuuung!

I felt his wounds, his ragged, piercing wounds.

I felt the blood. His warm blood trickled onto my open palms.

In that moment I was clean. Truly clean. The residue of evil was expunged. The stain upon my soul was gone!

Gone forever!

A fresh surge of joy broke loose. And as it did, the chasm within closed. Forever. The hollow man was full and overflowing.

I waited.

I waited for him to touch my feet. I tried to form the words, "Touch my feet too!"

But though I tried, the words would not come out. Then I remembered! I didn't touch his feet. I didn't nail in that spike.

Instead Jesus got up from my pinned right hand, and he moved to my head. I felt a rush of cool air across my face as he knelt down. Then he pressed his warm right hand to my forehead. But this was a yet more gentle hand—the hand of blessing.

Now it was peace that came! A wave of peace came crashing through. It surged around me. It overwhelmed my mind. Then it flowed within.

He came within. God came within.

He did not say a word, not a word. He did not need to. He already said all that needed to be said.

In due time he arose. And I heard his footsteps as he left.

But I lay in peace. Pinned open in perfect peace. How long I lay like this, exposed upon my earthy cross, I could not tell. Delicious joy—hot tears of joy—set no time limit.

But I was clean.

When I opened my eyes, the stars, ten thousand stars, shone down. They sang me to my feet, and I walked home, drunk with sober joy. I was new. I felt totally new from the inside out!

I crept up the creaking stairs and pushed open the boys' bedroom door. They slept on in sweet oblivion. I put my hand, my clean hand, first to Andrew's head. Then I moved over to my son Julius, where I did the same. The blessing flowed to them. I turned and pulled the door shut behind me.

Zelda was asleep too. She stirred a bit as I lay down but slept on. I joined her quickly. It was a blessed sleep, without interruption, the sleep of the newborn. The blond-haired girl did not visit. The solution had been found. It had been applied to my hands, to my heart, to my mind, and to my soul. Cleansing had come.

This year, at this Passover, unlike two years ago when Tara died, the death angel did not come to my house. The high priest's Passover lamb had been slain, and the blood had been applied—applied to my hands—to my heart.

I did have a future. Jesus, the donkey king, had given me a future, even as he said. And my future was in his hands. They were nail-scarred hands—scars I put there.

As the rooster crowed, Zelda pressed her warm body close to mine.

I smiled.

I rolled over and kissed her neck. She smiled back at me. I had so much to tell her, now that the book of life was open. Where should I begin?

I placed my left hand on her tummy. "There's a baby in there," I said with a smile of satisfaction, "and I'm so glad. Glad about so many things."

She placed her hand over mine. Then quite deliberately she meshed her fingers with mine. In that moment I knew that as a couple, we would rebuild our nest. Her love remained.

"God bless that little one," I whispered.

✠ ✠ ✠

Later that morning, in a great state of excitement, Renaldo called me over to his house.

"At daybreak there was a scream from the beggar boy's room," he explained. "I rushed in, and there he was, kneeling on the floor, rocking back and forth. He was holding his hand. The one that was cut off! But it wasn't cut off. It was fully attached!

"He kept repeating, 'Jesus came! Jesus came!' Then Lucas lifted both hands high and waved them in praise and joy."

This was no dream. It was reality. Moments later Lucas showed me his hand—the living proof. It was wholly restored, without defect, fully functional. Where it had been severed, only a faint line was now visible. In this moment, and for years to come, that line would testify of Herod's brutality.

But now this fully restored hand spoke of another king—a visiting king from heaven's realm.

Of course, Lucas had been right. He was right. This crippled boy vaulted over the wise ones of this world. He was right all along about this man—about the donkey king.

The kingdom of God had come with power!

Epilogue

Herod Antipas

Herod Antipas, the scheming Fox, despite his most valiant efforts, never regained control of his father's kingdom. In AD 39 the Roman emperor Caius Caligula called Antipas to account for his treachery. Herod had formed a secret alliance with Artabanus, king of Parthia, and Sejanus, a leading military officer. Arms for seventy thousand men had been laid in store for what was to be a coup attempt. Antipas was stripped of all his wealth and his ruling position as tetrarch. He was banished to Lyons in France (Gaul) and later died in disgrace in Spain.

Joseph Caiaphas

Joseph Caiaphas may be best remembered for his prophetic words regarding Jesus. Fearing Roman retribution against the temple, as the prophet's popularity grew, he said, "Don't you know it is better for one person to die for the people than for the whole nation to be destroyed?" (John 11:50 CEV). So for the good of the people, he had the Galilean prophet put to death. He chose the course that he thought best. But in AD 70, when the wood was dry, as Jesus had prophesied (Luke 23:28–31), the Roman army swept in. The entire nation and the great temple were destroyed. Not until 1948 was the Jewish nation restored. As for Caiaphas himself, his bones have been uncovered, and his stone ossuary is on display in Jerusalem today. A most ironic twist, since his archrival's bones have never been found, despite having spent good temple money on bribing Roman soldiers.

Pontius Pilate

The Roman procurator of Judea from AD 26–36 lost his position after waging a war against the rebellious Samaritans. The campaign was successful. However, the Samaritans launched a complaint to Vitellius, who gave oversight to the region of Syria. Pilate was called to account before the Emperor Tiberius. But Tiberius died before Pilate's arrival in Rome. Caius Caligula assumed the throne in AD 36. Apparently the governor of Judea lost his post and was then banished to Vienne on the Rhone in what is now France. The Christian historian Eusebius claims that not long after, "wearied with misfortunes," Pontius Pilate killed himself.

The Centurion

Neither the Bible nor history provides us with any account of the centurion's life after his confession before the cross that Jesus was the Son of God. However, it is worth noting that his confession of faith precisely mirrors that of the apostle Peter. It took Peter two years spent with the Christ to reach this point of faith. It took the centurion just six hours spent at the cross. Jesus went to extraordinary lengths to restore Peter after his threefold denial of the Christ during the trial before Caiaphas. Would the same Christ not show mercy to this centurion? In AD 40 the centurion, here named Marcus Longinus, was joined in his profession of faith in Jesus by the centurion Cornelius of Caesarea. The apostle Peter was instrumental in this conversion. It was a monumental event, a pivotal point in the history of the church and the world. God had broken through to the Gentiles. He broke through to a centurion. It meant the gospel message would encompass the globe.

Jesus of Nazareth

Two thousand years later, more than two billion people on this planet profess that Jesus is the Son of God. In every nation there are men, women, and children who freely bow before him. On the cross he caught a glimpse of his kingdom. It is a glorious kingdom!

Notes

Bold italic below indicates direct quotations from Scripture.

Chapter 1

p. 12, ***Hosanna to the Son***: Matthew 21:9.

p. 13, **I had watched many a triumphal entry**: Jesus's triumphal entry (Matt. 21:1–11).

Chapter 4

p. 24, **So what do you make of this Matthias**: After the Christ's betrayal, the Matthias mentioned here was chosen to replace Judas Iscariot as one of the twelve apostles. See Acts 1:15–26.

Chapter 5

p. 29, ***Rejoice greatly, Daughter Zion***: Zechariah 9:9.

p. 30, ***Jesus, Son of David***: Mark 10:47.

Chapter 6

p. 32, ***It is written***: Matthew 21:13 (NKJV).

p. 33, ***My house will***: Mark 11:17.

p. 35, **The wooden crutch clattered**: "The blind and the lame came to him at the temple, and he healed them" (Matt. 21:14).

p. 35, ***Blessed is he who***: Matthew 21:9.

p. 35, ***When the Messiah comes***: John 7:31.

p. 36, ***Hosanna to the Son of David***: "But when the chief priests and the teachers of the law saw the wonderful things he did and the children shouting in the temple courts, 'Hosanna to the Son of David,' they were indignant" (Matt. 21:15).

p. 37, ***Do you hear***: Matthew 21:16.

p. 37, ***Yes. Have you never***: Matthew 21:16.

Chapter 14

p. 79, ***We don't know***: Matthew 21:27.

p. 79, **Even some of my own men**: "Then some soldiers asked him, 'And what should we do?' He replied, 'Don't extort money and don't accuse people falsely—be content with your pay'" (Luke 3:14).

p. 79, **After reflecting a moment**: Jesus referred to Herod Antipas as the Fox in Luke 13:32. Whether Jesus was the first person to pin this title on Herod, we do not know. He certainly helped popularize it.

p. 80, ***So give back to Caesar***: Matthew 22:21.

p. 80, **Called them hypocrites**: Matthew 23 in its entirety is a scathing attack on the Pharisees and teachers of the law: "You snakes! You brood of vipers! How will you escape being condemned to hell?" (Matt. 23:33).

p. 81, ***The kingdom of God***: Matthew 21:43.

Chapter 19

p. 103, **I lost more than a Roman province**: "The Romans, for all their efforts to conquer Germany between 12 BC and AD 16, met with only limited success." Donald L. Niewyk, "Germania," in *Grolier International Encyclopedia* (Danbury, CT: Grolier Incorporated, 1991).

Chapter 20

p. 112, **If Barabbas is the soup**: "At that time a well-known terrorist named Jesus Barabbas was in jail" (Matt. 27:16 CEV).

Chapter 21

p. 118, **"Oh, yes," she'd said. "Almost"**: "Then he said, 'Go and wash off the mud in Siloam Pool.' The man went and washed in Siloam, which means 'One Who Is Sent.' When he had washed off the mud, he could see" (John 9:7 CEV).

Chapter 23

p. 134, **It was apparent that during**: "Then some began to spit at him; they blindfolded him, struck him with their fists, and said, 'Prophesy!' And the guards took him and beat him" (Mark 14:65).

p. 134, ***What charges are you***: John 18:29.

p. 135, ***If he were not***: John 18:30.

p. 135, ***Take him yourselves***: John 18:31.

p. 135, ***But we have no right***: John 18:31.

p. 135, ***We have found this***: Luke 23:2.

p. 136, **For some strange reason**: "While he was in Bethany, reclining at the table in the home of Simon the Leper, a woman came with an alabaster jar of very expensive perfume, made of pure nard. She broke the jar and poured the perfume on his head" (Mark 14:3).

p. 136, ***Are you the king***: Matthew 27:11.

p. 136, ***Is that your own idea***: John 18:34.

p. 136, ***Am I a Jew***: John 18:35.

p. 136, ***My kingdom is not***: John 18:36.

p. 137, ***You are a king, then***: John 18:37.

p. 137, ***You say that I am a king***: John 18:37.

p. 137, ***What is truth***: John 18:38.

p. 137, ***I find no basis***: John 18:38.

p. 138, ***Don't you hear the testimony***: Matthew 27:13.

p. 138, ***He stirs up the people***: Luke 23:5.

p. 138, **Then to Herod he**: "When he learned that Jesus was under Herod's jurisdiction, he sent him to Herod, who was also in Jerusalem at that time" (Luke 23:7).

Chapter 24

p. 146, **Now, change it to wine**: "When Herod saw Jesus, he was greatly pleased, because for a long time he had been wanting to see him. From what he had heard about him, he hoped to see him perform a sign of some sort" (Luke 23:8).

p. 149, **On seeing their moment**: "He [Herod] plied him with many questions, but Jesus gave him no answer. The chief priests and the teachers of the law were standing there, vehemently accusing him. Then Herod and his soldiers ridiculed and mocked him. Dressing him in an elegant robe, they sent him back to Pilate. That day Herod and Pilate became friends—before this they had been enemies" (Luke 23:9–12).

Chapter 25

p. 152, ***Crucify him***: John 19:15.

p. 155, ***Don't have anything to do***: Matthew 27:19.

p. 156, ***You brought me this man***: Luke 23:14–15.

p. 156, ***Therefore, I will punish him***: Luke 23:16.

p. 156, ***I find no basis***: John 18:38.

p. 156, ***But it is your custom***: John 18:39.

p. 157, ***No, not him***: John 18:40 (CEV).

p. 157, **Have him flogged**: "Then Pilate took Jesus and had him flogged" (John 19:1).

Chapter 26

p. 163, **When I shook my head**: "One of the conscripts picked up a pail of water mixed with salt and sloshed it over Jesus: the stinging brine was a routine way to revive a victim and help stem the flow of blood." Gordon Thomas, *The Trial: The Life and Inevitable Crucifixion of Christ* (London: Corgi Books, 1987), 176.

p. 164, ***Hail, king of the Jews***: Mark 15:18.

p. 164, **I ordered his hands bound**: "Again and again they [the soldiers] struck him on the head with a staff and spit on him. Falling on their knees, they paid homage to him" (Mark 15:19).

Chapter 27

p. 169, ***Look, I am bringing him out***: John 19:4.

p. 169, ***Here is the man***: John 19:5.

p. 170, ***Crucify! Crucify***: John 19:6.

p. 170, ***You take him***: John 19:6.

p. 170, ***We have a law***: John 19:7.

p. 171, ***Where do you come from***: John 19:9.

p. 171, ***Do you refuse to speak***: John 19:10.

p. 171, ***Don't you realize***: John 19:10.

p. 171, ***You would have no power***: John 19:11.

p. 172, ***If you let this man go***: John 19:12.

p. 173, ***Here is your king***: John 19:14.

p. 173, ***Take him away***: John 19:15.

p. 173, ***Shall I crucify your king***: John 19:15.

p. 173, ***We have no king***: John 19:15.

p. 174, ***I am innocent***: Matthew 27:24 (MLB).

p. 174, ***You yourselves see to it***: Matthew 27:24 (MLB).

p. 174, ***His blood be on us***: Matthew 27:25 (NKJV).

Chapter 28

p. 181, **Startled by my approach**: "A certain man from Cyrene, Simon, the father of Alexander and Rufus, was passing by on his way in from the country, and they forced him to carry the cross" (Mark 15:21).

p. 182, ***Daughters of Jerusalem***: Luke 23:28.

p. 182, ***The time will come***: Luke 23:29.

p. 182, ***Then they will say***: Luke 23:30–31.

Chapter 29

p. 188, **He would die naked**: "The cruelty of this form of capital punishment lay in the public shame and in its slow physical torture. Partly as a warning to other potential offenders, the condemned man was made to carry his cross, or the transverse part, along the public roads and to the execution ground, which was nearly always in a public place. There he was stripped of all his clothing. Affixed to the cross, he could not care for his bodily needs, and was the object of taunts and indignities of passers-by." Pierson Parker, "Crucifixion," in *The Interpreter's Dictionary of the Bible* (Nashville: Abingdon Press, 1962).

p. 191, **He took a sip**: "There they gave Jesus some wine mixed with a drug to ease the pain. But when Jesus tasted what it was, he refused to drink it" (Matt. 27:34 CEV).

p. 194, **To chants of "Raise him up"**: Jesus's prophetic words are about to reach fulfillment. "And I, when I am lifted up from the earth, will draw all people to myself" (John 12:32).

Chapter 30

p. 195, **But he was silent**: "He was oppressed and afflicted, yet he did not open his mouth; he was led like a lamb to the slaughter, and as a sheep before its shearers is silent, so he did not open his mouth" (Isa. 53:7).

p. 195, ***"Father,"* he gasped**: Luke 23:34 (TEV).

p. 196, ***Let's not rip it***: John 19:24 (CEV).

p. 196, ***"Ha!"* He wagged his head**: Mark 15:29 (CEV).

p. 197, ***Come down from the cross***: Matthew 27:40.

p. 197, ***He saved others***: Matthew 27:42.

p. 197, ***He's the king of Israel***: Matthew 27:42.

p. 197, ***He trusts in God***: Matthew 27:43.

p. 197, **He handed it to me**: "Pilate had a notice prepared and fastened to the cross. It read: JESUS OF NAZARETH, THE KING OF THE JEWS" (John 19:19).

p. 201, **I waited all day for some**: "Many of the Jews read this sign, for the place where Jesus was crucified was near the city, and the sign was written in Aramaic, Latin and Greek. The chief priests of the Jews protested to Pilate, 'Do not write "The King of the Jews," but that this man claimed to be king of the Jews'" (John 19:20–21).

p. 202, ***If you are the king of the Jews***: Luke 23:37.

p. 202, ***Aren't you the Messiah***: Luke 23:39.

p. 202, ***Don't you fear God***: Luke 23:40–41 (CEV).

p. 202, ***"Jesus,"* he gulped**: Luke 23:42.

p. 202, **He dropped back with**: "Adequate exhalation required lifting the body by pushing up on the feet and by flexing the elbows and adducting the shoulders. . . . However, this maneuver would place the entire weight of the body on the tarsals and would produce searing pain. Furthermore, flexion of the elbows would cause rotation of the wrists about the iron nails and cause fiery pain along the damaged median nerves. Lifting of the body would also painfully scrape the scourged back against the rough wooden stipes. Muscle cramps and paresthesias of the outstretched and uplifted arms would add to the discomfort. As a result, each respiretory effort would become agonizing and tiring and lead eventually to asphyxia." William D. Edwards, Wesley J. Gabel, and Floyd E. Hosmer, "On the Physical Death of Jesus Christ," *Journal of the American Medical Association* 255, no 11 (1986): 1461.

p. 202, ***Truly, I tell you***: Luke 23:43.

p. 203, ***Woman . . . behold your son***: John 19:26 (NKJV).

p. 204, ***Behold your mother***: John 19:27 (NKJV).

p. 204, **A total darkness descended**: "From noon until three in the afternoon darkness came over all the land" (Matt. 27:45).

p. 205, ***Eli, Eli, lema sabachthani***: Matthew 27:46.

p. 205, ***My God, my God***: Matthew 27:46.

p. 205, ***He's calling Elijah***: Matthew 27:47.

p. 206, ***I thirst***: John 19:28 (NKJV).

p. 206, ***Wait! Let's see if***: Matthew 27:49 (CEV).

p. 206, ***It is finished***: John 19:30 (NKJV).

p. 207, ***Father . . . Into your hands***: Luke 23:46 (NKJV).

p. 207, **The crosses began to vibrate**: "And when Jesus had cried out again in a loud voice, he gave up his spirit. At that moment the curtain of the temple was torn in two from top to bottom. The earth shook, the rocks split" (Matt. 27:50–51).

p. 207, ***He really was the Son***: Matthew 27:54 (TEV).

Chapter 31

p. 209, **The lead man among them**: "Because the Jewish leaders did not want the bodies left on the crosses during the Sabbath, they asked Pilate to have the legs broken and the bodies taken down. The soldiers therefore came and broke the legs of the first man who had been crucified with Jesus, and then those of the other" (John 19:31–32).

p. 210, **He pierced the skin**: "But when they came to Jesus and found that he was already dead, they did not break his legs. Instead, one of the soldiers pierced Jesus' side with a spear, bringing a sudden flow of blood and water" (John 19:33–34).

Chapter 32

p. 215, **My apology, Your Excellency**: "Now there was a man named Joseph, a member of the Council, a good and upright man, who had not consented to their decision and action. He came from the Judean town of Arimathea, and he himself was waiting for the kingdom of God. Going to Pilate, he asked for Jesus' body" (Luke 23:50–52).

p. 215, **"Hmm!" He rubbed a hand**: "Pilate was surprised to hear that he was already dead. Summoning the centurion, he asked him if Jesus had already died. When he learned from the centurion that it was so, he gave the body to Joseph" (Mark 15:44–45).

Chapter 33

p. 218, **In the interim Nicodemus**: "Nicodemus brought a mixture of myrrh and aloes, about seventy-five pounds" (John 19:39).

p. 220, **And quite the tomb**: "At the place where Jesus was crucified, there was a garden, and in the garden a new tomb, in which no one had ever been laid. Because it was the Jewish day of Preparation and since the tomb was nearby, they laid Jesus there" (John 19:41–42).

p. 220, **It was a tomb**: "He was assigned a grave with the wicked, and with the rich in his death, though he had done no violence, nor was any deceit in his mouth" (Isa. 53:9).

Chapter 34

p. 224, ***Sir, we remember that***: Matthew 27:63.

p. 225, ***So give the order***: Matthew 27:64.

p. 225, ***Take a guard***: Matthew 27:65.

Chapter 37

p. 247, **"No!" There was angry**: "There was a violent earthquake, for an angel of the Lord came down from heaven and, going to the tomb, rolled back the stone and sat on it. His appearance was like lightning, and his clothes were white as snow. The guards were so afraid of him that they shook and became like dead men" (Matt. 28:2–4).

p. 248, **These words brought only**: A full account of John and Peter's early-morning visit to the tomb can be found in John 20:1–9.

Chapter 38

p. 252, **But then maybe his disciples**: "Then Simon Peter came along behind him [John] and went straight into the tomb. He saw the strips of linen lying there, as well as the cloth that had been wrapped around Jesus' head. The cloth was still lying in its place, separate from the linen" (John 20:6–7).

p. 257, **The temple veil has**: "At that moment the curtain of the temple was torn in two from top to bottom. The earth shook, the rocks split" (Matt. 27:51).

p. 258, **"Now listen," he went on**: "Then the high priest tore his clothes and said, 'He has spoken blasphemy! Why do we need any more witnesses? Look, now you have heard the blasphemy. What do you think?'" (Matt. 26:65–66).

Chapter 39

p. 264, **A decision has been reached**: "When the chief priests had met with the elders and devised a plan, they gave the soldiers a large sum of money, telling them . . ." (Matt. 28:12–13).

p. 264, ***You are to say***: (Matt. 28:13–14).

Epilogue

p. 275, **Herod Antipas, the scheming Fox**: Merrill F. Unger, *Unger's Bible Dictionary* (Chicago: Moody Press, 1966).

p. 275, **As for Caiaphas himself**: W. Horbury, "The Caiaphas Ossuaries and Joseph Caiaphas," *Palestine Exploration Quarterly* 126 (1994): 32–48.

p. 276, **The Roman procurator of Judea**: Merrill F. Unger, *Unger's Bible Dictionary* (Chicago: Moody Press, 1966).

p. 276, **However, it is worth noting**: "He [Jesus] said to them, 'But who do you say that I am?' Simon Peter answered and said, 'You are the Christ, the Son of the living God'" (Matt. 16:15–16 NKJV).

p. 276, **In AD 40 the centurion**: The full account of the conversion of Cornelius the centurion is found in Acts 10.